M·U·R·D·E·R BY·THE·SEA

LAYNE LITTLEPAGE

W🌐RLDWIDE®

TORONTO · NEW YORK · LONDON · PARIS
AMSTERDAM · STOCKHOLM · HAMBURG
ATHENS · MILAN · TOKYO · SYDNEY

To Michael Keller and Sage Atkinson

> Murder cracks open the lives
> of people you don't know—
> like cracking open a walnut.
>
> —Enid Bagnold,
> *The Chalk Garden*, Act II

MURDER-BY-THE-SEA

A Worldwide Mystery/May 1989

Published by arrangement with Doubleday, a division of Bantam, Doubleday, Dell Publishing Group, Inc.

ISBN 0-373-26022-9

MURDER-BY-THE-SEA

CAST OF SPEAKING CHARACTERS
In the Order of Their Appearance

Vivienne Montrose	Carmel resident and former film star
Annie Watts	Box office manager of the Carmel Playhouse
Jonathan Patrick	Director and manager of the Carmel Playhouse
Matt Ross	Young writer from Los Angeles
Ted Reid	Jesuit priest on extended holiday
Hilliard "Hilly" Lawton	Carmel lawyer and member of the Board of Directors of the Carmel Playhouse
Medora Everett	Founder of the children's theatre troupe The Juvenile Leads, and mother of Edwinta Everett
Beatrice Brown	Wife of Oliver "Buster" Brown II of Pebble Beach
Celia Susan "Sisu" Potter	Carmel resident and amateur actress
Claudia Kellog	Stage manager of *A Classic Case of Murder*
Edwinta Everett	Granddaughter of deceased painter Edwin Everett and daughter of Medora and Thorson Everett
Hi Lo	Butler at Brown Hall
Helen Lawton	Ex-wife of Hilliard Lawton, and Gladys, the maid, in *A Classic Case of Murder*
Stephen Flanagan	Friend of Ted Reid's from Texas
Thorson Everett	Carmel painter and former stage director, only son of deceased painter Edwin Everett
Sandi	Teenage "friend" of Thorson Everett
Mrs. Kellog	Claudia Kellog's mother
Cortland Himber	Claudia Kellog's uncle and Chief of Police of Carmel-by-the-Sea

ONE

IN THE TWILIGHT of a beautiful August evening, Vivienne Montrose set out to walk from her house near the mouth of the Carmel River to the auditions being held that night at the Carmel Playhouse. The pine needles crackled slightly under her feet, and the herbs and summer flowers in the cottage gardens she passed perfumed the dry evening air with the last of their sweetness. The dusk held the crisp foretaste of autumn that always quickened something inside her. It was the beginning of a new season, and she was going to be in the new play at the Playhouse.

The new play at the Playhouse was never really a new play, since the Carmel Playhouse was thousands of miles from Broadway in every way. Fornication, four-letter words and exotic sexuality might reach Carmel via *Theatre Arts* magazine, but never across the boards of the Carmel Playhouse. The editorial page of *The Carmel Pine Cone* couldn't hold all the letters of outrage if one of the more shocking plays of the mid-1960s was produced in Carmel-by-the-Sea. Social and financial disaster would befall the Carmel stage.

That was fine with Vivienne Montrose. She loved a good old-fashioned play with characters you didn't have to be ashamed to portray. Shakespeare, Ibsen, Wilde, Coward—the Carmel Playhouse often managed to find an audience for some of their works. Vivienne didn't need the star part, either, especially now that her age was almost beginning to show. A good character role with some meat in it would keep her happy throughout an entire six-week run.

Rounding the corner of the street leading to the Playhouse, she passed a man and woman dressed in slacks, sensible shoes and ponchos—typical Carmelite. In typical Carmel fashion, they were walking a dog. A dog was *de rigueur* in Carmel-by-the-Sea, as was walking on the beach, wearing sensible clothes, burning driftwood in one's fireplace and avowing a distaste for tourists. This particular dog was large and golden and galloped ahead of the couple, obviously on his way to the beach. The man and woman smiled at Vivienne as though they knew her, and she smiled back.

Carmel had been good to her in the twenty years since she had moved north from Hollywood. The only celebrity she sought, she found acting in local little theatre productions, some of which were far more fulfilling than the films she'd made in the 1930s and early 1940s. The only problem was a small one: occasionally a tourist came sightseeing around her house by Carmel lagoon. They called it the Vivienne Montrose house ("Don't you remember her in *Song of the Heart* and *Star Over India*, Fred?"), and Vivienne hoped there were no plans to include it on a guide to Carmel in the near future

The new play at the playhouse was a murder my ery with several excellent women's roles. Jonathan Patrick, the director and an old friend, had told Vivienne there were roles in it for her and for her best friend in Carmel, Beatrice Brown.

A new play would be the perfect medicine for Bea Brown, Vivienne thought. Bea had been in the doldrums again; Vivienne knew the signs. Another love affair was ending or had ended, leaving Bea as she had been left so many times before—alone with her husband and fourteen Chinese servants in their mansion at Pebble Beach.

Like Vivienne, Bea Brown had spent her girlhood in Hollywood. While Vivienne had a career as a British ingenue in films, Bea had achieved considerably less fame as one half of a ballroom dance team. She met Oliver "Buster" Brown II in a nightclub and made what was termed a fortunate marriage. She assumed the roles of wife, mother, hostess and star of Carmel's amateur theatre, nearly in that order. Vivienne and Bea met almost twenty years ago in Carmel, and for two decades they had tried surpassing each other with horror stories of the Hollywood of their youth at lunches and teas in Carmel and at Pebble Beach.

The only forbidden subjects were Bea's love affairs. Vivienne had renounced romance before she moved to Carmel, and she considered it a weakness of Bea's to stay married to a man she despised and sleep with other men. At one time Bea had talked to Vivienne about her various romances, but gradually the topic had disappeared from their conversation. Surprisingly, their friendship hadn't suffered because of this. Vivienne loved to be amused and Bea loved to amuse. Bea's running joke involved her huge collection of detective novels, the sources of unending and ingenious plots to kill her husband Buster, or as Bea had long ago dubbed him, "the Toad."

The Carmel Playhouse was set into the slope of a hill several blocks above the beach. It was the lower part of a large cinema theatre which fronted on the block above it. Walking up the drive, Vivienne saw the gigantic Annie Watts, a Playhouse fixture, filling the box office window.

"Hello, Miss Montrose!" Annie shouted. She squinted at Vivienne through her thick eyeglasses. "Going to be in the new show?"

"I hope so, Annie." Vivienne wondered how old Annie was. The box office lady had skin that looked as if it had never seen the light of day and the ageless, sexless quality of the grossly obese. She might be anywhere between twenty-five and fifty.

Vivienne stopped, standing some distance from the box office. If you had a keen sense of smell, you avoided being too close to any area in which Annie Watts was confined.

Vivienne called out to Annie. "They do keep you hard at work here, don't they?"

"Oh, no, I'm not working," Annie bellowed. "I just like to be at the Playhouse. You know how it is, Miss Montrose."

"Of course," Vivienne shouted, "that's one of the reasons we all do this sort of thing. Nice to see you, Annie."

Vivienne entered the left double entrance door to the Playhouse, which stood slightly ajar.

The small theatre held a dozen people who had arrived in time for the seven o'clock auditions. The stage could be set up in the round, surrounded on four sides by an audience, or in three-quarters as it was this evening, with the colorful set of the summer musical leaning against the left wall. Jonathan Patrick, tall, slim and puckish, sat in directorial solitude in the center of the bank of seats opposite this wall. He was wearing his "professional in the theatre" look and bearing himself in the "above any personal ties" manner he used when holding auditions. Since Jonathan knew most of the people in the room far better than they may have wished to be known, his audition attitude was a strange contrast to the everyday Jonathan Patrick.

Matt Ross, the young writer from Los Angeles who rented Vivienne's guest cottage, was sitting near the door, and with him were two of the Playhouse regulars, Hilliard "Hilly" Lawton and Ted Reid.

"Uncle Hilly," as Jonathan Patrick dubbed Hilliard Lawton because of his genial, authoritative personality, was a local attorney and served on the Board of Directors of the Playhouse.

Ted Reid was an unusually well-dressed man in his thirties with fair hair and a languid, Anglo-Saxon face. He had played the dashing hero in the mystery play last season, doing a creditable job with the role. It had been learned that "Father Ted," as Jonathan call him, was a Jesuit priest from Dallas who had come to Carmel last year to "find himself." According to Jonathan, Ted Reid revealed his vocation to Sisu Potter, his platinum blond leading lady in last season's mystery and the person Ted Reid was "finding himself" with at the time. Naturally, word of Ted's vocation and avocation immediately got out to the rest of the cast and prompted Jonathan to quip that Ted seemed to be rehearsing for more than the role of Colonel Simmons.

Vivienne exchanged greetings with the three men. Matt Ross, usually very energetic and voluble, seemed subdued. Possibly this was due to Hilly Lawton's tendency to lead conversations.

"Jon asked me to come and read for the role of the family lawyer," Hilly volunteered. "Bad enough I was the killer in the mystery last year. If it turns out the lawyer is the murderer in this one, I can't do the part—it might hurt my practice. Besides, I bagged my quota last year."

"You haven't read the play yet, Hilly?" Ted asked.

"Never read the play unless I get cast. Then as little as possible afterwards. Except my lines, of course. And my cues. Otherwise you make enemies. You read it, Ted?"

"I did happen to glance at the script a couple of times." Ted Reid's mouth curled at one corner. "Just the role I'm interested in, of course. And my cues. But I did happen to notice that the lawyer isn't the killer. And he doesn't have many lines to learn either, so you're in luck."

"Jon *said* the role was perfect for me. Besides, no small parts, just small actors, right?"

"Jon may even use those very words tonight, but I hope not." Ted turned to Vivienne. "There's a role Miss Montrose would be perfect for—Persephone, the convicted murderess. A beautiful woman of mystery, just like Miss Montrose herself."

"It *is* a wonderful part," Vivienne agreed. It was the role she wanted. "You must be reading for the brother, Ted. I think you'd be right for it."

Ted smiled down at a leather button on his tweed jacket and twisted it as he talked. "It's an interesting role. A man with no real life of his own who's fascinated by the passions of others. A very repressed character. Should be perfect for me." He looked up at Vivienne, his eyes twinkling.

Vivienne was reminded of the considerable charm Ted had displayed when she'd talked to him on several social occasions. Unlike most men his age, he seemed comfortable talking to an older woman. Boyishness in a man in his thirties didn't often appeal to her, but Ted had a slight gaucherie guarded by a dry wit that was attractive. He was an intelligent man, sophisticated in his dress and manners, yet he stood with his toes turned slightly in, like a tall child in a man's clothes. She thought he must have been very successful in his former calling.

Vivienne made her excuses to the three men and walked across the small stage to find a place to sit and study her script. On her way to the other side of the theatre, she saw the darkly theatrical Medora Everett reading an open script on her lap. Several years ago Medora had founded The Juvenile Leads, a local children's troupe known to everyone in Carmel except Medora as "The Tiny Thespians." Medora had achieved minor celebrity from her former marriage to Thorson Everett, son of the renowned painter Edwin Everett, who had been Carmel's most famous personage. With her divorce, Medora had relinquished Thorson and retained a daughter as well as the Everett name.

Vivienne stopped near the chair where Medora sat, seemingly engrossed in her script, and spoke to her. "Medora, you're looking very well, as usual."

Medora raised her eyes slowly to meet Vivienne's and paused for dramatic effect. "Thank you," she intoned. Vivienne suspected Medora's plummy voice was the result of years of elocution lessons.

"How is Edwinta?" Vivienne asked. "I haven't seen her in months."

"Edwinta is an unusual child." Medora spoke slowly; her dark pupils moving to the left or to the right punctuated her mellifluous phrases. "She has very few friends. In fact, none that I know of. The other children can't bear a child with individuality. She can't help herself, of course. All that talent on my side and on her grandfather's." Medora snapped her script shut as if to conclude the subject.

"Please give her my love," Vivienne said, and moved away, slipping into the next row of seats. Her fondest memories of Winta Everett were of a precocious little devil who acted with her at the old Dockside Theatre before it burned down. Edwinta's father, Thorson Everett, had directed them both in a psychological thriller, *The Bad Seed*. Every few months Vivienne saw Edwinta, dressed in pale colors with matching roses in her blond hair, walking in Carmel. She supposed the girl must be sixteen or seventeen by now.

Jonathan Patrick rose to begin the audition. In the three years since becoming director of the Playhouse, Jon had held many such auditions. These occasions were among the few times he appeared absolutely serious. Despite being over six feet tall, Jonathan had a changeling quality, as though leprechauns had snatched the real John Patrick O'Shaughnessey from his cradle and substituted one of their own.

Jon first called on Medora Everett and Hilly Lawton to read a scene between the older sister, Artemis, and the family lawyer. They proceeded with laborious slowness to do so. Medora read as though she were listening to the sound of her own voice bouncing off the walls of the small theatre. Hilly was a slow reader and, true to his word, had not looked at the play. He got little meaning out of the lines and stumbled over the Greek names. Fortunately, the scene was short.

Three girls who looked like students from Carmel High School were huddled together in a corner of the theatre. Jonathan picked the most vigorous-looking girl to read Galatea, tne teenager, in a scene with Ted as the brother, Acis. Galatea would be the hardest role to cast.

The pair had been reading for a few minutes when the double doors on the left side of the theatre opened and Beatrice Brown made her entrance. Vivienne smiled in amusement as Bea paused in the doorway while the scene went on, standing well into the light in order to be seen. She was wearing a pale pink linen suit with matching beads, shoes and handbag. Pink was Bea's color, and the lines of the suit and the short skirt showed off her slim figure and still-shapely former showgirl legs. Her curly auburn hair was temporarily subdued in a smooth bouffant style.

As Ted and the girl finished reading, Bea made her way with conspicuous quietness around the theatre toward Vivienne and sat next to her.

"Impressive entrance," Vivienne whispered to Bea. "You look marvelous. Third girl from the left in *Footlight Follies*."

Bea grimaced and spoke in low tones. "Yeah. I planned to be a little late, but not this late. It hasn't been the greatest day."

"I thought Buster was away."

Still whispering, Bea settled back in the chair. "He is, thank God. He hopped up to San Francisco for some pow-wow with his toad pals." She sat up straight again. "Viv, something weird happened today that I—" She stopped, exhaled and crossed her long legs, wriggling against her short pink skirt.

The readings had started up again after Bea's interruption, and Vivienne leaned closer to her to speak quietly. "What happened?"

Bea opened her purse, brought out her playscript, and looked down at it. "It's not something you'd want to know about. Viv, believe me. I shouldn't have brought it up."

Vivienne didn't want to press the subject. Bea's love affairs weren't her favorite topic, and this sounded like a result of one of them.

Bea flipped through the script on her lap, giving a little shudder. "It sure scared the hell out of me," she added, "but it's probably just one of those freakish things that's never gonna happen again. Anyway, I think I can handle it if it does. At least now I'm prepared." She turned to Vivienne. "Look, Viv, with the Toad gone, I can stay out as late as I want tonight. Let's go to the La Playa later with Jon. I could use a few drinks and some laughs after today."

"That's fine with me," Vivienne said. "But what if Jon wants to discuss casting? He'll want to go to your place to do that."

"Forget Toad Hall for tonight. It's too dark and spooky out there, and it's too far away. We can all have lunch chez Toad tomorrow—tonight we go out."

Medora Everett was on stage again and reading with another of the high school girls. Vivienne was beginning to form a clear picture of how the play should be cast. Ted Reid was the only man with the right qualities for the brother, Acis. He had an isolated, introverted air about him. "A repressed character," he'd said, and she would agree.

Though he always auditioned poorly, Hilly Lawton would do well in the role of the family lawyer. She'd seen him in almost a dozen roles, and he was always good. Once he got his lines down, he was a natural on stage. His characterizations never varied much, but he was so believable you could forget he was acting. Vivienne wondered if he'd ever tried to make a career in Hollywood. With his rugged, straightforward good looks, Hilly would have been perfect for films.

None of the girls was right for the role of Galatea. They showed varying degrees of talent but none had the right intensity for the role of the eccentric, vulnerable teenager.

As for herself, Vivienne had her heart set on the role of the convicted murderess, Persephone. It was a fascinating role of great theatricality. The first entrance alone was worth the whole play.

That left Bea Brown and Medora Everett yet to be cast. Both would be excellent in either the role of the dominating older sister or the quiet sister with very few lines. But Vivienne knew Medora would never agree to play the lesser role, and, she suspected, neither would Bea. As director, the decision would be in Jon's hands. Although Bea would never mention it or try to use it in her favor, Brown money made up a major part of the backing of the Carmel Playhouse, and on occasions like this it was bound to affect casting.

Jonathan called for a break.

"Thank God! I don't know who I am anymore," Bea said, rising to her feet. Vivienne watched her as she made her way around the theatre, first stopping to embrace Medora Everett. She heard the irrepressible Bea asking Medora how her tiny thespians were doing. Vivienne turned away, smiling and saw Jonathan Patrick walking toward her.

"What do you think so far?" she asked him.

"It's going to be tough casting the girl's part. The most talented of those Carmel High girls looks like her big experience in life was hanging ten on a surfboard. Then there's the problem of the sister with no lines. We'll talk about it later over brandy at Bea's."

"We can't, Jon. Bea's set on going to the La Playa tonight. Buster's away, and she can stay out as late as she wants."

"Crackers and processed cheddar under the piñata again! How Bea can mingle with us hoi's and polloi's when she could be in that mansion is incredible to me. But I suppose it gets lonely out there in all that luxury with only half the refugees from Red China waiting on you hand and foot."

"She's invited us to lunch tomorrow at the Hall."

"Fantastic!" Jon's face lit up in anticipation. "We can sit on the lawn and watch the fog around the Lone Cypress. Unless by some miracle it's clear. Then we might actually *see* the Lone Cypress. You know, I don't think I ever *have* seen it, except on postcards." He leaned closer to her. They had been speaking in low tones, and now he spoke even more quietly. "Vivienne, a big favor. Could you and Bea wait for me while I lock up here later and walk me to the La Playa? Sisu Potter's going to show up tonight and try to corner me. If you two are with me, she'll stay clear. Sisu's impossible when she's trying to get a role. 'Instant Friend for Life, Just Add Water.'" He glanced up at the entrance doors. "Uh-oh! Brace yourself, show folk."

With a flash of bright yellow, Sisu Potter swirled into the theater through the left double doors.

"Eat your heart out, Loretta Young," Jon said under his breath. "Why hasn't someone told Sisu you can't twirl your skirts if you're wearing slacks?"

Sisu Potter leaned against the railing to one side of the double doors, awaiting recognition. She was dressed in more lemon yellow than one person should wear: lemon yellow slacks, a

lemon yellow short-sleeved angora sweater and lemon yellow
flats. She wore her platinum blond hair in a bouffant style, one
side pulled back with a lemon yellow bow. Sisu's face was
round, flattish and very pale. There was frosted pink lipstick on
her full mouth and a great deal of black eyeliner around her
small eyes.

"Jonathan, I'm late, I'm late!" Sisu shrilled across the theatre when she saw that no one was paying her much attention.
Approaching Vivienne and Jonathan, her voice dropped to the
husky, affected tones she used on the stage.

"Mommy and Daddy called from Tulsa, and you *know* how
impossible Mommy and Daddy are to get off the phone. I
mean, you've *met* them, Jonathan, you *know*." As she spoke,
her voice rapidly increased in shrillness until it was back to its
original high pitch. "But please, *please*, Jonathan, say you
haven't cast all the good roles yet!"

"No final casting until the end of the week, Sisu. Vivienne,
you've met Sisu Potter, haven't you?"

"Yes, of course," Sisu interrupted. "We met on opening
night of my play last year. I told Miss Montrose—Vivienne—
how I idolized her when I was a very young girl and used to see
her old movies on TV. I loved the one about the violinist, *Song
of the Heart*, where Vivienne was the sister of Natalie Carroll.
When was that movie made? Wasn't that way back in the
1940s?"

"Around that time," Vivienne answered coolly.

Sisu continued, seemingly oblivious. "Every time I've seen
it on TV lately, I've watched for that one little tiny scene you
have, but they've cut your part right out."

"Sisu, have you had a chance to look over the role I suggested to you yet?" Jonathan interposed quickly.

"The one with no lines? I did *glance* at it, but *frankly*, I was
hoping for something *weightier*. But I guess those roles are all
sewn up by those with *seniority*." Sisu flashed a smile at Vivienne, who did not return it. "With my temperament I really
am most right for the role of the teenage girl. What's her name?
But in such a small theatre I guess I couldn't play a role *quite*
so young."

They tore down the old Hippodrome, Vivienne thought.

"We'll be using a *real* teenager in this one," Jonathan said dryly. "But the quiet sister would be a stretch for you, Sisu. Athena, named after the goddess of wisdom. A character of great depth. I'm sure you'd find it a challenge."

Sarcasm was lost on Sisu. "Oh, I'll read for it, Jonathan, just to make you happy. But I want a chance to read for one of the *meatier* roles."

"Not to worry, Sisu. You'll get your chance," Jonathan said. Then he walked back to his chair near the center of the theatre.

"Intermission is over, ladies and gentlemen," he announced.

TWO

IF YOU WERE TO ASK Matt Ross why he went to an audition where the two male roles were as good as pre-cast, he would have answered, "It's great material!" It was all grist for Matt's literary mill. He had moved to Carmel-by-the-Sea a year ago to live in beautiful surroundings and have a peaceful place to write, never dreaming that the people he would meet there would prove ten times more intriguing than the film and television industry crowd he grew up with in Los Angeles. Carmel had once been an artists' colony, so maybe that explained it.

Renting Vivienne Montrose's guest cottage was a stroke of luck Matt still could hardly believe. Shortly after coming to Carmel, he had seen her walking down Ocean Avenue like a normal human being, doing her shopping. He followed her around on her errands, his heart quickening. She looked just as beautiful as she did in her movies. As beautiful, just not as young. Of course, he was too shy to speak to her then.

Matt was fascinated by the tangled web of lives encircling the Carmel Playhouse. There was plenty of characterization there, enough for several novels. He had auditioned for the mystery last year and was cast, only to die in the first act, but his quick demise gave him the opportunity to hang around backstage every night until final curtain, watching and listening. During the run of the show he got to know Bea Brown, Ted Reid, Hilly Lawton, Helen (Hilly's ex-wife), Sisu Potter and Jonathan Patrick. He was looking for a place to rent when Bea Brown told him about her friend Vivienne Montrose, who wanted to rent her guest cottage to some young person in the arts.

Matt's first novel was a saga of Hollywood in the Golden Age. He had been born into his background material: his mother and father were bit players. His mother died when he was ten, and his father, on hard times, put Matt in an orphanage. He tried never to remember the fear and the sadness of those long few years. Sitting in the dingy "playroom" of the orphanage and staring at the flickering television screen, he wanted to climb inside the black-and-white and glamorous world that didn't exist anymore, and never come out.

If they'd shown an old movie on Los Angeles television in the 1950s, Matt had seen it. He could recite the dialogue of dozens of them slightly ahead of the actors on the screen. He knew all about the old stars. Most of them lost their glow off the screen, but not Vivienne Montrose. She fascinated him. Not only had she been a star (or "sort of a star," as she put it) during the Golden Age, but she was second-generation Hollywood. Her mother and father were stage actors who had moved from London to New York, and then to Hollywood with the advent of sound and did character roles in all the old greats. Phoebe Lloyd played society ladies and royalty, and Talmadge Montrose played the colonel, the richest man in town, or the judge. If you watched old movies, you'd know their faces. Their talented young daughter, Vivienne, small-boned, ash-blond and hauntingly beautiful, had a minor career as an English ingenue.

Vivienne Montrose had to be nearly fifty, and she was still beautiful. She dressed simply, wore her hair in a chignon and used very little makeup, yet she turned heads wherever she went. She was unfailingly kind to people and polite even under the worst of circumstances. That was breeding. And her acting was something magical. She was especially luminous in a small theatre like the Carmel Playhouse. From this, Matt knew what a great film star she might have been if she'd been given a good role and a good director.

Matt was centering his novel around a character like Vivienne Montrose. She might suspect it, but he'd never told her. Getting information from her about her life in Hollywood wasn't easy: unlike most people, she didn't seem to enjoy talking about herself.

This last year in Carmel had been the best year of Matt's life. Not only was he getting fantastic material for his book; he was living in an earthly paradise. He loved walking on Carmel Beach, day or night. He loved the fog and the smoke from the wood fires that scented the end of each day. He loved standing in the center of town and seeing the ocean beyond the dark green cypresses. He loved the funny little houses and the Carmelites who inhabited them. Now that he lived here, he was a Carmelite, too.

He had been one of the first to arrive at the auditions. Stopping for a sandwich at the Village Corner, he met Ted Reid, also on his way to the readings, and they had walked to the theatre together. He knew Ted as well as anyone at the Playhouse knew him. Ted was a complicated man. Matt couldn't understand why anyone would want to join the priesthood, but everyone had his dream, and he supposed that had once been Ted's.

Jonathan and Hilly Lawton were at the theatre when Matt and Ted arrived. Hilly was telling jokes, which was what he did when he wasn't giving advice. The advice was usually good and the jokes were usually bad, but you felt Hilly was the kind of guy you could count on. That's why he was inspired casting as the mass murderer in last year's mystery.

Matt was surprised when Beatrice Brown arrived late; she was always on time to rehearsals. Bea was richer than anyone Matt had ever known, and completely unpretentious. Next to Vivienne Montrose, Bea was also the nicest person he'd met in Carmel. He could picture her in her youth—a wise-cracking chorine like Joan Blondell or the young Ginger Rogers.

During the run of the mystery last year, he and Bea discovered they shared a passion for detective novels. Matt had just finished a stack of mysteries she'd lent him on her last visit to Vivienne's house. Whenever Matt and Bea met, they discussed their latest favorite. The "method" was Bea's particular interest.

During the intermission, Matt walked over to a pretty girl who was sitting alone. She had short, curly brown hair and violet eyes and wore no makeup—unlike the girls from Carmel High with their heavy eyeliner and teased hair.

"Hi," he said as he reached her. "I'm Matt Ross—writer, amateur actor and Carmel Playhouse *habitué*."

"Nice to meet you. I think I saw you in the murder mystery last year."

"That was me. The first to die. I'm surprised you remember. I spent most of my time backstage waiting for the curtain call."

"I *remember* you from the curtain call," she said. "You took a little jump over the hassock."

"You *do* remember me." Matt was somewhat embarrassed. "I guess I tried too hard to be noticed. That's one of my faults, trying too hard." He sat in the chair next to her.

"It's good of you to introduce yourself," she said. "I don't know anyone here except Jonathan Patrick. And Hilly Lawton and now you. I'm Claudia Kellog. I'm going to be the stage manager."

"That's great! I wish you'd stage-managed the show last year. I would have had a much better time after I died if you'd been backstage."

Claudia reddened a little. "This is my first time. I know Hilly from our church. I help organize a lot of church functions. Hilly suggested I'd enjoy doing backstage work, so I thought I'd give it a try. It's quite a responsibility, but as Jonathan pointed out, there's only one set and just a few technical cues."

"And about four hundred props, plus all the furniture and the food for the first-act lunch. Do you have someone to help you with that?"

"Jonathan said Helen Lawton, Hilly's wife—ex-wife, I mean—would be doing that. She might do props and play the maid."

"You know," Matt said thoughtfully, "the more I listen to these readings, the more I want to be involved in this production. If you don't mind, I'm going to ask Jonathan if I can help out backstage. There may be more than Helen can handle if she has to worry about lines and entrances."

"That's very nice of you. I'm sure we can use all the help we can get." Claudia looked at him with her violet eyes, and Matt was increasingly aware of her unusual prettiness. "You know, I think Jonathan's getting ready to start. We should be quiet," she said.

"You're a born stage manager. I'm obeying already."

The readings continued, with the addition of Sisu Potter in the role of the sister who didn't say much. During her long silences, Sisu looked at Hilly or Ted and rolled her eyes to show her boredom. Matt noticed that Sisu only made faces when Bea Brown was reading and couldn't see her. As much as she tried to hide it, Sisu was intimidated by Bea. At least once per conversation Sisu liked to remind people of her rich parents in Oklahoma. During rehearsals last year, Sisu had reminded everyone that she was from a wealthy family right up through opening night when Bea threw a party for them at the Browns' mansion in Pebble Beach.

Bea referred to it as "Toad Hall," but Matt and those in the cast who had never been to Brown Hall were overwhelmed. It was the size of a small European kingdom and looked like the set of Alfred Hitchcock's *Rebecca*. A group of them went to the party together in Hilly Lawton's big car. As they passed the gatehouse and headed up the road toward the mansion, Sisu had suddenly stopped talking mid-sentence. She remained almost speechless all evening. Not surprisingly, the subject of the rich Oklahoma Potters never cropped up again when Sisu was around Bea Brown.

Matt hoped the auditions would end soon. It was almost ten, and everyone was tired and irritable. Sisu and a girl from Carmel High School read the scene that ended the second act. Dropping her voice to a husky whisper and then raising it to a loud screech, Sisu was not a very believable actress. Fortunately, when the scene was over there were no more requests to read.

The group was breaking up. Matt was about to ask Claudia if she would come to the La Playa when Jonathan was suddenly upon them and shaking Claudia's hand.

"Thanks for coming! We'll discuss all the details as soon as I've finished casting. By the way, would you like to come for a drink? It's just down the hill at the La Playa."

"Thank you, but I'd rather wait until I know the group better. Right now I'd feel out of place."

"Not true!" Matt said. "You know me, Jonathan and Hilly. Please come for a little while."

Claudia smiled at the two men. "I'll come as soon as I know the ropes a little better."

"That's a promise?" Matt asked.

"It will take me a while," Claudia said. "I really don't know much about the theatre."

"You'll learn!" Jonathan shouted over his shoulder as he dashed toward the light booth to shut off the lights.

THREE

SISU POTTER WAS PERCHED on a stool by the door, and Hilly Lawton stood behind her as she announced in her penetrating voice that they were taking her car and driving down to the La Playa.

Sisu gave a sidelong glance at Ted Reid and pursed her thickly painted, pastel lips. "If you want a ride, Teddy, you can sit in the backseat."

"Sisu, the La Playa is three blocks away. All downhill. I believe I can manage the walk, and so could you. No car will hit you in the dark in that yellow outfit."

"If you don't want a ride, fine. But spare me the insults," Sisu said as she climbed awkwardly down from the stool, clutching the railing in front of her. She was not well coordinated.

"Sisu, the last thing I'd ever care to do is insult you. I'm going to walk down to the La Playa. It's a gorgeous night, I'm in Carmel-by-the-Sea, and I could ride in a car in Texas." Ted turned to Matt, his pale eyes fixing on him as though calculating Matt's response before asking a question. "Matt, why don't we walk down there together?"

Matt looked across the theatre to where Bea Brown and Vivienne Montrose were talking quietly as they waited for Jonathan to finish closing up. "Sure," he said.

Matt and Ted started the short walk to the La Playa Hotel. It was indeed a beautiful night, warm and clear, with stars and a half moon visible above the tops of the surrounding pines. The lights of the Playhouse guided them down the rough wooden steps to the street.

Ted was always in the mood to talk.

"Mysterious goings-on between Sisu and Hilly lately—did you notice, Matt?" Ted always used first names. Matt thought it must be from being a priest.

"You're the one who's interested in gossip, Ted. And you're the one who knows Sisu."

"*Knew* Sisu, and restrain yourself from the obvious, please. And I never gossip. I discuss situations out of concern for the welfare of others." Ted seemed to be slowing his loping, slightly pigeon-toed gait to make more time for conversation before reaching the La Playa. "So you haven't heard anything?"

"I don't understand the attraction there, but who knows what goes on between two people? I don't know Hilly well, but he seems like a great guy—he acts like Sisu's big brother, and she obviously likes that. I just don't get the feeling they're attracted to each other romantically."

"Unlike you and our new stage manager. A very pretty girl, by the way. You know, Matt, I've known you for over a year, and that's the first time I've seen you show interest in a girl. You must feel you're getting over that unhappy love affair you had in Los Angeles."

Ted had a way of counseling when he talked that sometimes got on Matt's nerves. This was one of those times. Still, Matt told himself, this was the way Ted was accustomed to dealing with people.

"I never took a vow of chastity..." Matt stumbled a little. "What I mean is that it would take someone special to interest me. I don't want another romantic disaster. Besides, I've been concentrating on my writing. Maybe I haven't been looking very hard."

Following the lights in cottage windows, they walked along the dark street in silence for a minute. The salt smell of the ocean sharpened the night air.

Ted broke the stillness. "That brings to mind someone I suppose you must know pretty well by now. Vivienne Montrose."

"It does? Why?" Living in Vivienne's cottage was a responsibility Matt took seriously, and he was protective of her privacy.

"Celibacy. From what I've heard...I mean, from what anyone *knows*, Vivienne hasn't had a—a romance in almost twenty years."

Matt didn't respond.

"It's hard to believe," Ted continued. "She must have been hurt very badly to shut men out of her life. You know, as someone who has counseled many, many people, I'm always curious about these things. What do you think could have happened to her, Matt?"

"I haven't the slightest idea, Ted, and I wouldn't presume to guess." Ted was pushing too hard for information, Matt thought. Besides, talking to Ted about Vivienne would be like telling someone else's secrets in confessional.

The La Playa was before them. The small hotel was built in the bygone Mediterranean style of pink stucco, stone and red tile. The entrance was an arbor of honeysuckle vines and climbing roses, and the air was redolent with their fragrances. The men went through the lobby to the bar and chose a comfortable table by the wall, big enough for the entire group. The room was decorated with a south-of-the-border theme: cream stucco walls were hung with vividly colored folk art, and Mexican pottery held paper flowers in primary hues. A bright yellow piñata in the shape of a large dog hung over their table.

They sat and ordered drinks, and, as usual, Ted flirted with the waitress. He was having his customary drink, a Rusty Nail. Appropriate, Matt thought, as he ordered a Coke. He was beginning to feel as if he'd been with Ted for hours instead of minutes.

Ted jostled the ice in his drink with his right forefinger, then he lifted the glass and took a sip. "Matt, I don't want to pry, but I'm very curious about Vivienne Montrose."

Matt tasted his drink. You had to give Ted credit for persistence.

"After all, she's the closest thing Carmel's got to a real celebrity," Ted continued.

"Vivienne's a very private person, and even if I had any more information about her, which I don't, I wouldn't tell you."

Ted seemed to be weighing the evidence. "I was just asking because I find her so fascinating—there's something ethereal—unreachable—about her that appeals to me strongly."

"Madonna-like, you mean?"

Ted laughed. "Very funny. But seriously, a woman can seem aloof if she hasn't met the right man yet. Someone understanding and caring, who could get her to open up to love again.''

"I think you've been hitting the true confession magazines too hard, Ted." Matt paused. "But you may be right." He hadn't imagined Vivienne Montrose needing a man. Her isolation made her a more romantic figure in his eyes, but he was beginning to realize he sometimes took people too much at face value.

"I don't think she expects anything like that to happen," Matt said thoughtfully, "although I can see that it might be good for her. She has friends who love her, but at her age she might be feeling lonely. I don't know how likely it is she'll meet the right person, though. Carmel's a pretty small town."

Ted stirred the ice in his glass again and then looked directly at Matt. "Matt, you know her fairly well. Give me your advice as a friend. Do you think Vivienne might be interested in a man . . . considerably younger than she is?"

The idea was so outrageous that Matt hadn't caught on until now. "Don't even *think* about it! Ted, we're talking about Vivienne Montrose!" The shock was over, and Matt's anger was rising now. "She's not a Sisu Potter. She's not desperate. Why in the world would Vivienne Montrose want to involve herself with a Catholic priest who's twenty years younger than she is?"

Ted stared at Matt as though he was speaking a foreign language. "Easy, Matt." He took an appreciative sip of his drink. "Maybe she's just not interested in men. I understand she and Bea Brown have been close friends for years. Not that I've heard anything, but sometimes a woman who's been hurt by a man will turn to another woman. I've known a couple of cases where—"

"Jesus Christ, Ted!" Matt was so horrified he was almost shouting. "I can't believe you could even *think* of something like that. Jesus Christ!"

For the first time, Ted seemed embarrassed. "Sorry, Matt, but you know, as I priest I—"

"What's this I hear, Matt? Taking the name of the Son of God in vain in front of one of his anointed?"

Matt turned around in his seat. Hilly was standing behind Matt with Sisu at his side. He saw Jonathan, Bea and Vivienne just entering the bar from the lobby.

"Matt got a little upset at a remark I made," Ted explained. "I didn't mean it seriously. I enjoy speculating about people. I'm a student of human nature."

Sisu sat next to Ted. "Was Teddy being shocking again?" she asked. "He just loves to say things he couldn't say back at the monastery."

"Those are monks, Sisu," Hilly said, as he moved behind the table and sat next to her. "Matt, we trusted you to keep Ted out of trouble. He needs someone to protect him from himself. And we arrive to find you shouting at him in the name of the blessed Trinity!" The last was said in a Barry Fitzgerald brogue.

"What took you two so long?" Ted asked, smiling at Hilly and Sisu. "Car break down?"

Sisu tossed her head. "We were just sitting and talking... Oh, hello!" she said brightly to Jonathan as he reached the table followed by Vivienne and Bea.

Matt began to feel better. He loved these post-theatre sessions, when alcohol loosened the tongues of the people he so enthusiastically analyzed and recreated on paper.

The conversation, typically, revolved around absent friends. Matt wanted to learn more about Medora Everett, whose children's theatre troupe and juicy entanglement with the famous Everett family ripened her on the vines of Carmel gossip.

"Medora Everett impressed me," he said casually. "I've been in Carmel a year, but I've never seen her act in a show."

"Medora's only done a couple of shows since I've been here," Jonathan said, then bit into a large dollop of processed cheddar cheese on a cracker.

"Since her marriage broke up and Thorson Everett started...dating...young girls," Vivienne added delicately, "Medora's devoted most of her time to that children's troupe of hers."

"Stanislavsky goes grade school," said Bea.

"Bea, really?" Vivienne asked. "I've never seen one of their performances, but I've heard there are some talented kids in it."

"'Juvenile Leads,' my foot!" Bea exploded. "Those ham-hocks think they're the cutest things to come down the pike since Mickey Rooney left Boys' Town! And Medora encourages 'em. Or she encourages their parents. Them that pays the bucks for those acting classes Medora teaches—Margaret O'Brien 101 and 102.''

Sisu giggled.

Bea grimaced. "I sat through their Christmas show once. The one about the little star that couldn't find its way to Bethlehem." She reached for her drink. "I had to find my way to the ladies' room after that one."

"As an actress, I myself think Medora Everett is affected."

There was silence as all eyes around the table focused on the speaker: Sisu Potter.

Ted spoke. "Sisu, aren't you being a little harsh? Especially since your acting has been known to give the word 'affected' a new meaning?''

"*I* studied in New York!" Sisu's small eyes were flashing. "*I* was classically trained. Unlike *you*, Ted, who learned how to act on bingo nights calling out numbers to your flock in Texas."

"Jesuits don't have flocks, Sisu," Hilly interjected.

"Who asked you?" Sisu snapped. "What are you, some kind of goddamned religious expert just because you're alderman or altar boy or whatever the hell it is at your stupid church?"

"I think Medora is one of the best actresses in Carmel." Vivienne's crystalline voice cut through the bickering. "She has a beautiful speaking voice and perfect diction." Vivienne looked directly at Sisu. "And she moves gracefully onstage."

Jonathan, the mediator, moved quickly. "I agree, Vivienne. Medora is very gifted. I'd use her more often, but she'll only accept certain roles."

"The biggest role in the show," added Bea.

"I, myself, will accept a role of *any* size," Sisu said, undaunted. "I feel that when a person has talent, it shows, no matter how many lines a person has." One hand with small stubby fingers and bitten nails flew to her hair, a large sapphire ring sparkling on the fourth finger. "When I was doing off-Broadway, I once had a very small role. The maid. But I was definitely noticed."

"I'll bet she was," Bea said under her breath.

"I got a special mention in one of our reviews."

"Forty-seven, Sisu," Ted commented.

"What?" Sisu's voice crackled with irritation.

"That makes forty-seven times I've heard about your off-off-Broadway show in New York."

"So what?" Sisu said nastily. "I've heard about the agony and the ecstasy of the priesthood a few dozen times."

In his clumsy way, Hilly tried to play peacemaker. "The question is, Sisu, did Ted tell you when he was in agony or in ecstasy?"

"Very funny!" Sisu jumped up from the table, cigarette in hand, grabbing her purse. "You men think everything is so goddamned funny! I'm tired of being the joke around here!" She charged for the lobby.

Pure Shelley Winters, Matt thought.

Hilly stood up. "I'd better go apologize," he said, looking ashamed. "You know Sisu. Just a little girl under all that bluster." He reached for his wallet and pulled out some money. "I think this covers both of us."

"Looks like we have a new couple," Jonathan said softly as Hilly left the room.

"I cannot but be relieved," Ted said, after sipping his second drink. "The whip cracks, and the new dog scampers along with his tail between his legs—so to speak."

Bea Brown stood up quickly. "Well, everyone, I'm leaving now. Viv and Jon, I have a lot to do before we lunch tomorrow, and that includes actually *reading* the play!" She took money from her wallet and laid it on the table. "This is for the rest of us. My treat."

"To quote Sisu Potter: 'I, myself, should be going,'" Jonathan said, rising. "Thanks again, Bea. Vivienne, let me give you a ride home. And Matt—you too, if you want."

"Matt, why don't you stay a few minutes and we'll walk back together?" Ted asked. "I owe you an apology, you know."

Matt agreed. Ted did owe him an apology. "Okay. Thanks, Bea. And thanks anyway, Jon, but I'll stay a few minutes."

"Oh, make him apologize longer than that!" said Jonathan. "And buy Matt another drink while you're apologizing, Ted. Matt's a struggling writer. Spend some of those ecclesiastical dollars on him. He deserves it."

Ted was acting hearty and good-natured. "I wish I'd come West disguised as a truck driver! Good night and thanks, Bea." He looked directly at Vivienne and in a softer voice said, "Good night, Miss Montrose."

Farewells were said, and the threesome moved toward the lobby. Ted ordered more drinks. When he spoke to Matt, he was smiling.

"Now, Matt, please forgive me. I knew I'd said the wrong thing when you got so mad." Ted was turning on the shy charm, a variation of the technique he used on the waitress.

"I *am* exasperated, Ted. I'm a writer, I'm supposed to understand people, and I haven't got a clue about you. You're like someone from another planet. If being a priest makes you think the way you do, I can understand why you don't want to be one anymore."

The smile disappeared as Ted grew reflective. He picked up a fresh drink. "I know I'm not like a normal person. Being a priest, I can say things other people can't say and do things other people can't do. Of course, I'm not supposed to do some things other people *can* do." He toyed with the ice in his drink. "Sometimes it's like I'm playing a role and writing the script at the same time. That's why I love acting so much. You get applause for it." He took another sip. "I enjoy talking to you, Matt. Feels like I can say anything to you and it doesn't matter. You should have been a priest."

"Thanks, but I'm an atheist."

Ted chuckled. "A minor detail. Hasn't stopped a lot of good men." Ted was beginning to get drunk. It showed in the relaxing of his gestures and the realm of his conversation. "My mother wanted me to be a priest," he continued. "The old story, I guess. We were poor. That's how Mother made her mark on the world...my becoming a priest. I never knew what I really wanted. I was never allowed to know." Very slowly, Ted jiggled the ice with his finger. He caught Matt's eye, looking as though he was about to disclose the secret of the Sierra Madre. "I think if I could be anything in this world—anything I wanted to be—I'd be a professional actor." Ted was staring at Matt as if he expected him to be shocked.

Matt remained calm. "You have a lot of talent, Ted. You probably could do it if you stuck with it."

"That's the problem. Sticking with it." Ted looked slightly ashamed of himself. "I don't think I could take the struggle. In New York? With no money?" He looked down at his expensive clothes. "I'm used to having the best. And Carmel... I want to live in Carmel." Ted pronounced his desires as though his wishes were his rights. "But all I know how to do is...well, you know...and act in little theatre productions." He lifted his glass and swallowed deeply, then looked at Matt secretively, daring him to brace himself for another surprise.

Matt braced himself.

Ted had it. "I want to get married."

Matt stared at him. "Can you *do* that? What happens to a priest if he gets married?"

"He's no longer a priest. A priest is a priest for life, even if he never hears another confession or pronounces another absolution. The truth is, Matt, you can have sex with boys, girls or animals. You can even go to hell in a handbasket and practice birth control, but you're still a priest. Unless you marry." A mixture of excitement and fear crept into his voice. "If you marry—that's it. No getting back on the merry-go-round."

"What about Sisu Potter?" Matt asked. "If you want a wife with money, she's available, and it's obvious she's still crazy about you."

"Crazy is the word." Ted swallowed the rest of his drink in a gulp. "Sisu doesn't need a husband, she needs a keeper. I guess you could say I hurt her, but I never made her any promises." He waved for the check. "I know the whole story about her parents and what they're supposedly giving her if and when she suckers some poor guy into marrying her. But what man could stand her?"

The waitress brought their bill and Matt checked it. Ted downed the rest of his last drink. He was in a land beyond mathematics. Bea had left more than enough for everyone and a generous tip. The waitresses at the La Playa loved them.

Both men rose.

Ted hadn't finished. "Marry Sisu Potter, get the money, and then push her over Niagara Falls on the honeymoon."

"Isn't that a little extreme, Ted?"

They started for the lobby. Ted was walking unsteadily—surprising, since he had an unusual capacity for alcohol. Matt planned to file the evening away as another Carmel experience. He had to admit it was great material, but sometimes great material made him feel sick.

Ted wasn't talking. Sometimes there were blessings. The two men walked down the hill toward the cottage Ted rented by the ocean. They walked carefully. It was late, and the lights were out in the bungalows and beach houses they passed.

They reached the white picket fence surrounding Ted's cottage.

"Good night, Matt. Apologies for any insults."

"Don't worry about it."

Ted leaned on a white gate that glowed slightly in the faint moonlight. "Don't take this the wrong way—but your Miss Montrose—she *is* like a rose. Soon the petals start falling off. It's a waste."

Matt stiffened and started to speak.

Ted interrupted him. "I'm just observing, not participating. That's what I do best." He swung the gate closed behind him. "Men of the cloth drink too much," he said in farewell.

Matt watched Ted move through the shadows toward the small light over the door of his cottage. "Take it easy, Ted," he called out to him.

Matt walked down to the ocean, taking the long way home so he could be nearer the water. The half-moon rode high above Carmel Bay. The sea gleamed, reproducing the moonlight in dashes and dots. Except for an occasional car passing, he heard only the purr of the tide as it broke in waves on Carmel Beach. He cleared his mind of everything but the beauty of Carmel and walked home.

FOUR

THE NEXT MORNING, Vivienne, dressed in a blue shirtdress printed with tiny flowers and a straw hat to protect her from the sun, got into her yellow Mercedes sedan for the drive into town. She had a visit to make before lunching at Brown Hall in Pebble Beach

She took the curving scenic drive past Everett House, a modern structure of stone, steel and copper on a rock promontory south of Carmel Beach. It had been the home of the renowned artist Edwin Everett until his death five years earlier. Designed by America's most famous architect for America's most famous painter, it was now the residence of the son of America's most famous painter, Thorson Everett, who had moved his studio, personal effects and the first in a series of teenage mistresses into Everett House shortly after his father's death. His former wife Medora and his daughter Edwinta remained in their substantially smaller, humbler house near the center of Carmel. Today Vivienne was on her way to the smaller Everett house on Carmel Hill.

It was almost eleven o'clock when she drove up Ocean Avenue. The inn and motel crowd had burst, Continental breakfast-stuffed, onto the paths and sidewalks. Tourists were going in and out of doorways all along the avenue, wearing Bermuda shorts and other apparel named after the resort areas of the world.

Reaching her first destination, Vivienne parked her car on a side street on Carmel Hill and walked toward Medora Everett's house. It was a typical Carmel cottage: half-timbered and two-storied with a stone chimney, mullioned windows and a roof that was shingled but yearned to be thatched. Twining bushes of white roses grew over the gate to the front yard. Medora's car was not in the driveway. Vivienne might be in luck.

There was no answer when she rang the front doorbell. She walked on a stone path around the house, dodging more rosebushes drooping with enormous, fragrant blossoms and squeezing past lush, vibrantly colored hollyhocks and lilies. She envied Medora her garden on this sunny hill away from the damp and salt of the sea. Turning on the path, she reached the back of the house. A healthy green lawn bordered by a cypress hedge ran the width of the backyard. In the far corner stood a small gazebo made of rough-hewn branches.

Shading her eyes against the sun, she saw a pale golden statue lying overturned on the lawn near the gazebo.

"Excuse me!" Vivienne stepped back in surprise. The statue was Edwinta Everett, sunbathing.

The girl wrapped a towel around her herself and sat up, cross legged. "No problem. Just catching some rays. Are you here to see Medora? She split."

Since the girl didn't seem embarrassed, Vivienne lost her hesitancy. "No, Winta, I'm here to see you."

"Whatever for?"

Vivienne walked across the lawn and stood closer, looking down at the girl. Edwinta had grown into a beautiful young woman. Her hair was a pale, silky wheat color, hanging down her back, with bangs cut above her eyebrows. She had the face of a Beaux Arts sculpture: large, almond-shaped eyes, a wide classical jaw and Roman nose, and a small, full mouth. Her features and her perfect golden skin had the softness of youth. Her expression held the cynicism of jaded adolescence.

"They're casting a new play at the Playhouse this week," Vivienne said. "The first reading was last night. I think there's a role you're right for. I came by because I wanted to tell you about it in person."

Edwinta's eyes narrowed. "I heard about the show from Medora. She said there was a teen type in it, and Thorson's old girlfriends were woefully inadequate for the role. But she didn't say it was right for me." Edwinta had a rich speaking voice, low, but not as deep as her mother's. Her California kid slang was pronounced with Medora's exquisite diction and occasionally laced with one of Medora's exquisite phrases.

"Old girlfriends? Do you mean those high school girls? All of them?"

"Just Vicki and Suzi. Thorson only likes girls whose names end in 'i.'"

"Is that so?" Vivienne smiled in spite of herself. "If you're trying to shock me, you're doing a good job. In any case, I think it's something you'd enjoy and be awfully good at."

"*If* I still acted I might be interested. But like I don't tread the boards anymore." Edwinta remained sitting upright. "Sorry you made the trip up the hill for nothing."

"I'm sorry to hear that. I remember your performance when we were in *The Bad Seed* together at the Dockside."

"I was a kid then. Like it was all instinct. All children can act. Medora says so. Hence the Tiny Thespians."

Edwinta sat motionless on the lawn. Vivienne felt awkward, towering over the girl, but she wasn't about to give up. "I disagree, and I don't believe you think so either. I think you have a great deal of talent, and I think you know it. It's a shame it's going to waste while you ruin your skin in the sun."

Startled, Edwinta looked up at Vivienne and quickly looked away again. "My acting ability is a superficial talent. I inherited it from my mother, just like I inherited the ability to paint from my grandfather. I'm one of those unfortunate adolescents with too many talents. It's really a curse. But I'm also gifted with great looks which I don't have to do anything to develop except keep my tan even."

"Winta, I've known you since you were a little girl. I really enjoyed acting with you in *The Bad Seed*. I think I know you fairly well, under that tan."

Edwinta looked at her suspiciously.

Vivienne quickly took her script out of her handbag. "I'm going to leave this with you."

She held it out to Edwinta, who reluctantly took it and stared at it.

"The role of the girl, Galatea, is the one you might look at, if you're interested," Vivienne said. "It would be very challenging to play, but I think you could do it. If you'd like to audition, you can call me at home. Or you can call Jonathan Patrick at the Playhouse. He needs to cast the play by the end of this week."

Edwinta looked at the script in her hands and twisted one corner of her mouth down.

"I have to run now," Vivienne said casually. "If you're not interested, just drop the script off at the Playhouse one day."

The girl continued to look down at the script. Vivienne turned and began to walk away.

"Miss Montrose . . ."

Vivienne turned. "Yes."

"Who's going to be in this show? Is Medora?"

"It hasn't been cast yet."

"Well, I'll think about it."

Vivienne left Edwinta sitting on the lawn. Wrapped in a towel, the girl watched her as she turned on the stone path and circled the house.

FIVE

THE SEVENTEEN-MILE DRIVE wound through Del Monte Forest, past wooded cliffs and through meadows of golden poppy and purple lupin, slicing through the greens of golf courses and following the ocean shore. Thousands of tourists paid the gate fee to tour it year-round. The pearl of this huge area was Pebble Beach, site of Del Monte Lodge and the golf courses and mansions of the very rich, who had, by California standards, been very rich for a long time—at least one generation. Brown Hall was in a particularly dark and fog-frequented section of Pebble Beach on a small peninsula with a spectacular view of the Carmel coast, when the fog cleared.

Long gray tendrils of Spanish moss hung from the cypress branches clutching each other over the road. Dead cypresses stood like bleached, twisted skeletons intermingled with the dark green living members of their species.

Vivienne passed the Mortimer Mansion, a Moorish-style palace of stone and pink stucco that was the landmark before the turn to Brown Hall. Then she drove through a pair of high, open gates and waved at John Wong, the groundskeeper, who stood inside.

Around the first curve of the drive was a timbered English cottage, not the Hansel-and-Gretel variety usually found in Carmel, but a structure of wattle, daub and thatch lifted from the Sussex countryside, with smoke rising from its stone chimney. Two boys with straight black hair and very round faces waved to Vivienne as she drove past. She waved back.

The manor house loomed behind Bluebell cottage and the trees of the drive with the sea glistening behind it. Brown Hall had been built in the 1920s by the late Oliver Cleggston Brown, Senior, for his mother, wife and young son, Buster. Born before Peter began to be increasingly robbed to pay Paul, Oliver Senior had inherited some money and made a great deal more, surviving the crash of '29 and living into the 1930s with extensive holdings in six western states, which went entirely to Buster on his father's death. Buster was a multimillionaire.

"Toad Hall," as Bea dubbed the mansion after her nickname for Buster, remained almost unchanged from the day of its first inhabitation to the present. Three-storied, sprawling and sturdy enough to survive another great quake, it was as close a replica of an English manor house in the Gothic Revival style of the 1840s as its early-twentieth-century architect could make it.

Vivienne parked next to Jonathan's small red sports car in the wide drive before the mansion. She climbed the stone steps and, standing in front of the massive doors, raised her hand toward a nest of snakes surrounding a head of Medusa, their greenish undulations frozen in bronze like Medusa herself. Into the mouth of the gorgon, opened wide in a silent bronze scream, Vivienne thrust a finger, then quickly removed her hand from the vicinity of the head, giving a shudder. No matter how often she visited Brown Hall, she would never get used to the doorbell.

"Hi" Lo, the Browns' butler, opened the left door almost immediately. His small, dark-suited figure was dwarfed against the shadowed vastness behind him, but his face beamed at her out of the gloom.

"Miss Montrose, delighted to see you, as always." Hi Lo was from Singapore and had a British accent. "Mrs. Brown and Mr. Patrick are waiting for you in Mrs. Brown's study."

Vivienne followed the butler through the dark vestibule, past a standing suit of armor flanked by hanging weapons of ancient armed combat. Their heels alternately clicked on the polish wood or sank into Persian carpets. They walked the length of the great hall as light strained dimly through stained glass windows high in the vaulted ceiling overhead and to one side of them. The other three sides of the great hall were paneled in oak and hung floor-to-ceiling with portraits of Browns and non-Browns. Two of the portraits, one of Bea and one of Buster, had been painted twenty years earlier by Edwin Everett. Looking as vital and tense as a colt, a young Bea almost jumped off the canvas. A more subdued and smaller picture showed a heavy-lidded Buster, looking frighteningly like a toad wearing golf clothes.

Hi Lo preceded Vivienne into Bea's study. "Miss Montrose," he announced.

Both Bea and Jon rose as Vivienne moved into the room. Vivienne kissed Bea and hugged Jonathan, then sat near a small marble fireplace, lit against the constant damp of the ocean.

"Thanks, Hi," Bea called out cheerily as the butler left the room. "Jon, I know you're not quite as used to the formality here as Viv is. I don't mind it, actually, and the Toad basks in it."

"*Au contraire,* I'm eating it up. It was never like this in Butte, Montana." Jon slouched back comfortably on a green silk-upholstered sofa, smoking. "I'm still stunned by the great hall of departed progenitors out there. How many years back in the family do all those folks go?"

"They don't," Bea said, sitting again at her desk, as light from a green silk-shaded lamp glowed on her face, making her look slightly ill. "My family was dirt poor, and the Toad has no ancestors. His forebears go back a generation or two and vanish in the swamps. Out there we have portraits of God-knows-who."

Bea's study, also known as the morning room, was paneled in green silk and molded with gilded woodwork. An Aubusson carpet bursting with pale, flat flowers covered the entire floor of the room. Real flowers curved in profusion from crystal vases on the small tables, fighting for space with Bea's detective novels in their shiny paper jackets. Long windows opened onto the lawn and the bright blue sea beyond it.

"I hope you two already have your character assassinations out of the way," Vivienne said, "because we need to discuss casting, and no gossip is allowed."

"But we can't discuss casting a show without gossip," Jon said. "How else could we evaluate qualifications for a role?"

"Let's eat first," Bea prompted. "You're here on the one day in the year it's clear out, so we're on the lawn."

Bea opened the French windows. Descending the steps of the terrace, they passed a small zoo of marble-potted topiary cypresses. They walked across the lawn silently, awed by the clearness of the day and the huge expanse of shining ocean. In the distance along the rocky cliffs, the Lone Cypress clung to a precipice against the changing tides.

"Isn't this marvelous?" Bea asked, as they sat in lawn chairs around a wicker table.

The wine arrived, carried in an icy silver bucket by Hi Lo. His wife, Lily, brought them salads of avocado, tomatoes and black olives.

After the wine was poured, Jonathan raised his glass. "A toast . . . to *A Classic Case of Murder*!"

Bea struck her glass against the others and they drank.

"Now to business," Bea said. She took a large gulp from her glass. "The way I see it, our only problem is the kid. Viv and I are doing the two sisters with the lines, and Jon pleads with Medora Everett to do the sister who doesn't say anything. Ted Reid does the weird brother and Hilly does the lawyer. Perfect casting."

Jonathan swallowed his first bite of salad. "Bea, you have the gift of simplicity. Unfortunately, it's not quite so easy. Naturally, you'll play the dominant sister, Artemis. You'll be superb. And you, Vivienne, will do the Vivienne Montrose role. It was written for you. You should have done it on Broadway."

Bea speared a piece of avocado with a silver fork. "Jon, ease up on us, will you?"

He grinned. "The two men are perfect for their roles. Not the greatest actors in the world, but typecasting. Now . . ." He paused, took a bite of salad, chewed and swallowed.

Vivienne glanced at Bea. "Suspense," she said.

"Medora Everett will never play that role," Jon continued. "Not unless I rewrite it with a curtain speech in Act Two. My begging her would be to no avail, and it would embarrass me. That leaves Sisu Potter."

Bea made muffled sounds, her mouth too full to speak.

"I know you're not getting along with her, Bea, but Sisu is a hard worker, she learns her lines, she's the right age and she did behave herself during the mystery last year."

Bea finally swallowed. "She had to, she was dating a priest."

Jonathan ignored this. "If either of you could come up with anyone else, I'd love to audition them. I don't like bad feelings in a cast, and half the time Sisu irritates the hell out of me. I wish I could get someone the caliber of Medora Everett for the role, but this is Carmel, not New York City. Besides, Bea, I thought you didn't get along with Medora either." He raised a fork full of salad to his mouth. "By the way, this is delicious."

"Medora and I are not bosom pals." Bea twisted the crystal goblet of wine in her fingers and the sun caught the faceted prism in the stem, flashing a rainbow of light. "But I respect her acting ability, I respect her dropping Thorson like a hot potato when he started going after teenage girls, and, much as I hate to admit it, I even respect her gumption in getting together that god-awful kids' troupe." Bea tightened her hand around the stem of the goblet and doused the rainbow hues. "But I have no respect for Sisu Potter in any way, and we don't get along. If you have absolutely no other choice, then I'd go along with her, but remember, Jon," her eyes narrowed as she gave him a warning look, "it's a very *small* theatre."

"And getting smaller by the minute," said Jonathan.

"There's a possibility I might have the problems solved," Vivienne said. "Both of them."

"How, Viv?"

"I talked to Edwinta Everett today. Medora's daughter," she indicated to Jonathan. "Medora and Winta haven't acted in a show together in years. If Winta played the girl, Medora just might do the other part. That's a long shot, of course, but the important thing is that Edwinta is perfect for the girl's role, and I have the feeling she'd do it if we play our cards right."

"What do you mean, if we play our cards right?" Jonathan asked irritably. "This is Carmel, Vivienne. This kid may be the granddaughter of the immortal Edwin Everett, but she's not exactly Hollywood's hottest property. Any one of those high school girls that auditioned would love to get the role. Is this kid just like her mother? Do we have to get her to *condescend* to play the part?"

Vivienne's fair skin flushed. "I didn't mean it that way. It's just that she hasn't acted for several years, and I think she's hesitant about it for some reason. She might need a little coaxing."

"Just like Medora," Jonathan said darkly.

Bea chimed in. "Jon, she was brilliant in *The Bad Seed* with Viv. Terrifying! She scared the hell out of me as the psycho kid. She stole the show! Excuse me, Viv, but she did."

"Don't apologize. It's true. Winta Everett was the best child actress I've ever seen."

"Great, a teenage has-been," said Jonathan.

"Jon!" Vivienne exclaimed. "You're exasperating!"

"He works at that," Bea said.

"Okay, what's she like?" he asked. "Does she look thirty, like most teenagers?"

"She's small, with pale skin and blond hair—a lovely girl," Vivienne said. "She has a beautiful voice and perfect diction, like Medora's, only her voice is higher and younger. She's intelligent and very guarded. All her emotions are right under the surface, ready to jump out. She's studiously eccentric, undoubtedly the only way she could get any attention from Thorson and Medora. She—"

"Whoa! Hold on, Viv!" Bea exclaimed. "This kid really impressed you, didn't she?" They were eating abalone now, with a golden crust and served with lemon slices. Bea ate with relish.

"Yes," Vivienne said slowly, "she did. I see so much in her going to waste. Winta changed after her grandfather died. They adored each other, and he gave her tremendous encouragement. Thorson, Son of Thor, isn't much of a father to look up to, and Medora seems to ignore her... I'm sorry, I'm going off on a tangent that has nothing to do with casting. Bea, you know I can't drink wine in the middle of the day."

"Vivienne, it's settled," Jonathan said. "If you want her in the show, I will crawl to Medora's house on my hands and knees and plead with the kid to take the part. I just hope she lives in the vicinity so I don't have to crawl too far."

Vivienne's face lit up. "She lives up on Carmel Hill. But don't crawl, just let her audition for you. I told her to call either of us if she's interested. If she doesn't call—I'll think of a different tactic."

"I say the kid's lucky you're looking out for her, Viv," Bea said. "With Bozo the Clown for a father and Spider Woman for a mother, it's probably the best thing that could happen to the kid."

"Beatrice Brown, Girl Diplomat," commented Jonathan.

Bea took a sip of wine and continued. "So we try for Medora and Edwinta as a mother/daughter team. If that doesn't work, we go for Edwinta, former kiddie killer. Viv, seriously, she scared me so much in that show I've avoided her on the street ever since. I've always been afraid she'd set me on fire the way she did the handyman in *The Bad Seed*!"

"And if we can't get Medora," Jon said, "and we can't find anyone else who's right for the sister with no lines, do you two agree to Sisu Potter as a last resort?"

Bea spoke at last, staring at Jonathan as though reciting a litany. "Only if it's a last resort. And only if you keep her away from me. That means separate dressing rooms and different rehearsal times whenever possible." She paused for emphasis. "And only this once."

Vivienne's eyes sparkled. "I have another possible solution."

"What's that, Viv?"

"Either you or I give up our role and take the role of the sister with just a few lines, and either you or I give our role to Medora."

"Unfair, Viv!" Bea turned to Jonathan. "Vivienne knows me too well. She knows I wouldn't give up a good role to get Godzilla out of the cast. You've got me there, kiddo. As usual."

Dessert arrived, an open-faced tart covered with peaches and blackberries. Bea gazed at it longingly. She looked back at Vivienne and Jon. "Okay, go with Godzilla."

SIX

IT WAS NEARLY FIVE that afternoon when Vivienne returned home. As she opened the front door, the familiar smell of the house greeted her, a mixture of scents from the redwood walls, the driftwood ashes in the grate of the stone fireplace, and the dark green French candles she lit in the evenings.

She walked toward the kitchen with MacGuffin at her heels, who was barking and jumping as high in the air as a Scottie can jump. The dog had been a birthday present five years ago from Bea, who named him after Alfred Hitchcock's euphemism for a plot device. In one of his dashes across the living room, MacGuffin had turned up the corner of a large crimson and blue Persian rug, and Vivienne turned it down again as she passed.

She did not glance at the thirty-five-year-old version of Vivienne Montrose that gazed down at her from a wall near the fireplace. That Vivienne was wearing an evening gown painted in the hundreds of minutely varied blues of Edwin Everett's palette and stood before a shadowed background, facing the artist, with her body turned slightly to one side. Her blond hair was pulled back from her face in soft waves. Her face with its high cheekbones, curving mouth and wide-set slate blue eyes dominated even the vivid colors of her skin and her dress. Edwin Everett had imbued her features with a transforming warmth and passion. At times Vivienne would stand and gaze at the painting, marveling at the radiant woman on the wall. There were long periods of time when she didn't look at the portrait at all.

In the kitchen, she put food down for MacGuffin and began to make coffee. She thought of picking up the phone and inviting Matt Ross, who was a quarter of an acre away in the cottage, up to the house for coffee. Then the phone rang.

It was Jonathan Patrick. "Guess what?" he asked.

"She called?"

"You were right. She sounds exactly like a teenage Medora Everett."

"Jon! What did she say?"

"She said she hates acting and she burned the script in Medora's fireplace."

"Jon!"

"Teasing, Vivienne! She wants to audition. And if I can round up you and Ted Reid for seven tonight, we can read her."

"I'm free this evening, but why not have Bea read with us?"

"Vivienne, think about it. If it's you and Bea, Medora knows she's out of it immediately when the kid talks to her about the audition."

"I didn't think of that."

"I'll try to get Ted on the phone, if he's not out on a date—or praying. So come up to the Playhouse at seven."

"I'll see you there, Jon," Vivienne said. "And thank you!"

The afternoon seemed to pass slowly. Finally the time came for Vivienne to drive to the Playhouse; she arrived just before seven. As she was opening the door to the theatre, she heard a voice behind her.

"Miss Montrose!"

Vivienne turned. It was Edwinta, wearing a white dress and sandals with thongs that wrapped up her legs. She wore her watchful expression, but her eyes sparkled.

"I liked the part," she said.

"I'm glad you called Jonathan," Vivienne said as they walked into the theatre together. "It will be good to get the show cast as soon as possible."

Inside the Playhouse, Vivienne introduced Edwinta to Jonathan.

"I *have* seen you around Carmel," he said. "And your voice sounds a little like your mother's, but you don't look like her."

"I don't look like anyone," Edwinta said. "Shall I sit down?"

Vivienne caught the look of surprise on Jonathan's face.

"Yes, let's all sit down," he said. "I'd like to get to know you a little better, Edwinta. You come highly recommended. Why don't you tell me something about yourself?"

Edwinta was holding herself erect. "I came to audition, not to talk about myself." She spoke quietly, looking directly at

Jonathan. "I think I should read for you first. You might not want me for the part. Then the biography would be a waste of time."

"You're not shy at all, are you?" he asked.

"No." She gave him a small, rare smile.

"I would get us started reading, but we're waiting for one other person, and I'd prefer not to start until he gets here."

"Okay." A frown crossed Edwinta's smooth forehead. "I started acting when I was a kid. I was always the child if there was one in the plays Thorson directed. I've seen pictures of the shows, but I can't remember being in some of them. My best role was *The Bad Seed*." She crossed her small, perfectly tanned, sandaled feet and looked down at them for a moment. "Miss Montrose played my mother and Thorson directed. That was before the Dockside Theatre burned down. Since in *The Bad Seed* I set fire to the handyman, people thought I burned down the Dockside, but I didn't."

Jonathan always tried to remain serious during auditions. "I heard you were brilliant in that."

"I was eight." Edwinta looked hard at Jonathan. "I was too young to make a judgment."

"Well, everyone said—who saw it, that is . . ." Jonathan uncharacteristically fumbled for words and quickly changed the subject. "What else have you done?"

"Not much." The girl's voice had a bitter edge. "Medora started The Juvenile Leads when I was nine. I was a Tiny Thespian for a couple of years. Did you ever see the Christmas show? The one about the little star that got lost and couldn't find its way to Bethlehem?"

"No," said Jonathan, lying through his teeth.

"What a barfer! I was a lamb in that one, but I had a lot of wool on me, so I was well disguised. The poor kid who played the little star was wrapped in aluminum foil. The kid had zero talent, so the Alcoa was an improvement. The kid's mother came backstage after the show—she was crying! She said we captured the true spirit of Christmas. I mean, you're a kid, but even a kid has limits. So I told Medora the Everett side of my genetic composition was reasserting itself. I said I was giving up acting and going back to watercolors. And I did. Until now."

The three of them were silent for a moment. Vivienne felt a draft running through the theatre. Edwinta was watching her, her features held tight and expressionless while her eyes shone. Excitement and hope burned in this girl, and something Vivienne couldn't name.

"If you do this role, you'll be challenged," Vivienne said. "I think it would be harder than the girl in *The Bad Seed*. Teenagers are more inhibited as actors than children. And the girl is like you in many ways. There would be an easy way for you to play her, and a hard way."

Edwinta's eyes suddenly filled with tears, and she dropped her head quickly to hide them, her blond hair falling across her face.

Vivienne stopped. What an idiot I am, she thought.

The girl squeezed her hands together in her lap, still looking down. Her voice was muffled with the effort of speaking and holding back tears. "I want to do the role. I don't care if it's hard. I want it to be hard—"

The noise of the theatre doors banging open startled them. They all looked up as Ted Reid appeared around the corner of the railing.

"Hello, everyone! Apologies—I'm late!" Ted froze in place. "What did I miss?"

Vivienne felt her own cheeks burning. Edwinta had flung her head up at the noise. Her face was flushed and her eyes glittered.

Ted walked toward them with his boyish shuffle, toes turning slightly inward. He stopped and stared, first at Vivienne, then at Edwinta. "I'm reading with the two most beautiful women in the world!"

Jonathan made the introductions and asked Edwinta and Ted to read the first scene between Galatea and Acis. Ted, usually skilled, kept losing his place. Edwinta read easily and simply, but with some audition nerves. Then Jon asked Vivienne and Edwinta to read the end of Act II, a confrontation between mother and daughter.

"Sorry," Edwinta said when they were halfway through the scene. She pushed her hair back from her face in frustration. "I can't start yelling when I don't have the lines down yet. I don't have the technique. Let me try again."

Jonathan closed his script. "I'll let you try it again, Edwinta, but only in rehearsal."

"Why?" Edwinta asked. "I know I can do it better the second time."

"Because you can have the role, if you want it," Jonathan said.

"Why? How can you decide after just a few minutes?"

"I'm going to give you your first lesson in the theatre, Edwinta. When a director offers you a role, say thank you. It's obvious to me that you have what I need for the role. Do you want it?"

She smiled. "Thank you. When do we start rehearsing?" she asked, intent again.

"Sunday afternoon, one to five," Jonathan said.

"I'm delighted!" Vivienne said. "Now, can Jon or I give you a lift back home?"

"No, I'm going to walk, thanks."

"I'm walking back too, Edwinta," Ted said quickly. "Why don't we walk together?"

Edwinta regarded Ted as though he were a mangy dog trying to follow her home. "I'm going up Carmel Hill," she said.

"I'm going that way, too," Ted said. "For a few blocks, anyway."

"The city owns the streets." Edwinta picked up her bag and looked at Vivienne and Jonathan again. "See you Sunday," she said, and left the theatre with Ted at her heels.

Vivienne turned to Jonathan. "Jon, you did make up your mind about casting her awfully quickly. Even I was surprised, and I wanted her for the part. Why make such a fast decision?"

"She's the perfect type, I could see that instantly. She's heads above any of the girls that read. She'll be good, even giving the lines the way she read them. She might be great, with rehearsals and the right kind of direction, if I have it in me. No matter what, she'll be a challenge to work with. But above all," he paused and grinned at Vivienne, "I'm taking her on your recommendation. I trust your judgment."

"Jon, you're incorrigible!"

"Vivienne, my love, I need you to give me courage. Stay here for five minutes while I run into the box office and call Medora. Don't ever tell anyone I said this, but Medora scares the hell out of me. I've got to offer her that role so she can turn it down before Edwinta gets home. Can you wait?"

"Of course."

Jonathan disappeared into the passageway that led to the tiny front box office and returned a few minutes later, a look of strain on his face.

"She turned you down?"

"Needless to say, and managed to make me feel I'd insulted her at the same time. So now I have two enemies: Medora Everett for my not offering her a lead and Bea Brown for my casting Sisu Potter."

"If you only had two enemies in all of Carmel, I'd consider you a remarkably lucky man, for an amateur theatre director."

Arm in arm, they walked to the theatre doors.

"Jon, I don't like the way Ted was looking at Edwinta."

"How was he looking at her?"

"Like Humbert Humbert looked at Lolita. Edwinta's a minor! Ted is at least fifteen years older than she is."

"Not to worry, Vivienne. Ted falls in love on a dime. It means nothing."

"That's what I'm worried about."

"Vivienne, don't be a mother hen. In case you haven't taken a good look at Edwinta Everett since she was eight—the girl's a knockout! No pimples, no baby fat—the kind of girl all the girls hate and all the boys are in awe of." He paused and looked at Vivienne owlishly. "Believe me, Vivienne, that girl knows how to handle male attention. She probably cut her teeth on Daddy Thorson."

Jon began to walk Vivienne out to her car. "Besides," he said, "she and Ted have something important in common."

"What's that? The theatre?"

"No. Adolescence."

SEVEN

MATT ROSS HAD VOLUNTEERED for the job of prop master of *A Classic Case of Murder* and was scouring Carmel for furniture and props for the show. He was storing his finds and borrowings from various cast and theatre board members in what everyone called "the vault." This musty, cave-like back-stage area began behind the light booth and ran along the rear of the Playhouse. Seemingly endless, it extended into the pitch-darkness under the floor of the cinema theatre above. The repository had two entrances: one next to the light booth and the extra dressing area, and one leading onto a small ramp that descended into the audience on the far side of the theatre. Passage through the vault was lit by several dangling light bulbs which cast irregular illumination on sets, furniture and costumes of deceased productions lurking in the depths and dust.

A nasty surprise was also lurking in the vault for Matt one day when he thought he was alone in the theatre. As he was putting dishes and glassware in an ancient cabinet near the rear of the vault, he saw a pair of eyes glinting out at him from behind the darkness of a huge costume rack. He almost screamed aloud before he realized it was only Annie Watts, the enormous box office lady, peering myopically at him through her bottle-thick glasses. Although it would have embarrassed him to admit it, after that incident Matt tried to avoid going into the vault alone.

He went to the rehearsals of any play starring Vivienne Montrose as a pilgrim went to a shrine—regularly and religiously—and *A Classic Case of Murder* was no different. The show was shaping up well, although relations between several cast members were showing varying degrees of strain.

Bea Brown and Sisu Potter didn't speak to each other. This created an uncomfortable situation at the La Playa after rehearsal, especially since Hilly Lawton and Sisu were now a couple. Hilly tried to play ambassador, but never with any success.

Sisu also did not speak to Edwinta Everett. Most of the cast was bending over backwards to be helpful to "the kid," as Bea Brown called her—but not Sisu. She conspicuously ignored Edwinta, although once Matt caught her staring at the girl with such malevolent intensity it seemed she was counting the hairs on Edwinta's head with the intention of pulling every single one of them out.

The reason for this could have been Ted Reid's interest in her. Ted invariably took the chair next to Edwinta during rehearsals and walked her home each night, even though he lived in the opposite direction. Edwinta seemed to tolerate him glacially at first; then she warmed toward him. Finally, probably due to Ted's persistence, they were becoming inseparable.

Matt sat with Claudia Kellog every chance he got and usually walked her home after rehearsals. She was gentle, sensible and not at all theatrical—a refreshing change from almost everyone he'd known in his life.

Rehearsals were exhausting, even for an observer. Most evenings the group would troop down to the La Playa afterwards. Claudia came with Matt on a couple of occasions, but he would usually drop by after he walked her home. Ted always arrived later than the others, after his nightly walk with Edwinta up Carmel Hill. Jokes were often made on his belated appearance.

One night some three weeks into rehearsals, Hilly made a tired May-December joke when Ted arrived late. Matt saw a look of surprise and dismay cross Vivienne's face: it seemed she didn't know the extent of the Ted Reid escort service. As the gathering was breaking up, she touched Matt's arm and asked him if she could give him a ride back home.

Matt usually walked home from rehearsals or the La Playa, thinking over the evening and what he had written during the day, and Vivienne was aware of this. So Matt knew there was something she wanted to say to him when she offered him the ride.

He walked Vivienne to her Mercedes. Matt loved that car, a beautiful primrose-yellow 1958 model in perfect condition, with real leather upholstery. It wasn't a long ride home, but the night was foggy and Vivienne drove slowly.

For a reserved woman, Vivienne could be very direct. After they exchanged a few words about the rehearsal, she came to the point.

"Matt, I want to ask you about Ted Reid." She had both hands on the steering wheel and was looking ahead at the road as she spoke. "I must tell you his pursuit of Edwinta Everett disturbs me."

"I thought it would. I think it disturbs all of us, for different reasons."

"You know Ted fairly well, don't you?"

"I guess I know him as well as anyone in Carmel does." Matt thought of that night at the La Playa. "Ted's deceptive. He seems straightforward, but I don't think anyone knows him very well."

"Edwinta is a young girl with a famous name. It would be obvious to anyone who was interested that she'll inherit a portion of the Everett estate some day. Thorson is storing innumerable paintings of his father's in Everett House for later sale. That makes Edwinta an heiress." Vivienne paused, looking hard at the road. "So one could question whether Ted's motives might not involve more than the desire to guide a young soul down the path of righteousness."

They neared the house, and Vivienne pulled the car into the drive.

"Please come up for coffee." She turned off the ignition. "I don't want to put you on the spot, Matt, but this has been bothering me."

They walked up the front path and entered the house. Matt loved Vivienne's house: it was simple, yet in its way as luxurious as Brown Hall in Pebble Beach.

The dog trotted after Vivienne as she went into the kitchen to prepare coffee. Matt sat at the long trestle table in the dining room until Vivienne rejoined him while she waited for the water to boil.

Matt reopened the subject. "I had a feeling someone might start to worry about...the friendship."

Vivienne began slowly, gazing out the darkened window behind Matt. "I've known one or two men like Ted. In films and theatre one meets men who don't really have much to offer beyond what one might see in them on the surface. I was married to at least one of them." She made a small, rueful grimace. "And when one is a young, inexperienced girl, one doesn't have any idea—" She rose from the table suddenly and went toward the kitchen. "Be right back," she said.

She returned with a pot of coffee and cups on a silver tray. "Let's go into the living room."

They seated themselves near the fireplace, Vivienne in a deep leather chair and Matt on the large sofa, facing the portrait of Vivienne on the wall. Even partially shadowed and lit only by a small lamp nearby, the Vivienne of the portrait was a presence in the room. Vivienne handed a steaming porcelain cup to Matt.

He took several sips and set the delicate cup down carefully.

"I like to sit and stare at your portrait every chance I get," he said. "The colors are so vibrant—it almost has a life of its own. The portrait fascinates me. It's you and it's not you."

Vivienne gave a quick sidelong glance up at the painting. "I wish you'd been able to meet Edwin Everett, Matt. I still have a hard time believing he's dead." Her voice softened as though returned to another time. "Everyone referred to him as 'The Great Man,' in upper and lower case, and he was. When you were the subject of one of his paintings, you were the center of his world, his obsession. He was able to distill the essence of you onto the canvas. I found that a little frightening." She paused, her eyes returning to the painting. "When he'd finished with the portrait, he wanted it back. He was like that. He expected everyone to give him what he wanted." She gave a wry smile. "I wouldn't. Nor would I give the painting back to him. I don't give up what is mine to someone's whim." Her voice and expression had changed in a way Matt wasn't able to identify. "A part of me is captured on the canvas that I thought I'd lost. Now it's here to remind me, whether I like it or not." She glanced across the table at Matt. "As I said, it was an obsessive experience."

"That looking right into people—that girl, Edwinta, does that."

"Yes, she does."

"It's a little scary. And I get the feeling she expects people to give her exactly what she wants, just like her grandfather."

"It's interesting you should say that, Matt, but I don't see that in her." Vivienne looked down into the almost translucent porcelain of the cup. "She reminds me of myself at her age. She seems strong, but underneath she's extremely vulnerable. I hope she won't make the kinds of mistakes I made. What frightens me is that as a priest, Ted knows how to get people's confidence." She looked up at Matt again. "I think he takes unfair advantage of his training. And I hate to see the way he treats that woman now that their affair is over. She may be obnoxious, but they *did* have an affair."

"He told me he was never in love with Sisu. He said he was just attracted to her and she was a way for him to..." he trailed off, embarrassed.

"A way for him to do what?" Vivienne asked.

"Ted usually has a way of explaining what he does that makes it sound on a higher moral plane than it actually is—but from what he told me," Matt paused for a moment, still embarrassed, "his affair with Sisu was a way for him to have a woman for the first time."

"That's very disturbing! If he would pick a woman like that for that reason, the act must not have meant much to him. In that case, he wouldn't take the virginity of a young girl to mean very much either. And Edwinta is an innocent." Vivienne set her coffee cup down on the table abruptly, startling Matt.

"I don't know. Maybe that's what Ted wants. He told me he wants to get married and have children. A rich wife, he said." Matt looked at Vivienne with an embarrassed realization.

"Wonderful!" Vivienne rose and walked toward the dining room. "Do you want a glass of brandy?" she asked, over her shoulder. "I'm having one."

"Yes, a small one, please."

She returned with two faceted snifters.

He took the glass and weighed the heavy crystal in one hand, then swirled the liquid around, tipped it up and took a sip.

Vivienne sat down again, cupping her glass in both hands to warm it. The light from the lamp behind her threw a halo around her blond hair.

How beautiful she is, Matt thought.

"So now you know more of my secrets, Matt. Good for your book."

So she knew about being in the book.

"Edwinta is important to me," she continued. "I've given her advice about acting. But there's nothing I can say to her about Ted unless she asks, and I doubt she will. After all, it really is none of my business."

"I could talk to him. Tell him I don't . . . I don't know what I'd tell him. I don't think he'd listen anyway. Ted's the most selectively deaf person I've ever met. He thinks he's above everything, being a priest." Matt was feeling the brandy, doubly warming and soothing after the coffee.

"Christ's representative on earth," Vivienne said, turning the brandy around the bottom of her glass. "Very heady brew for a man to quaff regularly, even with a grape juice chaser and wafers to clear the palate."

She smiled delightedly as a look of surprise crossed Matt's face. "I shocked you, didn't I? You're also an innocent, Matt. The older you get, the more you'll realize things are seldom what they seem, especially in Carmel-by-the-Sea."

She tipped her glass up and sipped the last of the drink. Slowly and almost reflectively, she placed the crystal snifter on the table. "Now, good night, Matt. Thanks for coming up and humoring me."

They rose, and Vivienne preceded Matt to the door. He smelled the soft, flowery scent she wore, heady as a handful of carnations.

The brandy emboldened him. "How did you know that . . . that there's a character in my book based on you?"

Vivienne opened the front door for him. "I'm a good guesser."

She stood in the glow of the lamp above the door. The planes of her beautiful face were painted in chiaroscuro—light and shadow, like an old studio photograph. "See you tomorrow," she said.

EIGHT

THE NIGHT OF THE FIRST technical dress rehearsal, Vivienne went to the La Playa to meet Bea, Matt and Jonathan for dinner. Matt and Bea were sitting at a table overlooking the ocean when she arrived. Bea was chewing on a green cannonball of an olive from a tray of appetizers in front of them.

"Viv!" Bea exclaimed as Matt rose from the table. "We were just discussing the perfect crime. Matt's giving me advice."

Vivienne sat next to Matt. "You know, Bea, if anything ever happens to Buster, everyone in Carmel is going to think you iced him."

Bea exploded with laughter. "*Iced* him! Viv, you're amazing. I never know what's going to come out of your mouth."

"If Mrs. Brown was really going to murder her husband, she'd never ask my advice about it," Matt interjected, sitting again. "You can't act like Cary Grant in *Suspicion*, asking Isabel Jeans about poisons at dinner right in front of Joan Fontaine."

Bea chewed the last of her olive and placed the pit on the tray. "Naturally, I only talk about murder in front of you and Viv, Matt. Not in front of the—in front of Buster. Only Cary Grant has the looks to be that dumb." She was looking over Matt's shoulder at the entrance to the dining room. "Anyway, subject change. Jon's on his way across the room and looking frazzled. Let's put a moratorium on murder."

"Great title!" Matt said.

"What's a great title?" Jon asked as he appeared and sat with the rapidity of a veteran of the stage. "Bea, my love, I know you won't mind my taking a sip of your gin and tonic. I need it desperately." He raised the glass quickly and swallowed most of the drink.

"How are things at the theatre, Jon?" Vivienne asked.

"Fine, now." Jon flagged down a waitress. "Could you take our orders right away? We only have a limited time to eat. I'd like a drink, but in the state I'm in now, that would finish me for the evening."

"Have the rest of mine," Bea said. "I shouldn't be having it anyway."

"Marvelous! I'll have Bea's drink and a cheeseburger."

They all ordered light dinners.

"What a day!" Jonathan exclaimed. "Claudia Kellog's still up there practicing light cues. She's been a lifesaver! She knows the show inside and out—says the dialogue right along with the cast while she's up in the light booth." He took another large swig of Bea's former drink.

"Great," Bea said. "Next time I forget a line, she can yell it out of the booth. Maybe people will think I'm a ventriloquist."

Jonathan set his glass down. "Pretty, too. Those gorgeous eyes! Don't you think so, Matt?"

"Claudia's very pretty," Matt said, looking as though he wished the attention hadn't centered on him.

Jon held his hands together, his fingers pointing toward the ceiling. "Well, everyone, say them for tonight. First tech dress. The night before final dress and—sound the trumpets—opening night! This is the last rehearsal I'll be able to eat anything prior to." Seeing Bea make a face, he added, "Beatrice, we know you never have difficulty eating."

"It's true," Bea said, her hand halting midway in its journey toward another olive. "My appetite is disgraceful."

"Appetites, Bea, my dear, appetites," Jon said.

Vivienne changed the subject. "Regarding the opening night party, I wanted to check with all of you about who else to invite."

"Viv, I feel guilty about not having it at Toad Hall. It's so much work for you, even with Matt and a few of my servants helping out."

"Not at all. You've given the opening night party at the Hall so many times. It's only fair for me to take the responsibility this time. Especially under the circumstances."

"What circumstances?" Matt asked.

"Bea doesn't want to be in the position of having to invite a certain person—who shall remain unnamed—to her home," Jonathan said quietly.

"Once was too much," Bea muttered.

"Oh!" Matt said. "Of course."

"I've already invited Medora and Thorson Everett. Separately, needless to say."

"Including the teen paramour?" Jonathan asked.

"It would be tasteful of Thorson to restrain himself, but I'm not counting on it. I hope he only brings one."

"I don't know what Thorson's out to prove!" Bea said. "It's like he does it on purpose, to shock the hell out of everyone in Carmel. I hear his latest is pushing sixteen!"

"Now, Bea," Jonathan admonished, "just because his tastes have degenerated since your friendship with him."

"Degenerated! I'm amazed he hasn't been arrested for child molesting!"

"Let's change to a more pleasant subject," Jonathan said. "Sisu Potter."

Matt groaned, and Bea stiffened in her chair. She spit an olive pit into her hand and held it in her fist.

"I'm worried about tonight. Miss Potter's classical training at the 'Look Ma I'm Actin' School of Drama' has never been more in evidence. I've been sitting on her all through runthroughs, but when we get distracted with the technical stuff, she may go completely berserk on me. And if Hilly ever gets his fourteen lines down, it'll be a miracle. I'm thinking of requesting a novena from Ted, if he can tear himself away from the shrine of Edwin Everett's granddaughter."

After the light dinner was served and eaten rapidly, Vivienne left the others gossiping over coffee. The sun was setting fast, falling in bands of gold between the long shadows across the road as Vivienne walked up the hill to the Carmel Playhouse. Wood fires were beginning to scent the dusk. She went up the path to the theatre and opened one of the double doors.

Stepping inside, she closed the door quickly behind her and tried to accustom her eyes to the dark. A pinprick of light came from the booth where Claudia was practicing cues. The stage lights began to come up slowly, as if illuminating a play for ghosts, first irradiating the luminous tape marking entrances and exits and spots for furniture, then spreading across the floor of the stage until the empty seats circling the small performing area were finally dimly visible.

It was barely light enough to find her way to the dressing rooms. She had the first small room and Bea the second, which was even smaller. Sisu, Edwinta and Helen Lawton shared the third, and Ted and Hilly were in the fourth.

Vivienne opened the door of her dressing room and reached for the switch to the light fixture that dangled overhead. She started and stepped back. Someone was in the darkened room. Her heart stopped beating for an instant and then pounded again in fear. She switched on the light. Edwinta was sitting on one of the two small chairs.

"I didn't mean to scare you," she said matter-of-factly, looking up at Vivienne. "I know you get here early. I have to ask you something."

Vivienne closed the door and sat in the chair in front of the small dressing table. She noticed that Edwinta was already dressed in her Act I costume and wearing stage makeup. Her eyes looked enormous behind the mascara and shadow.

"Could I get dressed in here from now on?" Edwinta asked. "It's really bad in there."

"In the third dressing room?"

"Yeah." Edwinta bit her lower lip, chewing off some of her lipstick. "The vibrations are really bad. Like the worst. Worse than Sandi."

"Sandi?" Vivienne asked.

"Thorson's latest 'Save the Children' reject. It's like—let's say I wouldn't eat one of her Girl Scout cookies. Just like now."

"Winta, situations like this abound in the theatre—"

"I don't care! This theatre's too small! I just can't be in there anymore. Tonight I put my makeup on at home and changed into my costume when I got here. I sit in the vault where I can be alone, but I can't really be alone there, either, because—" Edwinta stopped.

"Yes?"

"Ted's always talking to me."

"Winta, this is absolutely none of my business, but I've been worried about that."

"About Ted? No problem—we're just friends." Suddenly she gave a little chuckle. "It's really true. At first I thought he was a creep. He kept hanging around me like this kid at Carmel High."

"You seem to be standing him well enough now."

"What happened was one day he seemed really upset, and when I asked him what it was, he told me he was afraid he wasn't doing a good job in the show."

"Oh, really?" Clever approach, Vivienne thought.

"Yeah. He said he felt so intimidated by all the rest of you...of us, I mean. Like everyone was so experienced and professional, and he just wasn't coming up to the level. Naturally, I told him he was doing just fine. I mean, his role isn't exactly Hamlet. Not that I told him that, naturally."

"Naturally."

"After that we started being friends. It's not easy for me to talk about things. Ted listens like he really understands."

"What do you know about him?" Vivienne asked.

"Not much. Ted doesn't really talk about himself. Just about acting. How much he'd like to be a professional actor." Edwinta fixed Vivienne with her intent gaze. "That's what I'd like to be! I'll be out of high school in June. Then I could go to New York! I know Medora'll throw a fit, but once I want something, I always get it." She paused and her eyes flashed away from Vivienne. "It's just that before..." She looked at the floor and spoke, her voice catching, "I didn't know what I wanted, so I pretended I didn't want anything." She looked up again and gave Vivienne a half-smile. "Then you brought me the script and got me in the play."

There were noises of arrival out in the theatre, and Vivienne spoke quickly. "Go on. Move your things out of the third dressing room now, Winta, before anyone gets here. I'll tell Jonathan about it myself. I'll alternate between here and Bea's dressing room. We'll make adjustments so each of us can have some privacy."

"Thanks. I won't forget it." Edwinta flashed her a look of gratitude as she jumped out of the chair and started to leave.

"And Winta," Vivienne said as the girl was about to go out the door. "Remember, you got yourself into the show."

NINE

VIVIENNE SAT IN THE HOUSE later that evening, awaiting her
first entrance at the end of Act I and working on her needle-
point as the scenes progressed. Jonathan Patrick was also sitting out front, jotting notes on his ever-present notepad. The
first tech dress was going smoothly thus far, with lighting cues
and props causing few problems. The cast was also pulling together, with the exception of Sisu Potter. Attempting to com-
pensate for her lack of dialogue, Sisu was performing intricate
maneuvers with parts of her costume and whichever props she
could get her hands on. At the moment, she was standing up-
stage of Bea Brown and Ted Reid, who were gallantly attempting to play their scene as Sisu toyed with a rose she had plucked
from a prop vase. After a lengthy smelling of the artificial
flower, she was now pantomiming a count of the petals; her lips
moving slowly as she pronounced each number, like a semili-
terate attempting to read.

Jonathan sat next to Vivienne and put his head in his hands
for a few moments. Then he looked at the stage. The petal
count was up to fourteen. "Vivienne, I don't know what to do
about her. The spirit of St. Vitus walks the Playhouse!" He
grasped his notepad resolutely. "I've got to stop this."

He rose. "Excuse me, everyone. I know I promised to hold
notes till the end of the act, but there are some things that just
can't wait."

He moved toward the stage. "Sisu, please try to give *less*. I
know you're used to acting in larger houses, but remember, the
audience is sitting right on top of you here. Try not to use so
much facial expression. Or so much movement. Don't touch
anything. Keep your hands as still as you can. Remember, less
is more!"

For once Sisu stood still, holding the artificial flower in one
hand. "But, Jonathan, I was really *feeling* it. Doesn't that *read*
from where you are?"

"Sisu," Jonathan paused as if to steady himself. "I'm afraid not. Please trust me in this. Think of it as film acting. If you try to make your face completely expressionless, it will be more dramatic, believe me." He started to turn away, then turned back with an afterthought. "Remember when Garbo was in *Queen Christina*—that wonderful close-up on the prow of the ship—and her director told her, 'Think of nothing.' When you're on stage during these long dialogues between the other actors, remember that. *Think of nothing*."

Jonathan sat next to Vivienne again as Ted and a seething Bea continued their dialogue. He looked up at the stage. Sisu's face was a study in blankness.

"Look at her, Vivienne," he whispered. "She's thinking of nothing. She looks like one of the living dead. *Why* did I say that?"

"Jon, why don't you block her so she's upstage with her back to the audience? How about looking out the window?" Vivienne suggested.

"For three acts? Vivienne, right now this show would have more dramatic value if she stood onstage with a brown paper bag over her head!"

The rest of the cast was almost climbing the set with tension. Bea slammed her prop book on a table and stalked off, stage right. Sisu, slowly and blankly, made her exit, stage left. Edwinta shot onto the stage for her scene with Ted, which they finished in record time.

Preparing for her cue, Vivienne circled behind the railing near the front of the house to go backstage for her first entrance. She brushed past Bea, who was waiting just offstage near the entrance door and shaking with anger.

"I'm going to kill her!" Bea hissed at Vivienne. "She's going to have upped her last goddamned stage when I get through with her. I'm going to chop her hands off at the wrists!"

"Courage," Vivienne whispered, squeezing her arm.

Helen Lawton pressed past them carrying the luncheon props on a tray. Bea stepped in behind her and made her entrance. While Bea was onstage as Artemis directing Helen as the maid in the placement of the luncheon things, Vivienne walked along the backstage corridor, past the light booth and into the darkness of the vault to ready herself for her entrance. At the far end of the vault, Hilly was dimly visible listening for his entrance cue.

Vivienne heard Ted Reid's voice from the stage, speaking angrily. "I don't like it! I'll never like it!"

"We hope so, dear," Bea gave her line coolly. "No matter what she's done, our house will always be open to her. After all, she's still part of our family."

Then Hilly disappeared through the curtained entrance and was onstage.

She heard the scrape of chairs as the cast sat down to lunch. Her entrance came just after the toast was announced and drunk. She picked up the suitcase that was the prop for the homecoming of Persephone and walked through the dim vault area to the far door. She waited in the darkened entryway just out of sight of the absent audience, holding the suitcase tightly and listening to the dialogue from the stage.

She heard Hilly begin his line in sonorous tones. "A toast to those dear to us who are far away."

Then Edwinta dove-tailed in with her line, "To Persephone!"

There followed a few seconds of silence during which Vivienne knew the cast was drinking the toast. She took a deep breath to time her entrance, delaying it until the last possible moment.

Suddenly she heard a scream coming from the stage. That's not in the script, she thought, and balked for a second, haunted by the actor's nightmare of walking into the wrong play. Then she stepped out of the vault door onto the small ramp leading through the audience and saw Sisu Potter half-standing and half-sitting, with a napkin pressed to her mouth that was beginning to show a small streak of red.

The rest of the cast held still for a few horrible seconds—as if they were posing for an ancient photograph—before Sisu began wailing into the napkin.

Sisu took the cloth from her mouth. "The glass! Props!" she choked out. "Props did it!" Then she began to sob hysterically. Jonathan hurried to her and took her by the shoulders, leading her backstage to her dressing room. Hilly followed immediately behind them. All at once, Helen and Matt came out of the backstage area into the house. They both began apologizing.

"It's my fault, I should have checked the glasses," Helen said in a frightened voice.

"No, Helen, it's my fault." Matt interrupted her. "I'm supposed to be checking all the props. And the glasses *were* fine the last time I checked them."

"It's probably just a scratch," Ted said. "It could have happened to any of us. Let's don't worry until we know what happened."

Bea walked over to Vivienne, who was sitting by the vault entrance.

"Is there a doctor in the house?" she asked, sitting next to Vivienne. "It couldn't have happened to a nicer fellow thespian." She glowered at Vivienne. "And I just said I'd chop off her hands, so don't get any idea I chipped that glass."

"I know. You've always maintained you couldn't hurt a fly," Vivienne said, and fought down an inappropriate giggle. Then Bea started to laugh, and turned hers into a coughing fit as Vivienne clamped her lips together tightly and held on to the seat of her chair.

Across the theatre, Edwinta looked as though she had caught the infection and was also trying not to laugh, while Ted walked toward the front of the house, as if needing air. Matt and Helen were examining the glasses and china on the table, and Claudia finally emerged from the light booth, blinking her violet eyes under the bright stage lights.

Jonathan came back through the stage right door and walked toward Vivienne and Bea. He motioned for everyone to join them. When all of the company except Sisu and Hilly were sitting together near the vault, Jonathan began to speak.

"Thank all of you for your patience. I'm very sorry about this. Hilly is going to take Sisu home. She really has just suffered a scratch. He'll make sure she's fine and then come back. We'll proceed without them and run the show as best we can until Hilly rejoins us. This unfortunate little accident was no one's fault and no one should feel responsible. And I'm sure Sisu...when she calms down...will realize that. Other than this, the rehearsal's going very well, and I'd ask for a round of applause for Claudia and our backstage crew, except—" He looked over his shoulder toward the door leading to the dressing rooms as Sisu emerged from it, a handkerchief over her mouth and leaning as heavily on Hilly as if she had broken a leg. "I don't think this is quite the appropriate moment," Jon concluded quietly.

Except for the shuffling of feet, absolute silence reigned in the theatre as Sisu and Hilly made their protracted exit through the farthest front door of the Playhouse. Everyone flinched slightly as the door slammed shut behind the pair.

"Understudy!" Bea muttered, *sotto voce*.

"Shh . . . Bea!" Vivienne attempted to hush her.

"It's all an act," Bea said contemptuously. "I've never seen anyone so desperate for attention. She probably cut herself on purpose!"

"Let's go on with the second act," Jonathan said.

TEN

MATT WENT UP to the theatre early on opening night to do a last check of props and furniture. Claudia Kellog was already there, practicing light cues and checking the luminous tape marking furniture placement, entrances and exits. He hadn't seen much of Claudia in the last few days. The minister at her church was ill, and she had been dividing her time between the Playhouse and her church. In a way, it was a relief. The magical feeling he had about her at first had faded. She was a very pretty, very nice girl from Carmel, but try as he would he couldn't make her into a romantic heroine. There was no mystery about her as there was about Vivienne Montrose. Claudia didn't even like old movies.

Vivienne and Bea were coping with masses of flowers that had arrived at the theatre for them, almost crowding them out of their tiny dressing rooms. Matt put the overflow on the makeup counter near the light booth. The combination of the autumn and hothouse flower scents gave the passage between the light booth and the vault the smell of a funeral parlor.

Sisu and Hilly arrived, followed shortly by Edwinta who, for once, was not trailed by Ted Reid. The reason for this became evident when Ted, beautifully dressed as usual, appeared at the theatre doors with a handsome and equally well-dressed friend. Ted and the stranger were standing behind the railing at the front of the house when Matt approached them.

"Matt, I want you to meet Stephen Flanagan. Steve—Matt Ross, one of my good friends in Carmel." Ted turned to Matt. "Steve's come all the way from Texas to see the show this weekend. With side jaunts down the coast to Big Sur and San Simeon, of course."

"The coast is spectacular," Matt said. "Have you been here before?"

"Several years ago Ted and I were here with a group of... well, a group, and both of us fell in love with the place.

Ted's the lucky one who's gotten to live here, though. I keep plugging away in Texas.''

"House is opening, everyone," Jonathan said to the three men as he walked through the draped door to the backstage area.

Ted and Matt went backstage before the theatre doors were opened to the public. Matt went to his duties at the prop table—his territory. Wedged in a corner of the narrow corridor that ran past the dressing rooms to the small backstage restroom and the equally small ticket office, it was laden with china, crystal, silver and prop food for the onstage luncheon in Act I.

Claudia began to knock on dressing room doors, calling out the minutes before curtain.

As he was checking the props, Matt noticed an unpleasant odor coming from the corridor. He attributed it to Annie Watts, who had just emerged from the restroom and gone back into the box office to sell tickets for the show.

In the dim light, he saw Sisu Potter approaching him. She walked to the curtained door near the prop table and fumbled around with the cloth until she found an opening, then pressed one eye against it. She shut the curtain quickly and stepped back.

"Who's that gorgeous man?" Sisu was using her husky but penetrating stage whisper. "Matt, you look—sitting on one of the stools—wearing a tweed jacket.''

Matt opened the drape a crack and looked out into the audience behind the railed area. "That's some friend of Ted's.''

"Oh, great. Another goddamned priest. It's a goddamned convention!" Sisu stalked away to her dressing room in disgust.

Matt looked out again at the audience through the draped doorway. The house was packed and chattering. He didn't recognize a soul. Suddenly he felt a cold hand pressed against his neck.

"Caught ya lookin' out!" a voice growled next to him.

Matt turned, his heart skipping a beat. Beside him was a chuckling Bea Brown, in place for her entrance at the opening of the act.

"Whew!" Bea wrinkled her face up in distaste. "I forgot how horrible it smells back here! How do you stand it?"

"I don't know if I *am* standing it. This is just the first night. I don't know if I can take this for the whole run of the show."

Jonathan appeared next to them, whispered "One minute! Break a leg!" and hurried back along the corridor to the light booth.

"Let me look," Bea said. She peered through the curtain and jerked herself back. "Jesus, Matt—they're all out there! Everyone in Carmel! I didn't think I was gonna get nervous, and I'm sick! It's not just the smell. I'm shaking all over!"

Music began playing in the theatre, the lights darkened in the house, and Bea was gone. As the stage lights went up, Matt heard her voice from onstage, speaking her lines into a prop telephone, sounding just as cool and commanding as she had in rehearsals.

After Sisu and Ted made their entrances, Matt went to the light booth to watch the first act with Claudia and Jonathan. The act went smoothly. Sisu did a minimal amount of wiggling, and the rest of the cast was "on." First night nerves were working in favor of the show. Hilly even remembered his few lines prior to the toast.

There was no need for Matt to be at the prop table until intermission, so he got to see Vivienne's Act I entrance from the light booth. Matt, Jonathan and Claudia held their collective breaths as the toast was made and drunk without a mishap. They finally exhaled as Vivienne, carrying a suitcase, made her entrance down the ramp from the backstage costume vault. She was dressed entirely in black, and her blond hair shone under the stage lights.

"She *is* this role," Jonathan whispered. "Look at her. She could have been in prison, she could have been in a nunnery— she's from another world."

Claudia dimmed the stage lights as the act ended to loud applause. "One down!" Jonathan said.

Matt waited during the applause for the actors to find their way off the stage via the luminous tape markings. Then he hurried along the corridor toward the prop table, in the midst of the normal backstage sounds of whispering, groans of relief and dressing room doors thunking closed.

He tidied up the prop table during the first intermission. He could hear the babble of people who had gone outside for the lukewarm free coffee the Playhouse offered its patrons under the eaves in front of the theatre, but he couldn't make anything out. Since Annie was outside serving coffee, the smell had blessedly disappeared from the area near the prop table.

After the first intermission, the actors walked onstage in the dark and resumed their places. Act II was Vivienne's star turn. When her character was revealed to be the mother of the character played by Edwinta, the theatre was hushed except for a few rustles and sniffs.

"Everyone's crying!" Jon whispered to Claudia and Matt in the light booth. "Now we've got 'em!"

At the end of the scene, the lights dimmed on the embracing Vivienne and Edwinta to the loudest applause Matt had ever heard in the small theatre.

As the second intermission began, Matt left the light booth to change the props for Act III. He passed Hilly standing next to the overflow of flowers. The audience was still applauding.

"We're a hit! Listen to that. They love us out there!" Hilly said loudly.

Sisu emerged out of the darkness next to Hilly. "*Vivienne's* a good actress," she hissed, pointedly ignoring Edwinta's performance. "Vivienne could carry *anyone*."

Matt saw most of Act III from the booth. The entire cast was onstage throughout the act, which culminated in the confession of the real murderess, the character played by Bea. Matt tried to ignore Sisu, who was slowly removing an incredibly long hair from the bodice of her costume during Bea's big scene. Inspired to her best, Bea was riveting in the most outstanding performance Matt had ever seen her give. When the applause began after the final blackout, Jon embraced Claudia, who was clinging to levers of the light board, and slapped Matt on the back.

"Great job! Great job, both of you! We're a smash hit!"

The lights rose again on all the actors. They all bowed and smiled and blinked under the stage lights, and then took their individual bows. When the cast finally left the stage, wellwishers from the audience began pressing their way into both ends of the narrow corridor to the dressing rooms.

Dodging the onslaught, Matt made a quick exit from the light booth and walked through the vault and out the far doorway into the house. Champagne was about to be served onstage, and the cast was expected to take part in the celebration, which would occupy Vivienne and the others for at least half an hour.

Matt was to drive Vivienne's car to her house and make sure everything was ready for the party. He left the theatre with some of the departing audience and stepped out into the balmy night. Walking along the street in front of the theatre, he heard the noise of the celebrants growing fainter in the distance behind him. Soon most of them would be rehashing the show at the party at Vivienne's house. Matt hoped no blows would be exchanged.

ELEVEN

SMALL LIGHTS WERE GLOWING in the trees and along hidden pathways around Vivienne's house, transforming the grounds into a fairyland of enchanted glades and bowers. In the kitchen inside, the less enchanting work of heating pots of veal stew and an oven full of sourdough bread was occupying Pearl, one of Bea's Chinese servants. Blossom, another of the servants from Brown Hall, was outside tending to the large tables laden with salads in huge crystal bowls and giant silver trays of appetizers. Near the tables, a third servant, Chang, was setting up the bar.

Matt found everything taken care of and nothing left to do—even the dark green candles had already been lit and wafted their cypress-scented perfume through the house. He was sitting in Vivienne's living room looking at her portrait when he heard the first car pull up outside. The front door opened and Bea Brown charged through the doorway, slightly flushed from the opening night champagne. Vivienne was immediately behind Bea, her eyes wide in warning.

"Matt, you're here!" Bea rushed across the room. "You'll tell me. Viv couldn't see—she had her back to that bitch—but I *know* you saw her from the light booth. What was that bitch *doing* during my speech in Act Three?" Bea's face was flushed to a shade almost as pink as her ruffled dress, and she gripped a small pink purse in both hands. "I know she was trying to upstage me with some asinine gimmick, and no one has the guts to tell me just what the hell she was doing."

"Well, it wasn't all that noticeable. I mean, I decided not to watch Sisu, just look at you."

"*What* wasn't that noticeable?"

"The hair on her costume."

"The *hair* on her *costume*?" The pitch of Bea's voice climbed and her grip on her handbag tightened.

"During your speech, 'I did it for Father...' Sisu had...well, there seemed to be a hair on her costume. Sort of stuck to her dress. I say 'seemed to be' because no real hair could have been that long."

"How *long* would you say the hair *was*?" Bea asked, as slowly as if she were questioning a mental defective.

"About a foot long," Matt said quietly, wanting to fade into the woodwork.

"She was pulling a *foot-long* hair off her costume during my big speech? What was I saying when she was doing it?"

"You were saying the whole speech."

Bea's complexion had reddened to a deep rose. "That speech is ten minutes long! She must have been doing it in some kind of goddamned slow motion!"

"That's a good way of putting it."

"That bitch!" Bea hurled her bag onto a nearby chair. "She's not going to *live* through this weekend. I don't know *when* I'm gonna to get her or *how* I'm gonna to get her, but she's gonna wish she was never *born*!"

"Bea, I'm sorry," Vivienne said. "I know how upset you are and I wish I could help, but I have to change. People will be here any minute now."

Bea clung to the back of the overstuffed chair on which her handbag rested like an abandoned nosegay. "Go ahead, Viv. I have to calm down. Matt, I need a drink. Where's the bar?"

"It's right outside on the lawn," Matt said. "Your people are great. Everything looks perfect."

"Good. Lead me to the champagne," Bea commanded. Matt thought it probably wasn't the wisest idea, but he led Bea there anyway.

Bea was drinking champagne near the bar and Matt was next to her eating steak tartare on toast when they saw Ted Reid and his friend Steve cautiously making their way from the front of the house through the garden.

"Who's that man with Ted?" Bea whispered to Matt as the men drew nearer. "He's a knockout! I saw him after the show, but I didn't get to meet him."

"He's a friend of Ted's. I think he's a priest."

"Good! I need a challenge! Get me a refill, will you, Matt, and I'll get the introductions out of the way."

When Matt returned with Bea's glass, Ted, Steve and Bea were talking.

"You surprised me so much in the third act," Steve was saying to Bea. "You were the last person I would have guessed was the murderess. Your acting was so intense. Even though there were other things happening onstage, I couldn't take my eyes off you."

"Oh, thanks!" Bea's eyes shone at the praise. Despite the dim and wavering light, Matt could see Bea's skin glowing. "I just found out that a certain cast member was trying to up-stage me during my final speech. I felt something going on, so I really threw myself into it." Bea gave a sidelong but intense glance at Steve from Texas. "Sometimes I need a challenge," she said.

Matt took this as his cue to go back to the house. Coming into the living room, he found Vivienne greeting Medora and Edwinta Everett. Vivienne had changed into a blue velvet dress and was wearing her hair pulled back from her face in the style of her portrait. Medora stood at least a head taller than her daughter. A striking, dark-haired woman with the posture and figure of a ballerina, Medora was dressed in a trailing purple dress and wore her hair in a bun. Edwinta was wearing her usual white, flowing clothes and sandals that laced up her legs.

Medora was complimenting Vivienne in her resonant tones. "Marvellous performance, as usual, Vivienne. Lovely dress you're wearing, too." Medora looked away from Vivienne toward the portrait on the living room wall. "As near the color of the dress in Edwin's painting as life can imitate art. Royal blue always was your color." Medora just noticeably emphasized the word "royal."

"Thank you." Vivienne seemed to ignore the emphasis. "You must be very proud of Edwinta. This was really *her* night."

"Of course. Edwinta's always had an extraordinary talent. One can't fight heredity. But I think this was her most challenging role." Medora glanced at the front door. She looked edgy. "Is everyone else outside?"

"So far it's only Bea Brown and a couple of people I don't think you know. Everything's set up. You remember the way, don't you, Medora?"

"Yes. The back stairs." Medora walked toward the small circular stairway that led to the rear of the house. "I'll be outside," she said to Edwinta as she disappeared down the stairs.

"Baaaa," Edwinta made a low, bleating sound.

Matt and Vivienne looked at her in astonishment.

The girl's face was expressionless. "That was my line in my previous challenging role of 'The Lamb' in *The Little Star That Couldn't Find Its Way to Bethlehem*." With that, she turned and walked to the stairs.

Matt and Vivienne watched Edwinta's blond head disappear down the stairwell, then turned to each other, smiles spreading across their faces.

"That Edwinta—she's a pisser!" Matt said, and to his dismay, felt himself turn bright red. "Excuse my language."

To his surprise, instead of taking offense, Vivienne laughed. "Tonight everyone's going to be saying things they'll regret the next day," she said. "I have to admit that's one of the things I enjoy most about parties."

The next arrivals were Claudia Kellog and an entourage consisting of her mother, father, a sister, several brothers, a man who seemed to be an uncle and several friends. Matt had already met Claudia's mother and father. He exchanged greetings with them and with Claudia and was introduced to the Kellogs he hadn't met. The only one in the family who resembled Claudia was her mother, who was small and had the same violet eyes and heart-shaped face. The rest of the family were tall, strapping and blue-eyed. Vivienne greeted them all graciously and directed them outside to the refreshments.

"I'm so glad they got here early and there are so many of them. Neutralizing factors," she explained to Matt after they had gone.

"Neutralizing?"

"I'm hoping a crowd will reduce the tension between certain cast members, and still to arrive are Thorson Everett and his girlfriend, with the accent on *girl*. I spoke to Thorson briefly backstage, and he said they'd be here tonight. Edwinta and the girlfriend despise each other, and I doubt Medora is too comfortable with her either. I hope I can keep them apart."

"I'll do what I can to help," Matt volunteered.

"Matt, if you could, I'd be very grateful. Just keep Thorson and the girlfriend away from Medora and Edwinta. Get him talking about himself. It won't be hard. The flower of humility doesn't bloom in Thorson Everett's garden."

"I guess having a famous name like Everett must have spoiled him."

"You've hit closer to home than you can know, Matt."

"Oh? What's he like?"

"Garrulous, expansive and absolutely no sense of humor. People say he has a huge ego, but I'd describe him as a man with a lot to prove. He used to direct plays, and now he paints. After a fashion."

They heard noises and a knock outside. Vivienne walked to the door and opened it. On the step stood a stocky man of medium height, dressed in a worn leather flight jacket and dungarees. His fair, longish hair was streaked with silver. Behind him stood an almost emaciated teenage girl with plumb-straight, bleached-blond hair. She wore a skirt that stopped at the top of her thighs and an angry expression on her face.

"Thorson, I'm so glad you came by," Vivienne said to the man.

"Couldn't miss it," Thorson Everett replied, striding into the room, followed slowly by the bleached-blond girl. "Lovely house. Haven't been here in years." He looked at the portrait on the wall. "The portrait, of course."

Thorson walked to Vivienne and took her hand in both of his, looking searchingly into her eyes. "Vivienne, in all the chaos after the show, I couldn't tell you how moved I was by your beautiful performance. It inspired me to direct again. I forgot what an extraordinary actress you are. I'd love to direct you in a Williams play, or maybe Chekhov, except I couldn't get a soul in Carmel to come and see it." He dropped her hand. "It's one of the regrets of my life that I've never been able to direct Chekhov in Carmel. The locals can't really appreciate much beyond *Time Out for Ginger*, with *Mr. Roberts* thrown in as an evening of high drama. Ah, Vivienne, you'd be perfect for Chekhov! All that overbred, repressed emotion. Madame Ranevskaya in *The Cherry Orchard*. 'Goodbye, dear orchard,'" he quoted. "You'd have them sobbing in the aisles! If we could get anyone to come, that is. By the way, have you met Sandi?" he added, belatedly acknowledging the girl behind him.

"I don't believe so. It's a pleasure," Vivienne said.

"For some people," Sandi replied with a scowl.

"Sandi has the engaging directness of youth," said Thorson.

Vivienne's eyes flew to Matt for help. "Matt, I want to introduce you to Edwinta Everett's father and...uh...Sandi, his friend. Matt is a very gifted young writer. Matt, if you could show Thorson and Sandi outside where the other guests are, I think you both would have lots to talk about. Matt's a playwright as well as a novelist, you know," Vivienne concluded hastily to Thorson.

"Just follow me," Matt said, taking his cue. He led Thorson and the recalcitrant Sandi down the stairs toward the rear of the house and the garden, racking his brain for a subject of conversation.

"Vivienne's told me a lot about your father, Edwin Everett. He must have been a remarkable man," Matt said.

"Wrong thing to say," came the voice of the teenager from behind them.

"Well, it's interesting," Thorson said, as though he hadn't heard her. "People rave so much about my father, and of course he was a great painter. Part of history. Unquestionably 'A Great Man.' No one could equal him *in his style*—which was more the style of the nineteenth century than the twentieth. *My* work, however, goes so far beyond the nineteenth-century Romanticism my father was schooled in that the viewer can barely have a flash of recognition that *my* work, indeed, is the work of 'The Son of Edwin Everett.' I speak not only in the technical sense, but in the sense of a unique vision..."

Sheesh! thought Matt. When can I get rid of this guy? He's as big a jerk as everyone says—maybe bigger!

Thorson Everett continued his expostulation on his unique vision as he, Matt and a bored and angry-looking Sandi walked out into the garden.

Matt saw two groups on the lawn: Claudia Kellog, her family and friends were standing on one side, and near the bar Bea Brown, Ted Reid and Steve from Texas clustered, joined by Medora and Edwinta Everett. To Matt's horror, Thorson made for the second group, with Sandi trailing ungraciously behind him. Matt, hastily bringing up the rear, tasted the defeat of his plan to keep Thorson and his girlfriend away from Edwinta and Medora.

Thorson hailed the night's performers. "Beatrice, my dear, and my dear child Edwinta! Words can't express what I felt about your marvelous performances!"

"If I hear the word 'marvelous' one more time, I'm heading for the john," said Bea, not quite under her breath.

Sandi stopped behind Thorson and was glaring at Edwinta. The two blond teenagers looked daggers at each other across the group.

Thorson didn't miss a breath. "I was amazed at how moved I was by the whole experience. It inspired me to direct again. How I'd love to direct the three of you in *The Seagull*! Beatrice as the actress, Madame Arkadina. And if she could ever tear herself away from her Tiny Thespians, Medora as the mysterious, moody Masha." Thorson finally acknowledged his former wife, who was looking far more moody than mysterious.

"And, of course, my child Edwinta as Nina! I can hear Nina's heartrending speech in the last act . . ." Thorson closed his eyes and cleared his throat slightly. "'I am a seagull!'" he quoted passionately. He opened his eyes, which were tearing, brushed his silver hair back from his forehead with one hand and gave an audible sniff. "God! There wouldn't be a dry eye in the house! If anyone showed up, that is."

There was a dreadful silence while Thorson helped himself to a glass of champagne. "I want to make a toast. To my child Edwinta's brilliant performance tonight!" He raised his glass with a broad gesture, and those in the group who held glasses raised theirs, some more eagerly than others.

Bea peremptorily bobbed her glass in the air and moved toward Thorson's girlfriend for a closer examination. "I don't believe we've been introduced. I'm Mrs. Brown. And what is your very young name?"

"Sandi," said the girl, tearing her gaze away from Edwinta, at whom she was staring with growing hostility.

"What an *unusual* name!" Bea boomed. The group had fallen silent, and the champagne Bea had consumed was increasing the decibels of her voice with every phrase. "Do you spell that with an 'e' at the end, or a 'y'? Or, no—don't tell me—let me guess! An 'i'?"

"That's right," Sandi said. "I changed it."

"Bea, you played Auntie Mame three years ago, didn't you? I suppose you never really get a role like that out of your system." Jonathan Patrick had made one of his surprising appearances from the darkness of the low trees beyond the bar. Helen Lawton and several of the board members of the Playhouse were following him, and bearing down on the refreshment tables as rapidly as her bulk would allow was Annie Watts.

"Helen and I finally got the theatre shut down." Jon gave a quick glance around. "Everyone seems to be here. Or almost everyone. Thorson, I haven't seen you in years."

"Didn't see you after the show, Jon."

"That's because Jonathan hides in the light booth until all the well-wishers depart. Especially other directors," Ted joked.

Thorson was startled into noticing Ted and Steve. "The two of you look familiar. One of you was in the play tonight, weren't you?"

"Yes," said Steve from Texas. "*He* was."

Thorson stared at the two men. "You bear a remarkable resemblance to one another. Has anyone else ever commented on it? Are you brothers?"

"In a manner of speaking," said Ted.

Jonathan glanced over at the backside of Annie Watts, who was not only making inroads on the refreshment table but blocking it from view. "If you'll excuse me, I'm famished, and I'm going to get over to the food while there's still some left," he said.

"Would you like something to eat?" Matt asked Sandi, hoping to remove her from the group.

"Is there any fruit over there? I'm a fruitarian."

"Let's go over and look. I didn't notice any fruit, but then I wasn't looking very hard. Or there may be some in the kitchen. But let's try the tables first."

Matt was delighted to get Sandi to the refreshment tables. He left her homing in on the fruit garnished on one of the trays.

He saw Vivienne and Hilly Lawton coming out of the house onto the lawn and went over to meet them. Hilly looked more genial than ever and Vivienne seemed ill at ease.

"Is everyone here?" Matt asked.

"Sisu's in the ladies' room," Hilly said. "If you'll excuse me, Vivienne, I'm starving. And I see the Kellog family over there by the food. My church, you know."

As Hilly walked away, Vivienne whispered to Matt, "They've been to a bar or two. At least Sisu has—she's the worse for wear already."

"So's Bea Brown. And Medora Everett's putting away a lot of champagne. There's just no way to keep people apart. I tried with Thorson's girlfriend, but it won't last. Once she eats all the fruit slices off the trays she'll be back with Thorson. And he's sticking near 'his child, Edwinta.' Talking about all the plays he wants to direct her in. Medora looks furious. By the way, do you have any fruit in the kitchen? Sandi's a fruitarian. Maybe we could get her into the kitchen for a while. After we lock Sisu in the bathroom."

Vivienne seemed possessed by a hostessly fervor. "Let me find Blossom and have her bring something out for the girl." She moved away from Matt toward the refreshment tables.

"Who's that *interesting* man with the silver hair?" A loud stage whisper in Matt's ear made him flinch. Sisu Potter put a hand on his arm and leaned on him heavily. "The one next to Little Miss Everett, I mean."

"That? That's Thorson. Thorson Everett."

"The painter? Isn't he the one who's dead?"

"That was Edwin Everett, his father. This one is the son—Thorson. He's Edwinta's father."

"Ugh!" Sisu staggered slightly. "He's the one who likes teenage girls. Don't introduce me. I'm going to find Hilly and those boring people from his church." She walked unsteadily away.

Jonathan was advancing on Matt with a plate of food. A look of mirth was on his face. "Cast parties are great material, eh, Matt? How are you enjoying the legendary Thorson?"

"I was warned, but nothing prepared me. He actually refers to himself in upper and lower case—'The Son of Edwin Everett'—like a horror movie!"

"All too fitting, since he came with the teenage bride of Frankenstein."

"Her name is Sandi. She's a fruitarian."

"Only in California could someone with no last name eat nothing but fruit. Come to think of it, over by the refreshment table I saw her trying to wrestle a lemon wedge away from Annie Watts."

"Jon...Annie Watts! Backstage tonight before the show, the smell near the prop table was terrible! You must have noticed it when you came by."

"If you'll recall, I didn't linger," Jonathan said. "It's not that bad, normally. Annie gets opening night nerves."

"Opening night nerves! She works in the box office!"

"What can I say?" Jonathan looked away. "She's a Playhouse fixture. Besides, she nannies for Mrs. Whetstone on the Board."

"Nannies!" Matt was horrified. "Someone would let Annie Watts near *children*?"

"Matt, it's Annie Watts." Vivienne was by his side with the latest party problem. "She asked me to have her steak tartare *fried*! I told her that's simply impossible. Then she asked me if she could go in the kitchen and do it herself?"

"Vivienne, don't let Annie in your house!" Matt was almost shouting.

"I told her that's the way you *eat* steak tartare—raw, with pepper and capers and lemon juice. Oh, that reminds me! I have to tell Blossom to put out more lemon wedges. Thorson's girlfriend ate them all!" With a look of distraction, Vivienne moved off into the crowd again.

Jonathan, chewing, swallowed quickly. "Matt, are we really here, or are we dreaming all this?"

"Look out, here comes my newfound teenage friend again," Matt said. Sandi was approaching, holding a lemon wedge and smirking.

"I think Claudia is more suitable for you," Jonathan commented.

"She's actually *smiling*." Matt said. "I hope nothing's happened to Edwinta."

If cows were rail thin and chewed on lemons, Matt thought, Sandi would look exactly like a contented bovine.

"I guess you don't like someone too much if you want her to be in a show about some guy who plays with himself," Sandi announced happily to the two men.

"Masturbation?" Jonathan asked wonderingly. "What an odd topic! There've been a lot of pretty shocking plays on Broadway lately, but I haven't heard of one about masturbation."

"That's right. Thor was talking about it. To *her*." Sandi made a face of disgust. "You know, about *her* being in it. But they couldn't do it in Carmel because it was about some guy named Ebson. He builds houses and he falls out of one at the end."

Matt and Jonathan looked at each other in disbelief.

"Ibsen," Matt said to Jonathan.

"*The Master Builder*," Jonathan said to Matt.

"I'm going to have a drink," Matt said. "People can take care of themselves. I'm going to forget about trying to keep them apart. Let them do their worst! And I'm going to talk to Claudia Kellog. *She's* sane."

TWELVE

MATT HAD DREADED talking to Claudia recently. He was embarrassed to have pursued her at first, then pulled back after he got to know her. It seemed that way with everything in his life: his imagination romanticized a person or a situation, and then reality set in and so did disappointment. Claudia hadn't turned out to be the mysterious, romantic creature her violet eyes and shy demeanor first led him to expect. Tonight, however, surrounded by the mild insanity of the party, he was drawn to her uncomplicated, sweet normality.

He walked towards the part of the lawn where she stood talking with her family and friends.

When Claudia saw him approach, she looked away instantly and then looked back again. She gave him a brief, shy smile and walked over to meet him.

"I thought you might like to take a walk down through the grounds to the lagoon," he said. "It's still clear enough so we can see the water in the moonlight."

Claudia seemed surprised by the invitation. "I'd enjoy that. It's such a beautiful night, and the moon is almost full."

As they navigated their way through the shrubbery down the slope of the garden, they didn't speak. They neared the lights of Matt's cottage. He had left all the lamps on inside to illuminate that area of the grounds, and under one of the trees nearby, they could see Bea Brown and Ted's friend Steve talking. Matt and Claudia walked past the cottage toward the lagoon. Near the edge of the grounds, they reached a wooden bench lit by one small stone lantern.

"Let's stop here," Claudia said. "I don't want to get too far away from everyone or they might worry."

Irritation was mixed with Matt's disappointment. He should have known better. There was no romance about Claudia and certainly no mystery. "I just thought you might like to see the lagoon at night," he said. "It's not that much farther."

"If you don't mind, I'd rather stay here."

Matt did mind, but he assented, trying to be a gentleman.

Claudia sat on the bench, and he sat next to her.

She turned to him. Even with the lantern light and the moon's illumination, her face was darkened, a shape only.

"Matt, I was surprised when you asked me to walk with you. I know you haven't wanted to talk to me lately. I don't think it's anything I did."

Matt didn't know how to respond. She was right. "It *isn't* anything you did..."

"I think at first you thought you liked me a lot more than you did after you got to know me. If that's true, I want you to know that I'm not angry at you. I know you've been feeling awkward ever since."

In thirty seconds Matt realized Claudia was much braver than he was. "You're right. I *have* been feeling awkward. I didn't know how to explain it to you. I still don't."

"If you could try, I'd like to know." Claudia's voice was soft, almost faint.

"I guess I've always been questing. I'm always looking for something more. For me to get involved with a woman, it has to be *right*. I don't know how to explain it to you, Claudia. You're so pretty and such a lovely person."

Claudia turned away.

"I mean it. It's just that for me, I have to have the feeling that the woman is the only right one for me."

Claudia's quiet voice stopped him. "Ted Reid says you're in love with Vivienne Montrose."

"That's crazy! She's twice as old as I am!" Matt was angry and embarrassed. "That's Ted! He can't keep himself out of other people's lives. Vivienne is—she's an idol of mine—she always has been. But it's crazy to say...I'm sorry, Claudia, I'm not angry at you. It's Ted." Matt was silent for a minute. He didn't want to hear the answer, but he wouldn't be able to resist asking. "What else did he say about me?"

Claudia swallowed. "He said he understood you because you and he were alike. I forget his exact words. I was upset by what he was saying, and I don't remember some of it. He said you would always have...have idols, not real loves. That you and he were alike in that way, but for different reasons." She paused. "That's all I remember."

Matt took a deep breath. He felt sick to his stomach. "I'm going back to the party, Claudia. Do you want to come?"

"I'm going to stay here for a few minutes. I'll be along soon." She turned away from him.

Matt left Claudia sitting on the bench in the moonlight, looking out toward the hills above the lagoon.

He didn't meet anyone on his way back, but he heard voices coming from various directions. He wanted to do some physical damage to Ted, but he thought it was probably a sin to hit a priest, and worse, it would spoil Vivienne's party.

He saw Vivienne across the lawn and made his way over to her.

"I'm back," he said to her. "What did I miss?"

"Matt, do you feel well?" she asked. "You don't *look* well."

"I'm fine. How's the party going?"

"There's a lull right now. Fortunately, Bea seems to have gotten quite interested in talking to that handsome friend of Ted's, so I don't think we have to worry about the foot-long hair, at least not for the moment."

"Steve is a priest."

"Oh!" Vivienne stared at him. "Oh, really? Well, then it all makes perfect sense, doesn't it?"

"It does?"

"Well, you know Bea." Vivienne hesitated. "I mean, she's so outgoing and enjoys new people so much. And if he's a priest, then it's all quite safe. I mean . . . limited."

"Like Ted Reid?"

Vivienne took Matt's arm. "Things could be much worse. Let's walk over to the bar. I want to make a quiet check on Thorson Everett. He's over there talking to some of the board members, and I think he must be on his twentieth glass of champagne." She glanced conspiratorially at Matt and squeezed his arm. "And please—no jokes about Thorson's finally being out of the 'teens."

Thorson Everett's champagne glass had found a permanent resting place near his elbow on one end of the bar, where it conveniently awaited Chang's frequent refillings. Standing next to him was Sandi, looking completely bored and chewing on a lime wedge. The small, rather frazzled-looking group around Thorson was necessarily silent as he continued what seemed to be a never-ending discourse centering on none other than Thorson Everett.

"Vivienne, come over here!" Thorson called out. "I was just recalling our wonderful production of *The Bad Seed*. You were marvelous, and Edwinta was truly brilliant. My own child, and she frightened me to death! What a pity she had to get involved with those dreadful Tiny Thespians of Medora's. That would put anyone off acting."

Behind Thorson and within earshot, Medora Everett approached the bar, empty champagne glass in hand.

Thorson took a swallow from his newly filled glass. "I'm delighted your group has gotten her back on the boards again, Vivienne. She's a natural. All of Medora's talent and more. I'm torn between wanting to direct her as Hilda in *The Master Builder*, or as Juliet. But we couldn't get a soul to come and see *The Master Builder*, and I have doubts about her rightness for Juliet. She's the perfect age, but there's a hardness about her. She's like her mother. There's more of a Lady Macbeth there than a Juliet..." Thorson's discourse ended in a sputter as Medora Everett, after placing her empty glass on the bar, picked up Thorson's full one and dumped its contents over Thorson's head.

"You're a joke, Thorson!" Medora said in her stentorian voice. "And tragically, you make a joke of the Everett name!"

Thorson seemed to be in shock. Champagne dripped down his face onto his leather jacket.

"You'll never direct Edwinta as Juliet or in any other role. You're all talk and no action." Medora threw a scathing glance at Sandi, who looked frozen, a wedge of lime in her mouth. "As anyone but a halfwit barely out of puberty can recognize." Medora looked back at her former husband, who was still staring at her in wet disbelief. "It really is a shame you gave up directing, Thorson. It's the *only* thing you ever did well. The rest of your life is a farce. Using Edwin Everett's paints and brushes doesn't make you a painter, any more than your moronic teenage tramps make you a man!"

Medora strode to Vivienne and took her arm, pulling her away from the stunned group of bystanders, and speaking to her in a slightly lower voice. "Vivienne, I'm leaving. I didn't realize how much it irritates me to be around him and that little lemon-sucking slut. And you don't need to look so shocked. I only did what everyone here would like to have done!"

Vivienne was visibly shaken and trying to recover her demeanor. "Medora... Why don't you let me see you to your car?"

"Where's Edwinta?" Medora demanded.

Vivienne's eyes flew around the bar area. "I don't know. I haven't seen her in some time."

"I suppose she can always walk home, or get a ride with that priest."

To the relief of the group around them, Vivienne and Medora started across the lawn toward the house. Chang began blotting up the champagne from Thorson's jacket. Those people near Thorson were unobtrusively drifting away, following the example of Thorson's teenage companion, who had vanished, lime and all.

Matt saw Jonathan Patrick standing near the refreshment tables and hastily made his way over to him.

Jonathan was obviously enjoying himself. "Gee, Matt, what do you think? Maybe Thorson and Medora'll get back together again!"

Matt looked at Jonathan in wonder.

"Sorry!" Jon said. "Bad taste! I really must try to take these things seriously. You realize this has *made* Vivienne's party. People will be talking about this for years."

"Jon, did you have any idea this was going to happen?"

"No. I'm just as surprised and titillated as everyone else. I've always found Thorson Everett an irritating boor, but this is the first time I've ever felt sorry for the poor bastard. Marriage to Medora must have been a hard row to hoe, if you'll pardon the expression."

"Have either of you seen Claudia?"

Matt and Jonathan turned to find Claudia's mother standing next to them.

"We haven't seen her since she went off with you, Matt," she said. "We're getting ready to leave now, and ..."

"I'll find her," Matt said, his heart sinking. He felt sick again. Claudia was probably still sitting on the bench in the dark, and he'd forgotten all about her. He started down the hill toward the cottage. The moon had gone behind a cloud, and it was much harder to find the way.

He started in fright as he saw a ghostly, white-clad figure with shimmering hair emerge from a dark clump of trees.

"Matt, stop!" The voice was Edwinta Everett's.

Matt realized he was almost running down the slope. He came to a halt. "Have you seen Claudia Kellog?" he called out.

"No. Have you seen Ted?"

"No. Not since the beginning of the party." He began to walk toward Edwinta.

"I've gotta find him." The girl's voice sounded high and very young. "I've gotta get out of here. Everything's been horrible. My mother and father had a fight, and my mother split. Ted said he and that creepy friend of his would give me a ride home if I needed it, and now I need it."

"Have you been down to the cottage?"

"No."

"I'm going down there." He took Edwinta's arm. She was shivering, and the sleeve of her white dress was damp. "You go back and find Vivienne. It's crazy for you to be out here alone in the dark. If I see Ted, I'll tell him you're looking for him."

Matt left the girl and continued on his way down the slope. Ahead of him were the lights of his cottage, but now the area around it was deserted. Bea and Steve from Texas were gone. The bench where he had left Claudia stood unoccupied, the small lantern still glowing near it. The fog had begun to come in across the lagoon, and the night sky had darkened. Matt opened the door of the cottage. No one was inside. He went back up the slope. It was eerily quiet, except for the infrequent, distant sound of voices coming from the direction of the party.

When he neared the house again, he saw Claudia's mother waiting for him. Claudia wasn't with her. Again, his heart sank.

Claudia's mother hailed him. "Matt, I waited to tell you. Vivienne said she saw Claudia starting to walk home. Claudia told her she needed the walk and the fresh air, and Vivienne said she told her to let us know she was going home. It's so strange she would leave that way, without telling us! That's so unlike

Claudia. Anyway, I wanted to make sure you knew before we left. You were so kind to go looking for her."

Matt felt as though a huge weight lay in the bottom of his stomach. "Mrs. Kellog, I feel terrible about this. I shouldn't have left Claudia alone down there. Please tell her I'll call her tomorrow. Can I walk you up to your car?"

Claudia's mother looked at him thoughtfully. He was reminded of Claudia's gaze. "Thank you, but I'll be fine," she said. "I'll tell Claudia you'll call." She turned and walked across the lawn.

Matt scouted the area, looking for Vivienne. Jonathan was at the bar with Helen Lawton, a few stalwart board members and Steve from Texas. Annie Watts was eating at the refreshment tables. There was no sign of anyone else.

He walked toward the house looking for Vivienne or Ted. He saw Bea, who seemed to be on her way back to the party. Bea's face was very pale, as though she'd removed all her makeup.

"Oh, Matt! What have I missed? I had to go take some aspirin and wash up. Is the party winding down? I can't go home till the bitter end, unfortunately. Where's Viv?"

"I was just going to look for her. Did you see the fight between Thorson and Medora?"

"I missed a fight? I wondered why everyone was milling around. I wasn't very... I was just heading right for the house and the aspirin, and I didn't pay much attention. God! Viv must be in a state of shock!"

Matt saw Hilly approaching them. "Hilly, have you seen Vivienne?"

Hilly looked ill and shaky. "No. I've been inside. Not feeling too well. Not used to champagne, I guess. Where's Sisu?"

Bea stiffened. "How would I know? The only reason I'd keep tabs on her is so I could stay away from her," she said huffily and quickly moved away.

Hilly gave a little groan. "I'm going to get something to settle my stomach and wait for her to turn up."

"I haven't seen Ted in a while. Edwinta was looking for him. Maybe they're together—Ted and Sisu, I mean."

"Probably," Hilly said, starting to move away. "Tell her I'm at the refreshment tables."

Matt found Vivienne talking to Ted in front of the house. Unlike most of the guests, Ted looked cheerful and refreshed.

"How's the party going, Matt? Vivienne tells me there was a little drama."

Ted's casual attitude irritated Matt. "The little drama was between Edwinta's mother and father, and I think she saw it. She's been looking for you. When I saw her, she was pretty upset."

"Too bad I missed the fracas. As I was just telling Vivienne, I went for a long walk on Carmel Beach. A lot has been on my mind lately, and—"

Vivienne interrupted Ted's ruminations. "Where did you see Edwinta, Matt? I think we ought to find her and make sure she gets home safely."

"I saw her down near the cottage about half an hour ago, maybe longer," Matt said.

"Maybe she went home on her own," Ted said, looking uncomfortable.

"She was looking for you, Ted. It seemed to be very important to her that she find you."

"Ted, there you are!" Hilly shouted. He was coming across the lawn toward them. "Where's Sisu?"

"I haven't seen her all evening, Hilly. Maybe she and Bea Brown are off slugging it out in the woods somewhere."

"Bea's at the bar with Helen and your friend Steve."

"We need to find Edwinta," Vivienne said.

"Don't worry, Vivienne. We'll divide up and look for both of them," Hilly said.

"You and Ted cover the grounds up here, and I'll go down to the cottage again," Matt said.

As if in a recurrent bad dream, Matt went down the slope. The garden around his cottage was still deserted. He opened the door. It was warm and comfortable inside, and he wanted to stay there, curled in the rumpled leather armchair next to his desk. Reluctantly, he shut the door and began to search the grounds outside. When he returned to the party, he found Hilly and Ted waiting for him, apparently already finished with their search. Neither Sisu nor Edwinta was in sight.

"Sisu's car's gone. Stupid of me not to have thought of looking there first." Hilly seemed to have recovered from the champagne and was holding a cup of coffee. "You know how she is—she might have gotten it in her head Bea would go after her for that upstaging she did in the last scene. She's a little scared of Bea, for some reason." He sighed, bemused. "It's hard to figure Sisu. She's like a little girl. Has to be the center of attention and can't face the music if someone's nose gets out of joint about it. No problem for me getting home, though. I'll catch a ride with someone. Maybe Jon can drop me off after he takes Helen home."

Hilly seemed almost as worried about Sisu's early departure as Ted was about Edwinta's disappearance, Matt thought. And he couldn't feel superior to either of them, because he'd treated Claudia in the same thoughtless way.

The remaining party guests were grouping around them as Vivienne approached from the house. She looked frightened. "I called Medora's number," she said as she reached them. "No one is answering the telephone. I know it's awfully late, but it seems one of them might answer."

"I speak as the voice of reason crying aloud in the wilderness—or something like that," Jonathan said. He took Vivienne's arm reassuringly. "It's time for all of us to thank our hostess for a lovely and truly memorable evening, and bid farewell till we all meet again—at the Carmel Playhouse, one half hour before curtain tomorrow night."

THIRTEEN

VIVIENNE AWOKE AT SIX the next morning after a restless sleep haunted by frightening dreams. The clash between Medora and Thorson Everett, a story to dine out on for most of the guests, had shaken her deeply. The unruly emotions of others had an unusual power to shock and disturb her, since she kept her own so carefully at bay. She was still worried about Edwinta, but it was too early to call Medora's house to reassure herself the girl was safely home.

MacGuffin was ready for his morning walk on the beach. Neither the fog, which moved in during the first hours of the morning, nor the walk through her trampled garden did much to cheer her, although MacGuffin jumped and ran happily, as if it were a sunny day.

The lagoon beach was a long, rising curve of sand fronting the place where the Carmel River met the sea. Except in the rainy season when it opened to pour the flooded waters of the river into the Pacific Ocean, the lagoon was a wide, shallow lake banked by hills on one side and edged on its other sides by marshes and sand. During the winter rains, trunks and branches of trees would wash down the river and out to sea; the tides brought the wood back again, drained of sap and filled with sea salt. From twigs to logs the size of telephone poles, the driftwood washed up on the lagoon beach to the delight of everyone in Carmel who had a fireplace and willing arms to carry it home.

More birds than usual were circling above the lagoon that lay dark and still beneath them. MacGuffin ran to the water's edge to get one of the thousands of driftwood pieces. He carried one to Vivienne and she threw it as far as she could, toward the reeds on the marshy side of the water. MacGuffin disappeared behind some of the reedy undergrowth and came back without the stick, his head thrown back and barking furiously. Vivienne picked up another piece of driftwood and threw it for him, but MacGuffin refused to yield his ground near the reeds where he stood shaking his tail and barking.

Vivienne walked over to him, treading on the crackling driftwood branches near the edge of the water. When she reached the dog, she had a glimpse of something pale behind a clump of reeds. Carefully picking her way through the reeds and driftwood, she rounded a jagged edge of the lagoon shore. Lying face down—half on the bank and half in the water—was the body of a blond woman in a white dress.

Vivienne felt her heart pounding in her throat as she tried to get her breath. A cry escaped her, and she began to run. She stopped next to the body and stood, nauseated and shaking, with her hands over her mouth. The tides had draped the muddy, bloated corpse onto the lagoon's edge like a piece of driftwood. The face was buried in the wet reeds, and of the head, only the blond hair, filthy and matted, was visible. At the same instant that Vivienne realized it was not a young girl's body, she saw a sapphire ring glittering on the hand of the limp right arm.

She turned and ran—along the beach, across the street, and through the grounds of her house to Matt's cottage. Gasping for breath, she knocked on the door.

There was no answering sound inside the cottage. She knocked again, louder, then over and over with both hands. The door was finally opened by Matt, who was still in pajamas and looked half asleep.

"Vivienne! What's wrong?"

She couldn't get her breath to speak. Just then, MacGuffin caught up with her and dashed into the cottage. Matt led Vivienne inside and forced her to sit in the big leather armchair. MacGuffin, panting, sat on the floor next to the chair. Vivienne didn't realize how bad she must look until she saw Matt's worried face.

"Vivienne, what happened? You're shaking all over! I don't have any coffee. Here, take this." He took a plaid lap robe from the back of the chair and tucked it around her.

"I'll be fine." Vivienne was shivering. "I have to call the police. I found—oh, Matt!" The vision of it flashed across her mind and she closed and opened her eyes to remove it. "There's a body in the lagoon. I think it's Sisu Potter. I couldn't see the face. But the hand has the same ring. And the clothes are what she was wearing last night. I think so, anyway. They're so wet and muddy it was hard to tell."

"Vivienne, I'm taking you over to the house so you can lie down. I'll call the police from there."

"But I'll have to go back. To identify the body." She stood up. "I found it."

"No," Matt said. "I'll go. If it's Sisu Potter, or anyone we both know, I can identify it."

Matt wrapped the blanket more tightly around Vivienne's shoulders and led her to the door. They walked up the slope and through the garden, across the trampled lawn and into the house, followed by the dog. Vivienne was still shaking. Matt took her up the stairs to the living room and pulled the blanket over her after she lay down on the sofa near the fireplace.

"There's coffee in the kitchen, Matt. Please help yourself."

Matt smiled at her, his face still anxious. "You don't need to be a hostess today." He disappeared into the kitchen and returned with a steaming mug. He went to the sideboard and added a dollop of brandy from a crystal decanter. He gave the mug to Vivienne and watched as she took a sip.

"Now I'll call the police. Don't move. And drink some more of that."

He walked back to the kitchen, and Vivienne heard his voice on the telephone. The words were indistinguishable. She closed her eyes. The image of the drowned body returned, and she opened her eyes quickly.

"I'm going down there now to meet the police," Matt said, back in the room again.

"I can go with you. I'm fine now." Vivienne sat up and swung her legs to the floor.

"No, please don't get up! It's damp and cold down by the lagoon, and you're still shivering. Just lie down again and rest. If I have to bring the police back here to talk to you, I will. But promise me you'll stay here."

"I promise." Vivienne took a deep breath. "I'll stay. I really don't want to look at it again. I'd rather be a coward and stay here."

Vivienne could hear Matt descending the back stairs as she stretched out on the sofa again and closed her eyes. This time, no image came.

THE SOUND OF A CAR outside awoke her. As she roused herself, she realized she must have been asleep for some time.

She sat up on the sofa as the front door opened. Matt Ross came in, followed by one of the previous night's party guests.

"You're Claudia's uncle!" She recognized the tall man standing behind Matt.

"I'm also the Chief of Police." The man was smiling down at her. "I'm Cortland Himber, Miss Montrose."

"Of course!" She straightened. "Forgive me. I must have heard your name last night. You looked familiar to me then, but I had no idea you were a policeman. I've lived in Carmel for twenty years, but I've never had anything to do with the police. Forgive me, I know I'm being incoherent, but I've just had a shock."

"A bad one," Cortland Himber said. "I need to ask you a few questions. I can do it now or later. Do you feel up to talking?"

"I don't think she should be talking to anyone right now," Matt said. "I think she should rest."

Vivienne was touched by Matt's protectiveness.

"Matt, thank you, but I can talk to Mr. Himber now. Or is it Chief Himber?"

"You can call me anything you like. Mr. Himber is fine." He turned to Matt. "I'd like to speak to Miss Montrose in private."

"Oh!" Matt did not seem pleased. He turned to Vivienne. "I'll be down at the cottage if you need me."

The police chief sat in a chair next to the sofa and faced Vivienne. He was a big man with thick, closely cut gray hair and sparkling blue eyes set in an intelligent face. He was wearing a sweater and slacks, not a police uniform. He looked at her intently for a few seconds before he spoke.

"How did it happen?"

Vivienne was startled. "What an odd question! I don't know how it happened. I only found her body. I wasn't there when she drowned!"

She felt herself redden as he observed her reply.

"Preliminary investigation," Himber said, and smiled at her disarmingly. "Get the subject off guard."

Vivienne looked away, confused. She didn't know what to make of this man.

"I should have gone back down there with Matt," she began. "I could have explained it to you then."

"You did just fine. I can see it was a shock for you."

She looked back at him. He was watching her sympathetically.

"It was," she said. "There were two guests missing from the party last night, and at first, when I saw the body, I thought it was a girl in our cast. Well, you must know—you saw the play."

"Yes."

"I thought it was Edwinta Everett."

"Why?"

"The white dress, really, and her vanishing like that. It was just a feeling. Then I could see it wasn't Edwinta. It was still horrifying, of course, but—"

"But you were relieved?"

"Yes. I didn't much care for Sisu Potter. I don't think many people did." Vivienne caught herself. That wasn't the right thing to say under the circumstances. "You must understand—that doesn't mean I wanted her to drown."

"I'm sure it doesn't. Tell me, I'm curious—after you saw the body wasn't that of Edwinta Everett, did you immediately recognize it as Sisu Potter's?"

Vivienne thought for a second. "Yes. That ring drew my eye. A sapphire ring. After I saw it, I guessed the body was Sisu's, but I didn't examine it closely."

"Why not?"

Vivienne felt herself shudder. "Looking at it made me ill."

"You didn't like Sisu Potter?"

"No one really did. To varying degrees, she antagonized almost everyone. Except Hilly Lawton, of course, and he—oh, no! Someone must tell him! They were very close, he and Sisu. In fact, they were almost going together, as they say."

"We'll make sure he's told."

"How awful for him! I dread seeing him tonight!" Vivienne froze with an awful realization. "The show can't go on tonight, can it? I'm sorry, that's such a trivial thing to say after there's been a death, but . . ." She stopped.

"The show can go on if you have an understudy for Sisu Potter."

Vivienne thought of Bea saying, "Understudy!" as Sisu left the theatre on the night of the cracked wine goblet. She almost started to mention the incident but thought better of it. "No, we don't have understudies," she said quietly.

Chief Himber watched her silently for a moment. "When did Sisu Potter leave the party?"

"I don't know. No one knew. She and Hilly arrived later than most of the guests. They were both a little under the weather."

"They'd been drinking?"

"I think they'd been to a bar after the champagne at the theatre. Sisu, especially, looked as if she'd drunk too much. Then there was . . . a great deal to attend to. I don't recall seeing her again. Hilly came looking for her, and no one knew where she was, so the men went to search for her and Edwinta. Then we realized Sisu's car was gone, so everyone assumed she'd just gone home on her own. She was that kind of person. Temperamental, prone to stalking off in a rage, except . . ." Vivienne trailed off, thinking.

"Except?"

"Come to think of it, Sisu was the kind of person who would stalk off in a rage only if everyone could see it. She had to have an audience. Otherwise, there would be no point; she wouldn't enjoy it."

"I got that impression from her performance. The upstaging, the posing, all of that."

"Yes, exactly! It would have been obvious to someone in the audience. We were almost used to it. So you can see how it doesn't make sense that she would leave without attracting attention to herself. Only none of us thought of it that way at the time."

"What about Edwinta Everett? Did anyone check to see if her car was gone?"

"She came to the party with her mother, and Medora . . . left early. Left without her."

"After the rumpus at the bar. I saw it from a distance. A little excitement I'm sure you weren't expecting."

They were silent for a few moments.

"Did Sisu Potter seem depressed to you recently? Any mood changes, anything different about her?"

"She struck me as a person who would be quite moody, if one got to know her. But she seemed the same as usual, only she'd had more to drink."

"Was this usual?"

"I have no idea. I was never at another party with her." Vivienne thought of Bea Brown. Bea hadn't wanted to invite Sisu to Brown Hall again, or she would have given the opening night party instead of Vivienne.

Suddenly she remembered Edwinta Everett. She glanced at the clock on the mantel. It was now ten-thirty and late enough in the morning to call. "I need to make a phone call. May I? In all of this, I forgot about calling Medora Everett to make sure Edwinta got home safely."

"Go ahead. Take your time."

Vivienne rose and walked to the small table which held the living room telephone and her address book. She looked through the book, found Medora's number and dialed it.

She heard the phone ringing and then Medora's voice, even deeper in the morning than in the evening, coming on the other end of the line. "Everett residence."

Oh, no! Vivienne thought. She actually answers her phone "Everett residence!"

"Medora, this is Vivienne Montrose. I'm sorry to disturb you this early in the morning, but I wanted to make sure Edwinta got safely home last night."

"She must have, because she just had breakfast and went out for a walk."

Vivienne, relieved, fell awkwardly silent, not knowing if she should apologize for inviting Thorson and his girlfriend to the party, and hesitant to talk about the drowning. Either subject seemed fraught with danger. Suddenly feeling stronger, she opted for the latter topic.

"Medora, there won't be a show tonight. Jonathan will have to call everyone, but perhaps you'll want to break the news to Edwinta."

"No show? What happened?"

"Sisu Potter died."

"No!" Vivienne could hear Medora's shock over the wires. "How?"

"She drowned in the lagoon." Vivienne was surprised by the coolness with which she was able to report the information. "I found the body this morning."

"My God! What a shock for you! Why do you suppose she did it? Ending it all after her performance? Isn't that a bit melodramatic? She could at least have waited for the reviews to come out."

Vivienne, startled, glanced over at Cortland Himber. He stood with his back to her, looking out the window toward the ocean. She was sure he was listening to every word.

"I don't know, Medora. It *was* a shock, but I guess I'm over the worst of it now, if I can talk about it like this."

"What a surprise! Well, I'll tell Edwinta. She'll be delighted. She despised the woman. Good-bye, Vivienne."

Vivienne heard the click as Medora hung up the phone. She stared at the receiver for a minute and then hung it up. She turned and found Cortland Himber watching her.

"A surprising conversation?"

"A surprising person. You never know how people are going to react to death. I suppose if it's someone you don't know, you might be quite flippant."

"Like Mrs. Everett?"

Vivienne thought better of relating the conversation, so she changed the subject. "I have a question, Mr. Himber. Do you think her drowning was accidental?"

"Do you?"

"A question with a question with a question." She looked at him. He stood watching her, as though waiting for her to move. "Please sit down again," she said. "May I get you some coffee?"

"No, thank you," he said quietly. He sat again in the same chair.

Vivienne again sat on the couch. "I suppose I asked because I've been rehearsing *A Classic Case of Murder* too long. No one really liked Sisu. There's a book I remember reading—a whole group gets together and murders someone they all dislike so no one person can be found guilty."

Chief Himber spoke in a voice that seemed deliberately soothing. "Miss Montrose, you've just recovered from a shock, probably on top of very little sleep last night. Matt Ross told me you were shaking uncontrollably when he found you. Sometimes after a person has been very disturbed by an event, they try to become an expert on it. Try to get a feeling of control over something uncontrollable. I'm not Sigmund Freud, but I've seen it happen. I think what you really need is a rest, a good meal and a good night's sleep."

The phone rang.

Vivienne jumped up, paused a moment to show Chief Himber she was in perfect control, then walked over and answered it.

"Vivienne." It was Jonathan Patrick's voice.

"Yes, Jon."

"Vivienne, brace yourself. Are you sitting down?"

"No, but go ahead."

"Medora Everett just favored me with the weirdest phone call I've ever received in my life. I think Thorson and the teen-age chippie finally drove her over the edge."

"What did she tell you?"

"She said—brace yourself for this—I'm quoting: Sisu Potter was depressed over her performance last night and committed suicide by drowning herself in that lagoon next to your house. You tried to save her, but by the time you got to her, she was dead, and you had to pull her body out of the water!"

The horrible vision of actually touching that body flashed through Vivienne's mind and she shivered. With an effort, she gained control.

"Well, that's not really accurate, Jon. I found her body, but I didn't know she was going to commit suicide. In fact, I'm not even sure she *did* commit suicide. She did drown, though, and the police chief is here now, talking to me about it."

"My God, Vivienne, I can't believe she's really dead! Sisu! This is awful!"

"As for what Medora said, you know how people can confuse a story when they're upset—"

"Just let me get hold of myself for a minute, Vivienne."
Jonathan audibly took a deep breath, then exhaled. "I still
can't believe it. No, Medora wasn't upset. She sounded utterly
calm about the whole thing. She said she thought I knew about
it already. Oh, I almost forgot! The reason she called—brace
yourself again—she volunteered to take over Sisu's role so the
show could go on!"

"My goodness! I'm stunned. What did you say?"

"I couldn't say anything. Medora Everett volunteering to do
a role with ten lines! I thought she'd cracked up! I said I'd call
her back. Now that I think of it, maybe it's her way of making
amends for last night."

"Someone has to call everyone in the cast and tell them, Jon.
Especially Hilly Lawton. He's going to be devastated, and I
think you should tell him rather than a stranger."

"God! I don't envy myself! I'll have to call off the show this
weekend, that's for certain. And maybe for good. Let me think
about this, Vivienne, and make the calls. I'll call you back."

She hung up the phone and turned back to Cortland Himber, who had risen.

"I realize your telephone is in constant use, Miss Montrose,
but I'd like to deprive you of it for a minute."

She smiled at this gentle sarcasm. "Certainly. Go ahead."

He dialed, then spoke into the receiver. "Hi. What's up?"
He listened for a minute, then said "Okay, I'll be there," and
hung up. He turned to Vivienne. "We found her car in the
parking lot of the lagoon beach. Her purse was inside with her
keys and identification. I have to meet one of my men at her
house and inform her next of kin."

"I understand she has parents in Oklahoma."

"We'll be in touch with them. I may come back to ask you a
few more questions, if you don't mind. Don't worry," he
smiled. "No earlier than tomorrow."

"Any time you like," Vivienne said. She extended her right
hand to him.

"Thank you for your help." He took her hand and looked
down at her. "I appreciate it. You weren't feeling well, and it
was a strain for you. Please take my advice and get some rest.
Don't worry about any of this. It will all be taken care of."

"I hope so, Mr. Himber." She saw him to the door and watched as he walked toward the police car parked in front of her house. She closed the front door and slowly walked back toward the windows that overlooked the lagoon. She took in a quick view of the dark hills in the distance and the fog beyond them concealing Point Lobos and looked away. She hoped the place wouldn't always be haunted for her.

I should take his advice and rest, she thought. She walked down the stairs to her bedroom. MacGuffin was curled on the end of her bed, sound asleep. The excitement had been too much for him. He didn't stir as she sat next to him, his small, furry body rising and falling almost imperceptibly as he breathed. She lay flat on the bed with her head on a soft pillow, staring up at the beamed ceiling for a long while, her breath coming in deeper spasms as her emotions continued to churn inside of her.

The phone rang again. She reached for the receiver on the small table by her bed.

The caller was Jonathan Patrick. His voice had the hard edge it took on when he was under strain. So did his humor.

"This wasn't in my contract with the Board of the Carmel Playhouse, but I've spread the word. I've told everyone but Hilly Lawton. Even *I* am not up to that—Ted's going to break it to him. He's a priest and used to things like life, death and amateur theatre. If he can't handle it by himself, he can take Boy Beautiful with him. They can do their Bobbsey twin routine and perk Hilly up. Ted was very upset, by the way. Said she didn't seem depressed and he couldn't understand it. Secretly, I think he's relieved as hell."

Vivienne laughed in spite of herself. "Jon, you see everything, don't you?"

"It's the gift of omniscience, and it's a curse, but yes, I do." His tone changed. "Vivienne, I think you should call Bea right away. I'm worried about her. She's very, very upset. I thought she'd be delighted—you know how much she hated Sisu. But she sounded beside herself. Hung up on me and wouldn't come to the phone when I called back. Some Chinese answered, not the one that sounds like Leslie Howard—another one. 'Missy Brown out now, no talkee.' The whole thing begins to feel like a bad Charlie Chan movie. I guess that's redundant, isn't it? I know I'm blithering. By the way, Medora Everett's dead serious about doing Sisu's part. Anyway, we'll see what happens when the dust-to-dust settles. There I go again! I have to get off the phone now, Vivienne. You know how I am—I'll just get worse. Don't forget, call Bea.''

FOURTEEN

As was usually the case, the clouds that settled on Carmel had thickened into a fog in Pebble Beach. Vivienne turned her car slowly around the dark curves of the Seventeen-Mile Drive. The cypresses along the sides of the road were black with moisture, and soggy moss drooped from their twisted limbs. Waiting for the high gates to Brown Hall to swing open for her, Vivienne glanced around the grounds. The windows of Blue-bell Cottage were shuttered, the children were nowhere to be seen, and the only sign of life was a thread of smoke fighting its way out of the stone chimney.

Toad Hall rose up into the mist, dark with a cold damp that penetrated its stones and timbers every time the fog came in and never really left until the coming of a rare dry spell. Vivienne parked her car and, stepping carefully to avoid slipping on wet granite, climbed the stone slabs to the huge doors. She rang the Medusa bell and waited. Several minutes passed before Hi Lo opened the door.

"Good day, Miss Montrose." Although Hi Lo seemed surprised to see her, his greeting was subdued, as if the weight of the atmosphere was pressing down upon him.

"I'm here to see Mrs. Brown, Hi. I wasn't able to reach her by telephone."

She looked at the butler, waiting to receive an answer, and he looked back at her, giving none.

"She's not expecting me, but I'm sure she'll see me if you let her know I'm here."

Hi Lo hesitated a moment.

"It's very important that I see Mrs. Brown," Vivienne insisted.

"Yes, of course, Miss Montrose. I'll announce you." He turned and led her through the entryway into the great hall. When the fog was as heavy as it was today, no sunlight passed through the stained glass windows of the great hall, and all the lamps blazed.

The butler knocked on the door to Bea's study. The sound of Bea's voice, muffled and distant, came from inside.

Hi Lo faced the door and bellowed, "Miss Montrose to see you!"

After a few moments of silence, there was a click from the lock, and the door opened several inches. Bea stood behind it in the green light of her study, looking pale, ill and frightened.

"I guess you talked to Jon," Bea said. "Come on in."

Vivienne stepped into the room, and Bea closed the door behind her and locked it. The door beyond Bea's study leading to the library was open, and crates lined the floor of the study and the library. Vivienne could see the nearest of them was filled with books.

"My crime library," Bea said with a gesture toward the crates. "Have some coffee?"

"No, thank you."

"Then I'll have some." Bea went to a silver service set up on a large table and with shaking hands, poured coffee from a giant urn into a small teacup. She was wearing a flowered dressing gown, no makeup and huge reading glasses perched on her upturned nose that made her look like a very frightened child.

"Bea, what are you doing?"

"Getting rid of evidence."

"What evidence—books?"

"My murder mysteries—all of them. Otherwise they're gonna think I killed her."

"Bea, dear, I want you to sit down. Stop drinking that coffee. It will just make you more nervous."

"You're right. Okay. I'll stop." Bea put down the cup and sat abruptly in a green chair near the coffee service.

"Now, Bea—think about what you're doing. Everyone knows you read murder novels. Everyone in this house, everyone at the theatre, everyone in Carmel! Packing them up in crates and giving them to the Salvation Army won't make any difference. And why in the world would anyone think you killed Sisu Potter?"

"I'm not giving them away," Bea said vehemently. "I'm gonna burn 'em!"

"Burn them! You could keep a foundry going for a week with all those books for fuel!"

"You're right." Bea looked taken aback. "That doesn't make sense. You're right. I can't burn them." She peered at Vivienne intently through her glasses. "What can I do with them?"

"Call someone and have him put the books back on the shelves."

"I can't do that! None of the servants know what the crates are for. I just called for them to be sent up. I've packed half the books already. I can't ask one of them to put them all back on the shelves! What if the police talk to them? They'd have to tell them everything they knew!"

"Why don't you let me put them back?" Vivienne used her most soothing tones. "It can't take that long if you packed them this morning. You go upstairs and rest and I'll—"

"They have to go in alphabetical order!" Bea jumped up. "You can't, Viv! *I* have to do it! Otherwise, if they're in the wrong way, someone might notice and ask questions."

Vivienne wondered what could possibly have Bea so frightened. She walked to her and put her hands on her friend's shoulders. "Bea, dear, you're terribly upset, and you're behaving irrationally. I don't understand why anyone would think you killed Sisu Potter."

"Because I hated her!" Bea burst out. "Because I wished her dead over and over. She was a vicious bitch, and I'm glad she's dead! I don't care how horribly she died—I'm glad!" Then her face wrinkled up behind the huge glasses and she began to cry.

Vivienne made Bea sit in the nearest chair. She knelt next to her and held Bea's head close to hers, stroking her hair. "Listen, dear, I want you to calm down. Everything is going to be fine. I'm going to ask Lily to get a hot toddy for you and put you to bed. Don't worry. While you're resting, I'll put all your books back—in alphabetical order."

Bea stopped sniffling and glared at Vivienne. "You can't, Viv. You'll be an accomplice if they suspect me."

"No one's ever been sent to Alcatraz for putting books on a shelf."

Bea started to cry again. "Viv, you don't know. You're my best friend, but you don't know what kind of a person I am."

"You're a wonderful person!" Vivienne took Bea by the shoulders and shook her gently. "The best in the world! And you absolutely did not kill Sisu Potter or anyone else. You couldn't kill a fly. So stop pretending there's any possibility you could!"

Bea took a large, lace-edged handkerchief from the pocket of her dressing gown and blew her nose, almost losing her glasses in the process. She pushed the frames back on her nose again. "I can't go up and lie down, Viv. I'll just lie there and worry myself sick. I've got to do something. I'm gonna put the books back on the shelves, like you said. If you want, you can help me. But you don't have to."

"Of course I'll help you." Vivienne realized the best thing for Bea might be keeping busy. "We'll do it together. Let's go in, and you can show me where they go."

"Okay." Bea rose. "But first, I *am* going to have that hot toddy sent up. Do you want one, too?"

"No, but I'd love a hot cup of tea."

Bea pulled the green brocade bell rope that hung against the wall. In a matter of seconds, there was a knock on the door of the study.

Bea flipped the latch, opened the door a crack and spoke through the opening. "Hi, tell Blossom to make some hot tea for Miss Montrose and a hot toddy for me. Also some sandwiches—chicken and ham and whatever roast you have around. And some pastries and fruit and a cold salad. And some cheese, too—a couple of kinds, with crackers. But make sure the drinks get here as soon as possible. Thanks." She closed the door again, locked it and turned to Vivienne. "I'm beginning to get my appetite back."

Vivienne laughed in relief. "Oh, Bea—I was so worried about you! At least you're feeling better!"

"So far," Bea said grimly, looking at the floor. She looked up quickly. "Let's go into the library and get started."

They walked past the crates near the library door.

"Let's get these back in," Bea said. "They're *A* and I hauled them out here after I filled the crate."

"Why don't we each take an end of the crate and carry it?"

The two women picked up a crate that Bea, and her furious energy, had earlier moved by herself. They carried it back into the library and set it down near the shelves that had been emptied.

The library of Brown Hall was a rectangular room with walls paneled in blood-red wainscotting and fronted with high mahogany bookshelves filled with mostly untouched sets of the great works as they were bound and sold in the early part of the century. The section housing Bea's mystery novels in their vividly colored jackets stood out from the rows of Harvard Classics, Shakespeare, Dickens, Kipling, Thackeray and Austen the way Bea stood out from Brown Hall: bright and flamboyant, but lining up with the long-established order of things.

As they came back into Bea's study for the other crate, they heard knocking at the door.

"Just a second, Hi," Bea said. "Viv, let's get this crate in there and close the door. That way he can serve us in here and not see what's going on with the books."

They hauled the second crate into the library and returned to the study. Bea closed the library door behind them. Then she walked to the door of the study, unlocked it and opened it wide. Hi Lo was standing outside with a silver tray that held a porcelain tea set, cups, saucers, and a drink steaming in what looked like a cut glass vase. He carried the tray into the room and set it next to the coffee service.

"I'll take this away, if you wish," he said, gesturing at the coffee things. "And Mrs. Brown, Blossom asks that you hold the toddy with a cloth at first. It's extremely hot."

"Thanks, Hi. You can take the coffee away."

The butler picked up the tray holding the coffee service and left, closing the door behind him.

"Thank God!" Bea said, reaching for the toddy. "I hope Blossom washed this after she took the dozen long-stemmed roses out of it!" She picked up the huge glass after wrapping a linen napkin around it and took a sip. "Tastes great!"

Vivienne poured tea for herself, and with beverages in hand, they went into the library to resume work.

They started shelving, working silently and swiftly. By the time they reached John Dickson Carr, Bea had finished half of her drink and a knock on the library door told them the food had been served in Bea's study.

"Let's take a break," Bea said. "This guy was nothing if not prolific. Anyway, we've got Agatha Christie coming up, and I'm starving!"

Vivienne was also hungry. They went back to the study to find a feast spread before them: piled on silver and porcelain serving dishes were stacks of sandwiches, mountains of cakes, great rounds of cheese, dozens of crackers and enough fruit to feed Thorson Everett's Sandi for a year. They sat near the table bearing the banquet and began to eat.

Bea silently put away three sandwiches to Vivienne's one and ate several crackers with cheese and a small bunch of grapes before she spoke again.

"Viv, I can't thank you enough for doing this. I was crazed this morning. I don't know what I would have done if you hadn't come over."

"I was very worried about you. Very. I've never seen you like that before. I still don't understand why this has upset you so much. You barely knew Sisu."

Bea raised her glass in a toast. "To Toad Hall—my home sweet home! Nothing and no one is gonna make me lose all this." She sipped her drink and set the big crystal goblet on the table next to her. "And if there was a scandal, Viv, or even any kind of publicity or gossip that got to the Toad, it could happen. The Toad doesn't care what I do, as long as he doesn't know about it and no one he knows tells him about it. He's never been crazy about my being in shows. None of the wives of his snotty golf buddies do anything like that, but he tells his pals it keeps me out of his hair, and it does. I know you can't understand, Viv. I can see it on your face. You've never been able to. You're so goddamned independent and self-contained you can't imagine how anyone else can be different. That's not a criticism. I admire you for it, even more because I'm not that way."

"Why would there be a scandal? The only people who know you have...affairs are friends like Jonathan and me. Even if anyone would talk about it by accident, we're not in the same circles as Buster and his friends."

"Viv, you know I signed papers before I married Buster. That old bitch who spawned him is responsible—Buster was too hot to trot to think of it back then. If I go, I go with nothing. My clothes and my jewels—and how long could I live on that?" She took a gulp of her drink and clutched the goblet, looking down at her pink, polished nails. "Everyone thinks I'm so casual about being rich. If they only knew! I gotta have the clothes, I gotta have the jewels, I gotta live in Brown Hall. *Then* I can be casual about all of it." She took another swallow and set the glass down. "Take all this away and I'm just Beatrice Fenstermaker, tap-dancing wonder from Youngstown, Ohio. Oh, sure, if I was Ginger Rogers I could go out and do club dates and be on TV. But I'm not. I took my good looks and my twinkle toes and I married bucks with 'em. And now I'm stuck. I can't go anywhere else but here, and I'm not going to. No one's gonna get me out of here either!"

Vivienne felt the ache in her friend's pain. "Bea, I know you think I don't understand, but I do."

"Viv, I envy you." Bea's eyes were starting to tear up again behind her glasses. "You're so strong. You could work in the five-and-dime on Ocean Avenue if you had to, and you'd still be the same. You'd be behind the cash register, and a bunch of old movie fans would be queuing up to get your autograph!"

They both laughed, Bea through her sniffles. Then she looked at Vivienne intently. "I'm not like you. Take all this away and put me in a tract house out in Seaside and I wouldn't be the wonderful person I am today. I mean it."

Vivienne didn't speak.

"So I stay here and have affairs. I criticize Thorson Everett for his teenage girlfriends, but I'm no better. I just go after boys of all ages. I fall in love with every goddamned one of them and it never lasts." Bea took off her glasses, laid them on the table beside her, and ran her hands through her hair, pulling it back from her forehead. The skin of her face lifted and smoothed, and she looked like a sad teenager.

Vivienne felt a lump in her throat and turned her gaze away.

"There were a few times I thought I could leave it all for love," Bea said.

Vivienne looked back at her.

"But they didn't come off." Her mouth twisted down. "Not after I told the guys the facts of life about the Brown bucks."

"Bea, I can't eat anything more. Let's go back to work." Vivienne rose and started for the library. Bea got up to join her, and Vivienne stopped, turned and hugged Bea. The two women clung to each other for a minute.

"Bea, I really understand. And you know you've always got me for a friend. No matter what happens." Vivienne squeezed Bea's shoulders and stepped back. "And if you ever need money, it's yours—just ask me."

Bea wiped her nose on one of the napkins and picked up her glasses. "No. You're the greatest friend anyone ever had, but no. I'll never ask you for money."

They walked back into the library to finish off John Dickson Carr. They shelved until they reached Agatha Christie.

"She's my favorite," Bea said quietly. She put away *The ABC Murders* and *And Then There Were None*. "I had a dream about her last week—really vivid. She was real as life—kind of portly, with white hair and that long English nose." Bea stared into the distance in recollection, while Vivienne listened and continued shelving the titles. Bea's voice took on a gently hypnotic quality, and in the dim light from the sconces high above them in the musty library, Vivienne could almost see the scene as Bea described it.

"She was wearing a baggy tweed suit and a kind of cream-colored blouse held together at the collar with a cameo. She was sitting at a big desk and writing on a yellow lined pad with an old-fashioned fountain pen. You know, the kind with a lot of silver curlicues on it—real old. She kept scribbling on the pad for what seemed like hours. Finally, when she'd finished writing, she handed the pad to me across the desk. I took it and read what she'd written. It was the perfect way to murder Buster and not get caught! I mean, not the slightest suspicion. It was brilliant! Then she spoke to me in a high-pitched, English voice—she sounded just like Agatha Christie would sound. 'Take it, my dear,' she said. 'It's yours to use as you see fit.' I ripped the sheet off the pad and folded it up and thanked her. Then we started to talk about her books. I asked her about the ones I really loved and how she ever thought up those plots. It seemed like we talked for hours. Then my maid came in with the breakfast tray and I woke up. Needless to say, I forgot what she wrote," Bea concluded in disgust. She picked up *Easy to Kill*, gave a loud "Ha!" and shelved it.

Vivienne thought the best comment was no comment. They continued shelving the Christie books for a few minutes, Vivienne taking them out of the crate and giving them to Bea, and Bea placing them on the shelf.

Vivienne handed Bea *Murder on the Links*, and Bea, musing, held it for a moment. "Maybe someday I'll figure out how to commit the perfect crime," she said, placing the volume on the shelf. "He plays golf at Cypress Point or Pebble Beach every day he's here. Tough figuring the trajectory of a golf ball, though, with all that wind out there."

"If you haven't come up with something so far with this research library at your fingertips, I don't hold out much hope for you, Bea."

"I know. I want to murder Buster. I wish he was dead, I really do. I dream about him kicking the bucket. I had a dream that I chopped him up in little bitty pieces. All that was left of him were little matchsticks and two little round things like that kelp—sea grapes—you find washed up on the beach; you step on them and they pop. I popped them, and that was the end of him. Pretty obvious, huh?"

"Pretty obvious." Vivienne pulled *Partners in Crime* out of the crate and handed it to Bea. "And don't let this give you any ideas."

Bea stared at the cover of the book for a moment, then put it on the shelf.

"I know you couldn't kill Buster." Vivienne reached down for another book and continued speaking. "The only reason I put up with your plots to bump him off is because I know that's all they are—plots. Outlets for your frustration. I know you could never go through with any of them, and not because you're a coward, but because it's terribly wrong. If you take a life, I believe you should have to give up your own in payment. I don't approve of murder."

Bea let out a yelp of laughter. "To quote Matt Ross—great title! You beat all, Viv, you really do. That's why I love you so much—you're like someone out of one of these books."

"No, really, Bea. In your dream, Agatha Christie outlined the perfect crime for you and told you to use it as you saw fit. And you forgot it! You see? You're not a murderess!"

"Good. You can testify for me someday," Bea said under her breath.

They made a concerted effort and reached *Witness for the Prosecution and Other Stories*.

"That's Christie!" Bea triumphantly slid the book onto the shelf next to the others. She turned to Vivienne. "You look exhausted, Viv. Why don't you go home and let me finish up? I've gotten my second wind. And there aren't that many more to put back—I was only up to Doyle when you stopped me."

Vivienne hadn't realized she was beginning to look as tired as she felt. "If you don't mind, I think I do need a good night's sleep. It seems like I've lived two lifetimes in the last twenty-four hours."

"I don't mind, if you don't mind my not seeing you out. I'm on a roll. If I stop it'll be hard to get started again."

Vivienne walked toward Bea's study.

Bea called out to her. "Wait a second, Viv! What's going on with the show? Are we canceling it or getting a replacement for what's-her-name?"

"Didn't Jon tell you? Medora volunteered to do the part."

"Vivienne, you're joking, aren't you?" Bea looked stunned.

"I'm not. Jon told me."

"Jesus! Medora Everett doing a role with all of ten lines. Why? What the hell does she have up her sleeve?"

"Why don't you call Jon? He's under a lot of strain, having to call everyone about this, and he was very worried about you after you hung up on him."

"Okay, I'll call him as soon as I'm done. Drive home safely, Viv. It's scary out there around those curves on a day like this."

"I will." Vivienne walked into the study for her purse.

"Maybe I'll call you later," Bea shouted after her. "After my heart-to-heart with Medora!"

Vivienne turned and came back into the library. "What do you mean?"

Bea straightened after she retrieved another book from the crate. "Since she's taking over Sisu's role, I just want to warn her about foot-long hairs," she said, widening her eyes. "They can be fatal."

FIFTEEN

THE HEADLINE of Monday morning's *Herald*, the daily newspaper of the Monterey Peninsula, read: "Woman Drowns at Carmel River Mouth." Matt stood by the newsrack in front of the Village Corner and stared, surprised by the shock he felt at seeing the news in print. He bought a copy and walked through the restaurant to the patio. Sitting at his favorite table in the morning sunshine, he began to read. The story was brief.

The body of a 37-year-old Carmel woman, Celia Susan Potter, was found early Sunday morning washed ashore at the mouth of the Carmel River. Miss Potter had been a resident of Carmel for the past year. According to Carmel police, it is believed she drowned late Saturday night or early Sunday morning after appearing in a play at the Carmel Playhouse (see review on page 23) and attending a cast party following the performance at a house near the river mouth. Presently, the Carmel River terminates in a lagoon or large pool of landlocked water blocked by the sand of the beach from flowing freely into the sea.

The article, presumably for lack of information about Sisu, went on to discuss other recent deaths by drowning in the Carmel area.

Great, Matt thought, no mention of Vivienne's name. That was a relief. All she needed was a mob of death-crazed tourists prowling around her house.

He flipped to the second section and found page twenty-three. "New Star on Carmel Stage" headed the review of *A Classic Case of Murder*. Matt skimmed it. The new star on the Carmel stage had not drowned in Carmel lagoon.

He went to the pay phone inside the restaurant and called Vivienne.

"The review's out," he said.

"I know. Gushing and inane, as usual, but very good for the show. Gruesome, though, to say the least, with the connection to the front-page story."

"That policeman did you a favor by not giving the paper your name."

"I know—I'm grateful. But I suppose I'll have to go to the inquest." Vivienne sounded slightly hopeful.

"I haven't heard anyone mention anything about an inquest! And if there *is* one, *I* can go. We can say I found the body."

"That would be lying, Matt."

"If they have an inquest, I don't think you should go. I'll bet that policeman doesn't think so either."

"Well, they'll notify me if they need me, I suppose." She sounded wistful. "It seems like they would. To give evidence, you know. I think it would be interesting."

"Interesting—Vivienne, it would be crazy! You know how upset you were. It would just bring back bad memories."

"I was upset *then*, Matt. But I'm fine now." Irritation was creeping into her voice. "It's not as though I'm unstable and it would send me over the edge!" Her voice softened. "Matt, are you home now?"

"No, I'm up at the Village Corner."

"Jon and Bea are coming over this afternoon for drinks or tea, whichever anyone wants. If you'd like to come, you're welcome."

"Sure." Matt was eager to hear more discussions about the drowning and whether or not the show would go on.

"I wondered if you might be seeing Ted Reid today?"

"I don't see Ted that often. We're not best friends."

Vivienne was silent at the other end of the line.

"But I could," he said. It was obvious everyone wanted to know how Hilly Lawton and Ted Reid were taking the death, and Ted had been the one to break the news to Hilly and to Sisu's parents. "I'll call him and see if he wants to get together. Knowing Ted, he probably will."

"Thanks, Matt. You read my mind. I didn't want to inconvenience you, but Jon doesn't know quite how to handle this and with the show up in the air right now, we're all curious about—"

"Vivienne," Matt interrupted in spite of himself. "Next time, just ask me if you want a favor. I don't mind doing anything you need me to do, but you don't have to hint around. You're too polite for your own good. Just ask."

"Okay, I will." Vivienne sounded a bit surprised. "We'll see you around four, then."

Sheesh! Matt thought as he hung up the phone. I just talked to Vivienne Montrose as if she were a normal human being! Aware of some new dimension to his personality, he returned to his table and ordered breakfast. He read the review of the show once more, this time at his leisure.

After the headline, the reviewer outlined the play without giving away any of the surprises, and praised Jonathan Patrick for his "Broadway caliber" direction. Matt skimmed down to where the players were mentioned.

Formerly Hollywood's and now Carmel's own Vivienne Montrose gave a gripping performance as the accused murderess, Persephone Braithwaite, with a breathtaking entrance at the end of Act I and a powerful scene in Act II. Another of the Peninsula's leading ladies, Beatrice Brown, was at her finest in the taxing role of the eldest sister, Artemis. Playhouse regular Hilliard Lawton contributed one of his excellent characterizations in the role of Philip Winfield, the lawyer. Ted Reid, a relative newcomer to the Playhouse stage, captured attention as Acis Braithwaite, the eccentric younger brother, with Sisu Potter making much of the small role of Athena Braithwaite, and Helen Lawton playing Gladys, the maid.

The surprise of the evening was a young lady this reviewer recalls from the Dockside Theatre some years back. Granddaughter of Carmel royalty Edwin Everett and daughter of theatrical luminaries Medora and Thorson Everett, Miss Edwinta Everett has grown into a young actress of remarkable promise. As the wayward child, Galatea, she fascinated the audience with her beauty and unique stage presence. Watch for her—this talented local girl will go far!

Although embarrassing, the review would be good for business. Matt went to the pay phone again and called Ted Reid.

The phone rang several times before Ted answered it.

"Ted, it's Matt Ross. How are you doing?"

Ted uttered his platitudes in what seemed to be relatively good spirits. "I think I'm over the worst of it now, Matt. It's always a shock when a young person dies, no matter how many times you see death."

"I guess it's hard for anyone to handle," Matt said. Even a priest, he thought to himself. "Ted, have you had breakfast yet? I'm up at the Village Corner, and I thought you might want to come up if you haven't eaten."

"I'm sending Steve off by himself. Sisu's father's arriving late this afternoon and I have to be around. Why don't you come down here around noon and we'll take a walk on the beach."

"The beach?" Matt immediately thought of the lagoon beach. He hadn't been there since the discovery of the body.

"Give me credit for a little tact, Matt. I meant Carmel Beach."

"Noon is fine. See you then."

Matt returned to his table and finished breakfast. Then he pulled out his notebook and began to add to a series of recollections he was making about the opening night party while it was fresh in his mind. He strolled around Carmel for an hour or so, thinking about his next novel. As it neared noon, he headed down to Ted's cottage.

"Glad you're here early, Matt," Ted said when he opened the cottage door. He stepped onto the porch next to Matt and closed the door behind him. "I won't invite you in—most of Steve's bags are here and the place is a mess. He went down the coast to San Simeon. This hasn't been much of a vacation for him. To top it off, Sisu's father is coming tonight. That isn't something anyone who didn't know Sisu should have to endure."

He and Matt walked through the small front yard, and Ted opened the gate to the street. They walked along the block toward the nearest street that would lead them down to the beach.

"I remember the two of us walking somewhere and discussing Vivienne Montrose," Ted said, shuffling slightly with his pigeon-toed gait. "It seems like a million years ago. When was that?"

"Right after the first audition. We were going down to the La Playa from the theatre."

"Of course. It *was* a million years ago. How's Vivienne taking this? Someone told me she found Sisu's body."

"I think she's all right. She was in shock at first, but now she's talking about going to the inquest! I've told her that's crazy—she still has a famous name, and she'd hate that kind of publicity. She's just not thinking about that now."

"She's a very honest woman, isn't she? Strong moral principles—black or white—no gray areas."

They turned the corner and saw Carmel Beach and the ocean spread out before them. The breadth and brilliance of the water always awed Matt, no matter how many times he saw it.

"Yes, she is," Matt said.

"I hear she had quite a past before she moved to Carmel. Since we talked about her last time, I've heard a few things."

"That was a long time ago, Ted." Matt was getting angry. "And it's none of your business. While we're on the subject, Claudia Kellog told me you'd been giving her your professional psychological opinion of me. That's none of your business either."

Ted balked slightly, staring ahead of him. "I don't remember anything like that. What did she tell you?"

"She said you were making some kind of comparison between the two of us. You and me. That neither of us could handle a romantic involvement."

Ted stopped, feet pointing toward each other. He looked at Matt. "Well, that's true, isn't it? But I don't remember saying it. I tend to forget half of what I say—that's why I always tell the truth."

"It may be true as far as you're concerned. Just don't include me in your comparisons."

"Apologies, Matt. I have the world's biggest mouth, sometimes. You're right. Look, let's get down to the beach and breathe some salt air and you'll get over it."

It was hard to stay mad at Ted after he did his repentant bad boy act—he was so convincing at divorcing himself of any responsibility for his own words and deeds. Besides, Matt wanted more information for the tea party later.

The two men walked down the narrow granite and stone staircase to the beach, Ted in the lead. They hit the dry sand at the top of the beach and trudged through it down to the firm, wet sand at the ocean's edge. The glare from the water was strong with the hot noon sun directly over their heads. Gulls swirled in front of them, and small bevies of sandpipers trotted past them as they walked in the direction of the cliffs and golf courses of Pebble Beach.

Matt led into the subject. "I'm sure you're not looking forward to seeing Sisu's father tonight."

"I hope the worst is over, but it probably isn't. I talked to him on the phone yesterday. It's the mother who's really broken up, I hear. Sedated, with a nurse, the works. So far, the hardest part was breaking it to Hilly." Ted put a hand to his forehead, shielding his eyes from the sun.

"What happened?" Matt asked.

"I called him Sunday morning, woke him up—that must have been around eleven. Jon just wasn't up to calling Hilly, and I understood that. It was a terrible shock at first. I still can't believe it, Matt. She wasn't depressed or despondent. I think she must have just taken a walk and slipped and fallen in the water. She couldn't swim, you know."

"I remember we had a cast party for the show last year at some board member's pool and Sisu didn't go in."

"She used to joke about it. She'd had every lesson in the book, and she still sank like a stone as soon as she hit the water."

"God, what a thought!"

"Exactly. Anyway, *I* wasn't over it enough to handle it by myself and I took Steve for moral support. We went over and broke the news to Hilly. He's taking it very hard. I don't think he really believes it yet. He looks like an old man—like it broke something inside of him." Still screening his eyes from the sun, Ted stopped and looked out at the water. "Did you know they were talking about getting married?"

"Who—Hilly and Sisu?"

"Yes. They were keeping it a secret until the show was over. Sisu hinted about it to me once, but I didn't catch on."

"Why keep it a secret?"

"Partly me, I guess. Sisu never really stopped coming after me. Partly other people in the cast, too—Helen Lawton being in the show. They're divorced and everyone's the best of friends, but maybe they felt it would be awkward. And I think Sisu was intimidated by Bea Brown."

"Bea Brown! Why? The foot-long hair?"

"No, that was just the tip of the proverbial iceberg. Bea's money was part of it. It's sad about Sisu. She didn't have any friends here except me and Hilly, and neither of us are going to the funeral. Her father will be taking her body back to Oklahoma all alone."

"Why aren't either of you going? Especially Hilly, if they were going to be married?"

Ted began to walk again, and Matt followed his lead.

"I'm not going because I have a houseguest," Ted said. "Also because I have a show to do, if it goes on, and frankly, because I don't have the stomach for the whole sad scene. Hilly told me he's not going because he has to help out at his church, but I personally think he's just not up to the Potter parents' grief and the whole scene either."

"Claudia told me their pastor's been sick and everyone would be busy helping out this week."

"The church is a convenient excuse and one I know well," Ted said. "Matt, do you think Jon will reopen the show? I'd hate to think of all our work going down the drain. And I'm sure the Playhouse needs the income."

"I don't know yet. I'll be talking to him later this afternoon. Maybe he'll have some ideas. I think everyone is in a position to do it except Hilly."

"Hilly doesn't have that many lines. Jon could do the part. And Hilly could come back into the show in a couple of weeks, once he's feeling better. You can't stay in mourning forever, and it would be healthy for him to keep busy with the show once he's up to it. I think Helen could do Sisu's role and Jon could easily find another maid."

"That's a good idea about Jon filling in for Hilly. And about Sisu's role—Medora Everett apparently volunteered to take over."

"Oh? That's a surprise!" Ted seemed apprehensive. "Very attractive, but I hoped I'd never have to get to know her personally. I heard she caused quite a scene at the party; I'm glad I missed it. I imagine I was walking right about here when she dumped the champagne on her ex-husband's head."

"Ted, whatever happened to Edwinta Everett that night?"

"I don't know." Ted looked away and began talking into the wind and Matt missed his first few words.

"I didn't hear you," Matt yelled in Ted's ear.

Ted turned his head back toward him. "I just said, I haven't seen her since the beginning of Vivienne's party. I know you'll think I'm a coward, Matt, but sometimes it's just easier to let things ride. I'm not good at involvements. It was wrong of me to spend so much time with that girl—she's just a child. When Steve got here, I realized how dependent on me she'd become. She assumed I was going to pay her all the attention I used to before I had a guest visiting me."

"How immature of her!"

"That's what I mean," Ted continued, entirely missing Matt's sarcasm. "If we start doing the show again, I've got to have a talk with her." Ted's steps quickened, and Matt hastened to keep up with him. "I hate situations like this! I don't handle them well. Edwinta scares me at times. She has an intensity that's frightening." He stopped and stood still, thinking. "It'll be a challenge for me to deal with her. Maybe I'll write her a letter."

"Jesus, Ted! You spend weeks practically drooling over that girl and following her around like a dog, and then when you've got her affection, you drop her like a hot potato!"

Tex fixed Matt with his pale eyes. "A dog and a hot potato," he repeated thoughtfully. "To counter your two similes with one metaphor: 'People in glass houses shouldn't throw stones.' I don't think you're in any position to condemn me, are you, Matt?"

"At least I picked someone over eighteen!" Matt felt himself flush with fury. "And I didn't drop Claudia. I've been trying to talk to her ever since the party, but she's been too busy with the problems at her church to see me."

"I wasn't asking you to confess the details of your personal life, Matt; I was just defending myself."

"On the contrary, Ted! I think you'd love to know the details of everyone's personal life so you could repeat them to everyone else you know and psychoanalyze the hell out of them as you do it!"

Ted seemed abashed. "You're right, Matt. I need to learn to keep my big mouth shut."

"I'm not in the mood for your cute schoolboy apologies, Ted. Maybe this thing has put more of a strain on me than I'm used to, but I just don't have the patience to deal with you." Matt turned away from Ted, who was staring at him in surprise, and looked toward the other end of the beach where the sand ended at the rocky point of Everett House. He looked back at the priest. "I'm going to walk down to the rocks down there and try to cool off. I'll see you around, Ted."

With that, Matt started down the beach, leaving Ted behind him. His last glimpse of Ted showed him a man who looked as if he'd lost his best friend in the world. But Matt wasn't worried. Ted was resilient.

SIXTEEN

By MID-AFTERNOON MONDAY, Vivienne had mixed a pitcher of martinis, put it in the refrigerator to chill and was arranging the cakes she'd bought earlier in the day for the tea at four. She expected everyone to partake of the cake and tea, with the martinis kept ready for Jonathan and Bea. A knock at the front door surprised her; it was too early for any of her guests to arrive.

Vivienne opened the door to find the police chief, Cortland Himber, standing outside.

"I hope I'm not disturbing you," he said, smiling down at her. "One of the nice things about being a policeman is that you don't have to be invited over. I find I can drop by any time and most people will let me right in."

"Please do come in." Vivienne again found herself being charmed by the big policeman. "You're not disturbing me. I'm expecting a few guests later, but I have time to see you. Can I get you some tea or coffee?"

"No, thank you. If we can sit down for a few minutes, I promise you I won't take much of your time."

They sat in the same places they had occupied on his previous visit—Vivienne on the sofa and Chief Himber in the armchair across from her.

As soon as they were both seated, he began to speak. "Miss Montrose, regretfully, I'm ordering an inquest into the death of Miss Potter."

"You mean it isn't routine?"

"The coroner can hold an inquest on any given case—that's his prerogative. Or the county sheriff or the chief of police can order one. Ordinarily, no inquest would be held in this case."

"Why not?"

"Drownings are not normally inquested in this county. Swimming and surfing accidents are all too common. And in this drowning there appear to be no signs of what might be called foul play. Miss Potter drowned, but every sign points to an accidental death.''

"Then why order an inquest? And why did you say 'regretfully?'''

"You're going to be subpoenaed to give evidence. You, Matt Ross and I will all be testifying—that much I can tell you. Even though we're going to try to keep as low a profile on it as possible, there's always the chance of publicity.''

"If this is something that has to be done, I don't mind about publicity.''

"I mind," he said. "This business of an actress in a murder drama dying on opening night hasn't touched off the wire services yet—we're too small-town and it hasn't been noticed. But it could, and I wouldn't want to see that happen.''

"It seems as if it would only be a small blurb in the papers somewhere—one of those odd coincidences the papers like to pick up and give a paragraph or so to.''

He settled back in the chair, regarding her with what Vivienne thought must be a policeman's eye. "Miss Montrose, you're naïve. You've lived in Carmel for a long time now, so maybe you've forgotten what the press is like. The local papers are quiet and conservative, and they respect privacy. But let the big boys get onto this and it's another story. There's quite a little tale here for those jackals if they ever get hold of it.''

"What do you mean?''

"First of all, there's Vivienne Montrose—you're still a well-known name. The party she disappeared from was at your house and you found the body. 'Film star finds body of drowned actress.' 'Suicide at star's party.' Headlines of that ilk. Then there's Mrs. Brown—wife of one of the richest men in California, mansion in Pebble Beach—more fodder for the carrion-feeders. I understand she and Miss Potter were enemies. And to cap it off, we have the granddaughter of a famous painter, a girl whose father who could be in jail for molesting a minor if any of the mothers of the girls he's squired around pressed charges. A pretty girl, whose picture would look good in the tabloids. This teenager, who doesn't even look sixteen to me, just happens to be dating a Catholic priest. Those animals would tear each other apart for a story like that.''

Vivienne thought of Bea and Edwinta as she looked at the man sitting opposite her. "Yes, I see what you mean."

"Good," he said gently. "I'm not trying to upset you, but I do want you to see how things are."

"Where did you hear all of this—from Claudia?"

"A while back she described your rehearsals to me. Some is local gossip. I've also talked to one or two other people in the cast since Miss Potter's death."

Vivienne sat in troubled silence for a few minutes. "It just seems to me that when a life is involved, none of the other things mean as much—the publicity and all that—if there's any question about whether or not it was accidental. Ironically, any publicity would affect two of the people I care most about in the world. Beatrice Brown is my best friend and Edwinta Everett is like a daughter to me. I don't want them to be hurt. And I didn't like Sisu Potter, not at all. But, you see," she looked up at him, "they're alive and she's dead. Maybe it's because I found that—that pitiful body—that I feel I owe her something."

He was still studying her with his inscrutable gaze. "I'm glad to hear that," he said. "I regret ordering this inquest because I don't think it will prove much, one way or the other, and as I told you, it may do more harm than good."

"Then why did you?" Vivienne asked, leaning toward him.

"Everyone I've talked to who had anything to do with Sisu Potter thinks she was murdered, but you're the only one who's suggested it to me. Everyone else thinks it, but they're not saying it. I have to listen to that. There's a lot of fear in the air about this and not much sorrow. I have the feeling some people are afraid they might be suspected of killing her." He looked at Vivienne for a few seconds and then stood up. "You have guests coming."

Vivienne also rose. "When will the inquest be held?"

"Probably in several weeks."

"That's a long time from now. Why is that?"

"A lot of tests have to be completed—microscopic work, toxicology, blood alcohol. I'd estimate two to three weeks."

"And you said you'll be there?" Vivienne asked.

"Yes, but you won't see much of me."

"If I need to ask you anything, do I just call the Carmel police?"

"Yes, that's what you do." He began walking toward the door.

As Vivienne followed him, the front door opened, and Bea Brown came into the room. She stopped, and her eyes brightened when she saw Chief Himber.

"Hi! You look familiar! I'm not being rude by barging in— I'm like family here—I never knock." She extended her hand. "I'm Bea Brown."

"I'm Cortland Himber." He shook Bea's hand. "If I look familiar, it could be because I'm Claudia Kellog's uncle. I was at your opening night. You gave a great performance—both you and Miss Montrose."

"Oh, thanks! It's a fun play to do. We're going to figure out today if we can reopen it. With an improved cast." She winked at Vivienne, and Vivienne glared at her. "I'm not interrupting anything, am I? You look like you're leaving."

"Yes, I am. Nice to have met you, Mrs. Brown. Thanks for your help, Miss Montrose."

"Miss Montrose! How formal!" Bea blurted after the front door had closed behind Chief Himber. "Nice guy. Kind of a rough diamond. What did he mean, 'Thanks for your help'?"

"Bea, he's the Chief of Police."

Bea blanched. "Oh, my God, Viv! What did I say to him? No wonder you gave me that look. Oh, Jesus Christ!" She started to walk toward the fireplace and then turned back, pacing.

"Bea, don't worry about it. He's not investigating a murder. You're not a suspect. He just came over to tell me I'll be subpoenaed to testify at the inquest."

"Inquest! Oh, God!" She stood still, staring at Vivienne.

"Don't worry. He says it will all be over quietly—that there was no sign of any foul play. He doesn't want publicity any more than the rest of us."

"An inquest! Subpoenaed!" Bea's shoulders sagged. "God, Viv. I came over here early 'cause I wanted to eat some of those great cakes you always get, and now I don't have any appetite. I'd almost forgotten about it. I was just thinking how much fun it would be to do the show without that bitch. I don't feel good,

I really don't.'' Looking drawn and anxious, she sat in the nearest chair.

"There's nothing to worry about, Bea. He says he wants to keep what they call a low profile on it. In a few weeks the whole thing will probably be forgotten. Why don't I get you a cup of tea?''

"I need something a hell of a lot stronger than that.''

"I've made martinis for you and Jon to have later.''

"Great, I'll have half of one.'' Bea followed Vivienne into the kitchen. "Where's MacGuffin? He's usually all over me when I come by.''

"He's outside. I have to take him for a walk later. I've been taking him to Carmel Beach instead of the lagoon beach ever since Sunday.''

"No wonder,'' Bea said, helping herself to the pitcher of martinis. She poured some into the glass Vivienne gave her and took a swallow. Vivienne took the pitcher from her and replaced it in the refrigerator, then began to make tea.

"This is great,'' Bea seated herself at the kitchen table. She took another sip. "I have an alibi, you know.''

Vivienne turned to look at her. "You have what?''

"In case anybody asks, that's all. I have an alibi. I was with a priest.''

"Bea—''

"Father Stephen Flanagan. I was confessing.''

"Bea!''

"It's true! I was with him for almost the whole party. That's why I had to go to your bathroom and wash up. I cried and my makeup ran and I got a terrible headache. I always do when I cry. So I had to take some aspirin. I even ran into Matt Ross when I was coming out of the house. So, see—I have an alibi.''

"Although it's none of my business, Bea, if you were with him for the whole party—''

"Oh, it wasn't like that! Girls aren't a priority in his life; I saw that right away. Of course, they're not supposed to be if you're a priest, but you know what I mean. It's not that I'm a Catholic. I just needed someone to talk to. I told him all about my whole life—Buster, Toad Hall, the men—everything. That's why I started crying.''

Vivienne shook her head, at a loss for words. "Bea, I don't know what to say."

"You don't have to say anything. I'm just telling you I have an iron-clad alibi."

As they looked at each other, Vivienne became aware of the repeated, distant sound of knocking coming from the front door.

"It's Jon! I wonder how long he's been knocking? It's so hard to hear from here." She walked through the living room to the door and let him in.

Jonathan Patrick practically exploded into the room. "Vivienne, I have news! Where's Bea?"

Bea appeared around the corner of the dining room, her martini glass raised high. "Here I am!"

"The phone is ringing off the hook at the theatre! Annie and I can't keep up with it. Everyone in Carmel wants tickets for the show. Where's the cake?"

"In the kitchen. I'll bring it right out for you."

"No tea, just cake. After that I'll have whatever Bea is drinking at this very early hour."

Vivienne went into the kitchen and prepared a tray with tea, china, silver and a plate of cakes. Bea and Jonathan were sitting on the sofa when she returned. Bea was whispering something to Jonathan and stopped as Vivienne entered the room.

"Just telling Jon about the police chief being here when I came over," Bea said, as Vivienne placed the tray on a low table before them.

"The cakes look wonderful!" Jon exclaimed, helping himself to several. "I've saved all my news until you got back in the room, Vivienne. We're going on with the show. Medora Everett, of course, will do Sisu's role. And either I will do Hilly's role, or he'll do it himself—more of that later. I'm also setting up a system of understudies for everyone."

"Understudies!" Bea exclaimed. "Who else are you expecting to die?"

"Bea, please. Just for illness, that sort of thing." Jonathan popped one of the small cakes into his mouth and chewed vigorously. They waited in suspense for his final swallow.

"I'll understudy and possibly do Hilly's role," he continued, picking up another cake. "And Matt will understudy

Ted—he just doesn't know it yet. If he doesn't want to, I'll understudy that, too. Claudia Kellog will understudy Edwinta, and Medora Everett will understudy you and Vivienne. Helen Lawton will understudy Medora.''

"Why do I feel my days are numbered?" Bea wailed. "I don't feel good about Medora understudying me. She's already in the goddamned review as a 'theatrical luminary' and she wasn't even in the show."

"Oh, yes. She and Thorson."

"If those two are luminaries, the light must be pretty dim!"

"Now, now, Beatrice, we're all going to pull together on this one. It'll be necessary, because we're going to start doing the show—with everyone's permission, of course—on summer schedule, Wednesday through Sunday. But this coming weekend we'll start on Friday."

"It's fine with me," Vivienne said.

"It's okay with me, too," Bea said grudgingly. "I'm just planning to stay real healthy. And I'm not sending Medora up front to get me any coffee at intermission!"

"What do you mean about Hilly Lawton? That he may or may not do the show?" Vivienne asked.

Jon swallowed his second cake. "I finally got up the nerve to call him. He didn't sound as bad as I thought he would—maybe relief is finally beginning to hit him, too."

"Huh?" Bea asked.

"Well, Vivienne and I have a theory that Ted Reid may be a bit more relieved than he'd like to let on that Sisu is no more—"

"That wasn't my theory, Jon. That was yours. I really don't know Ted that well."

"Anyway, Hilly's not on top of it yet, and he's not sure he wants to come back into the show right away. Mcmories, all that. So we're going to leave that up to him. And I haven't asked Ted if he'll agree to the summer schedule yet, but I don't think it'll be a problem. He has plenty of free time."

"Matt was going to talk to him today," Vivienne interjected. "He should be here any minute now. Matt, I mean."

"Is he going to testify at the inquest, too?" Bea asked.

"Inquest? What inquest?" Jonathan, excited, halted on the way to putting a third cake in his mouth.

"It's in a few weeks, Jon. I have to testify because I found the body."

"You know, she couldn't swim," Jonathan said thoughtfully. "And I can't picture Sisu committing suicide. Not that way—she wasn't the type. I could see her taking sleeping pills and calling everyone in Carmel including the rescue squad to say she was checking out, but she wouldn't have drowned herself. It had to have been an accident."

"If it was an accident, what I don't understand is why she would have gone for a walk by herself," Vivienne said. She hadn't meant to bring the subject up; it had come up in spite of her. "She wasn't the kind of person to leave in the middle of a party, especially at night, and go off walking alone. I could see Ted as the sort of person to do that, but not Sisu. Unless someone went with her, or someone followed her, or someone arranged to meet her somewhere—"

"And then pushed her in!" Jonathan concluded enthusiastically. He had been listening to Vivienne with a rapt expression on his face, absorbed in her speculations. "You're right! But you said the policeman told you there were no signs it was anything but an accident. That would mean—what would it mean?"

"It means that she wasn't bashed over the head, that there weren't any bruises on her arms from being shoved in or marks on her neck from being held under the water, and most important, there was no banana peel by the edge of the lagoon with the murderer's fingerprints on it," Bea said. "Look, as far as I'm concerned, if there was ever anybody who's better off gone, it was her. The day that broad stepped into the pond out there and went 'glub, glub,' she performed a civic service for all of us."

"Bea, please! You forget, I found her body."

"Only glad it wasn't me," Bea muttered. "I would have left it there."

They heard a knock on the door. Vivienne went to answer it, and Matt came back into the room with her.

"Matt, you missed our true crime stories," Jonathan said. "Have some cake. I'm ready for a martini now. Don't get up, Vivienne. I'll help myself."

"I'll come too," Bea said. "I need a refill."

Bea and Jonathan went to the kitchen while Matt sat near Vivienne and, scowling, helped himself to tea and cakes.

"Don't mind me," he said. "I'm in a terrible mood. I'm recuperating from a scenic walk on Carmel Beach with Ted Reid. I went back to the cottage and wrote it all down verbatim to get it out of my system. I'll let you read it sometime—after I expurgate it!"

"Was it that bad?"

"For a person as self-centered as Ted is, he has an amazing ability to find someone else's sore spots and poke them with his finger. You just want to punch the guy, and then he does this 'Ah, shucks' routine and you want to punch him even more, but you can't. It's like he's wearing glasses and a turned around collar and weighs ninety pounds. You were so right about him—righter than you knew!"

Vivienne was about to speak, but stopped as Bea and Jon returned with their drinks.

"Matt, do you have any objection to doing the show on summer schedule and understudying Ted?" Jonathan asked.

"Well, no, I guess not. Not if it's for the good of the show."

"It is. We're getting calls like crazy. The review and the story in the paper did it. And we can really catch the Playhouse up financially, maybe even get ahead. We'll do three shows this weekend and start again on Wednesday next week. Do you think Ted'll mind doing the extra nights, Matt?"

"Call him yourself, Jon. But I did get the feeling he was eager to do the show again."

"What about the kid?" Bea asked. "Did anyone ask her?"

"I told Medora, so I assume she's passed the news to Edwinta," Jon said. "I'll start blocking Medora into the show this week, and we'll reopen on Friday. She's a trouper; she'll just need a couple of blocking rehearsals and she'll be fine. I can't get new programs until next week, so we'll make an announcement of the cast change before each performance. By the way, the new program will have a printed tribute to Sisu in it. 'In Memoriam: Celia Susan Potter'—something like that."

"Oh, spare me!" Bea groaned. "This time I'm really gonna be sick!"

"I think that's so revealing," Vivienne said. "Celia Susan Potter—'Sisu.' She went through life using her baby name."

Bea put down her drink, clutched her throat with her hands and made gagging sounds.

Jonathan pointedly ignored Bea's action. "Hilly suggested the tribute in the program, and I think—pardon me, Beatrice—that it would be a nice touch. So until we get the program printed up, we'll just insert a little slip of paper into each one with 'In Memoriam' on it."

"A cute little note with black edges? I can see it now—they'll fall out of the programs and lie all over the floor—like dandruff!"

"Now, Bea, a little kindness toward the dead."

"Kindness, ha! I have to be on my best behavior now that I have Spider Woman for an understudy!"

"Matt, Bea has this notion Medora is going to poison her throat spray."

Bea threw Jon a pained expression. "How esoteric! I was thinking more of my old-fashioned down at the La Playa." She picked up one of the little cakes and regarded it suspiciously. "I still don't understand why the hell she wants to do this show in the first place. There's something going on there."

"As I told Vivienne, I think she wants to make it up to everyone for the scene at the party. And to give Edwinta a chance."

"Are there no other women in Carmel who can walk around stage and say a dozen lines?"

"Bea, you know Medora," Jon said. "That ego's so huge she probably thinks she's the only one who can do the role justice."

"When are you rehearsing her, Jon?" Vivienne interrupted the interchange.

"Wednesday and Thursday nights. Just me and maybe Claudia. I don't feel I can ask the cast to rehearse the show again, and Medora's a trouper. Friday's our reopening."

"It's too mysterious," Bea continued, still speculating unhappily. "I didn't like it when I heard it. There's something I don't trust about Medora. She has too many secrets."

"Don't we all?" asked Jon.

For an instant, the four of them sat in an awkward still life, not meeting each other's eyes. Vivienne broke the silence by rising from her chair.

"Excuse me, I need to make a phone call."

Vivienne heard Bea's voice behind her as she walked through the dining room towards the kitchen: "Too close to home, Jon!"

Vivienne picked up the kitchen phone and dialed the operator for a Carmel number, then dialed the call. She let the phone ring eight times, then hung up. There had been no one at the other end to answer "Everett residence."

SEVENTEEN

THE TEA PARTY BROKE UP shortly thereafter, with Jonathan leaving for the Playhouse and Bea going back to Brown Hall for dinner. As the sun set over Point Lobos far beyond the large windows of the living room, Matt and Vivienne sat drinking tea and eating the last of the cakes. Vivienne, slowly nibbling on a cake and seemingly lost in thought, suddenly looked up at Matt.

"I have an idea, and I wondered if you'd be willing to help me with it," she said.

"Sure, what?"

She set her fork down on one side of the porcelain plate. "Let's both keep our eyes and ears open about this. About Sisu Potter's death."

"I thought the police were supposed to do that."

"If they can, Matt. But the police chief told me he was afraid he wouldn't be able to find out anything. Or prove anything."

"You mean, prove it wasn't an accident?"

"Yes. He said something to the effect that he got the feeling everyone he talked to thought Sisu had been murdered, although I was the only one who actually voiced the suspicion to him. He said there was a lot of fear in the air and not much sorrow."

"I've felt that myself. That's very perceptive. I wouldn't have expected that of him."

"Why not? He's an intelligent man. He just doesn't know the people involved the way we do. Except for Claudia, of course."

"People *have* been acting strangely," Matt said thoughtfully. "As though they were trying to make sure they had alibis."

"Which people are you talking about?" Vivienne leaned forward.

"I guess Ted is the only one I meant," Matt said, watching her. "When I was walking on the beach with him, he said something about being right there—at that spot on Carmel Beach, he meant—when Medora poured the champagne over Thorson's head.''

"Did it seem to you he was acting guilty?''

"Ted seems to be guilty of everything and innocent of everything at the same time. I think it comes from being a priest.''

"Undoubtedly," Vivienne said dryly. "What did you mean about my being right about him?''

"Oh, that. Ted's doing exactly what you said he would about Edwinta Everett. 'It was wrong of me to spend so much time with that girl—she's just a child. When Steve got here, I realized how dependent on me she'd become...' That kind of talk. By the way, has anyone spoken to Edwinta yet?''

Vivienne tensed and clasped the arms of her chair. "I'm sorry, Matt, I feel very angry about the way that man has behaved, and it's disturbing me. I've tried calling Edwinta's house several times—I did so less than an hour ago when I went out to the kitchen. No one was home. The other times, Medora answered.''

"When I ran into her the other night going down to my cottage, she was very upset. I don't know whether she saw the fight between Medora and Thorson, but she knew about it and she wanted to leave. She was looking for Ted. She said 'he and that creepy friend of his' had promised her a ride home. And you know," Matt was hit with a sudden recollection, "the sleeve of her white dress was damp. I felt it when I touched her arm.''

"What do you mean?''

"Not that I think Edwinta would—would kill anyone, but if someone pushed Sisu Potter into the water, wouldn't their clothes get wet, or at least damp?''

"Matt, it's impossible that Edwinta would kill anyone!''

Seeing Vivienne's eyes flash, Matt felt an immediate need to qualify his suspicion. "I know that and you know that, but didn't she play a child murderess in *The Bad Seed*?''

"That was a play!''

"But maybe she feels she's under suspicion, since she and Sisu didn't like each other, and everyone knows she played the 'bad seed.' Didn't the 'bad seed' push someone into a lake and drown them?''

"Yes, a little boy," Vivienne looked toward the window, where the setting sun streaked the sky behind Point Lobos with pink and gold. "You're probably right, Matt. She feels under suspicion. That explains why she's nowhere to be found. That and Ted's desertion."

"If we were looking for people who had it in for Sisu, objectively we'd have to include Mrs. Brown."

Vivienne was up in arms again. "That's impossible, Matt! Bea couldn't kill a fly—you know her! She's been plotting to kill Buster for years and it's all a game."

"But suppose she saw Sisu walking toward the lagoon—I'm just speculating now—and suppose she followed her and maybe, on the spur of the moment, pushed her in. Or saw Sisu fall in and didn't try to help her."

"Someone could have done that. But not Bea. Besides, she was with that priest, Steve, for the whole party, right up until she ran into you as she was coming out of the house."

"You couldn't have a more perfect alibi than being with a priest, I guess. But suppose—I'm just playing devil's advocate now, because I don't think Bea Brown would harm anyone— suppose someone murdered Sisu by drowning her *after* the party, not during it?"

"After everyone had gone home, you mean? In that case, Bea is still safe, because she went home with her servants, all the way out to Pebble Beach."

"But if Sisu died during the party, the people who disappeared for a while, like Ted, would really be in trouble," Matt mused. "We could make up a time chart showing where people were at different times during the party."

"I don't see how we could possibly keep track of everyone. People were back and forth, and I was in and out of the house so often."

"Before we try figuring all this out, we need to find out what time she died," Matt decided. "That's primary. Can you find out from that policeman?"

"He might tell me, but why should he?"

Matt had to explain a simple fact of Carmel life to her. "Because you're Vivienne Montrose," he said.

"Oh!" Vivienne looked taken aback. "Do you really think that's reason enough?"

"It's reason enough for anyone in Carmel. Why don't you try? Call him tomorrow and ask him to stop by. Tell him some of what we've been speculating about and find out what he knows. What time she drowned, whether she could have been held under the water, or pushed, or what."

"All right, I'll try."

"And I'm going to talk to Claudia tomorrow if it kills me. Every time I call her house her mother says she's over at the church, helping out. Anyway, I'm going to find out what she knows."

"She's a lovely girl, Matt." Vivienne was regarding him almost inquisitively. "I think she cares for you."

Matt looked away in embarrassment. "I haven't treated her very well. I owe her an apology."

"If you haven't, I would agree with you," Vivienne said, rising. "I don't mean to rush you off, but I plan to make it an early night. I haven't quite caught up from that party."

"Oh, sure!" Matt jumped up. "I have some writing I have to get to."

"One more thing," he said as they walked to the door. "Ted told me Hilly and Sisu were planning to get married."

"Not really!" Vivienne stopped and looked at him. "Poor Hilly, no wonder he's been devastated. I didn't know it was that serious."

"According to Ted it was. He said Sisu hinted about it to him, but he didn't catch on. I asked him why they were keeping it under wraps and he said he thought Helen Lawton might have felt awkward about it, being in the show with them. He also dropped the fact that Sisu was still coming on to him, but you know Ted's ego."

"You told me you wrote down your talk on the beach with Ted. I'd like to read it sometime soon."

They reached the front door. Matt was well aware he was playing Watson to Vivienne's Sherlock, but he didn't mind.

"I'll drop it by tomorrow," he said in farewell.

EIGHTEEN

VIVIENNE TOOK MACGUFFIN to the lagoon beach early the following day. Since the ill-fated morning after opening night, they had been taking their walks on Carmel Beach, where there were pebbles and seaweed but no driftwood. Now MacGuffin was running and jumping in joyous anticipation of playing the driftwood game at long last. They descended the steep stairway from the road to the beach. MacGuffin hopping down the steps in paroxysms of dog delight. When they reached the sand, both Vivienne and the dog ran toward the ocean.

They crossed the smooth, wet sand at the water's edge, dodging the surf. MacGuffin frisked along, frightening the birds digging for food in the shore, making them half run, half fly away. Vivienne backed away from a big wave and moved up to slightly higher ground. She looked around for her dog. He was lagging behind, playing with the birds. She called out to him and he ran toward her, leaving the prints of his paws next to the prints of her feet in the damp sand.

Together they ran up the dunes toward the lagoon. MacGuffin couldn't wait to get to the driftwood, and Vivienne's curiosity had at last overcome her fears of visiting the spot again. They came to the top of the rise and saw a calm lake encircled by the marsh, the sandbank and the hills. The ocean's sounds were muffled there, leaving them in a cocoon of stillness, broken occasionally by the clacking and cooing of a dozen water birds floating near the far shore of the lagoon.

On impulse, Vivienne left MacGuffin scuffling in a pile of driftwood and walked back toward the parking lot, which lay between the upper part of the scenic drive and the beach. She studied the stretch of coarse sand leading to the lot. It was blackened from campfires, littered all over with small pieces of half-charred driftwood, and pitted thousands of times with small valleys that were the indentations of many feet.

She walked back toward the lagoon and saw MacGuffin charging her, a stick in his mouth. He dropped the stick at her feet and looked up at her expectantly. She threw it for him and began searching the area for another piece of driftwood. She finally found a long tree branch, smooth and bone-dry, and holding it, she picked her way across the sand toward the spot where she had found the body.

When she stood there, she found herself repressing a shudder, but all was still, as if neither human life nor death had touched the place. The water lapped gently against the reedy promontory near her feet. She reached out with the stick and poked it down into the water, finding a shallows extending several feet out.

She began to walk along the embankment toward the ocean side of the lagoon. Stopping by what had once been the trunk of a good-sized tree, she took off her shoes and placed them on top of the big bleached log.

She went back to the lagoon shore again, lifted up her skirts and stepped in, going as deep as she could while holding her skirts high enough to keep them dry and reaching with the driftwood stick to test the depth of the water. She waded along in the shallows close to the embankment, testing the depth with the stick as far as she could reach.

At the point where the lagoon met the white sand of the ocean, the shoal fell away sharply. She climbed out of the water and circled the smooth sandbank until she reached the rocks below the cliffs on the other side. She stepped from rock to rock as far as she could go, pushing the stick down into the water. The boulders were part of a rock shelf that extended from the foot of the cliffs down into the water. She looked up to the top of the cliffs some twelve to fifteen feet above her. If there were no bruises or marks on the body, she doubted Sisu Potter could have jumped or fallen from their heights.

Finally, girding herself for the most difficult task, she walked back to the spot where she'd found the body, lifted her skirts and stepped down into the shallow water. Shivering as much from revulsion as from the cold of the lagoon, she waded out several feet until she felt the shore dropping away, then turned and began to scramble back onto land.

She heard a voice calling out something indistinguishable. She flung her skirts down and looked up.

A man was coming toward her across the dunes, walking with big athletic strides. It was Chief Himber.

"Were you calling me?" she shouted. The sound of her voice seemed to disappear into the wind.

"Yes," he shouted back, almost reaching her. "I said— 'You're doing my job!'"

"Then you saw me?" She felt herself blush, wondering how long he had been watching her wading in the water with her skirts up to her waist.

"I witnessed your investigation of the depth of the shoreline of the lagoon, yes," Himber said. "I stopped by to see Matt Ross. He'll have to be subpoenaed to testify, too. He told me you wanted to see me. He said you were down here with your dog."

"MacGuffin! I got so absorbed I completely forgot about him! I do want to speak with you, but I have to get him first. He's probably found some kids to play with, or a dead seagull to roll in." Vivienne started down the slope toward the beach, calling the dog's name.

MacGuffin was also absorbed—in chasing birds near the surf. Vivienne ran down to the shore and retrieved him. She started back up the rise again, but stopped when she saw the police chief walking down to meet her.

"MacGuffin. Unusual name," he said when he reached her side. "*Is* he?"

"A MacGuffin?" Vivienne smiled. "No. He's always been exactly the way he seems. Dogs are."

"They're reliable that way, unlike some people. Too bad they can't talk. They'd make great witnesses." He paused. "So what are your findings?"

Vivienne and Chief Himber fell into stride, walking along the beach in the direction of the hills beyond the lagoon, with MacGuffin trailing behind them.

"The shoreline is shallow several feet out, then it drops," Vivienne began. "Except where the lagoon meets the sandbank. Then it drops quite sharply. Where I found the body—in that area—it seems impossible that she could have slipped in and drowned accidentally. Unless she panicked and got turned around and stumbled into the deeper water. It's hard to say. If she fell near the sandbank, it would have been much harder to get out. The water seems quite deep there, while the sand on the bank is smooth. When you were there that morning, did you notice signs that anyone had walked there or might have slipped in?''

"The tide had been in the night before, but not that high. There were some footprints in the bank—more like small troughs in the sand—but no sign that someone had slipped into the lagoon.''

"You mean, if she had slipped off the sandbank into the water—''

"There would be signs of it. The smooth dune formation would have been broken.''

"It's shallow by the rocks over there, too. Under the cliffs, I mean. The moon was out that night, and you could probably have seen to walk on the rocks, but would she have gone walking on the rocks at night if she couldn't swim? I wouldn't. And she couldn't have fallen off the cliffs, could she, if there were no signs of that on her body?''

The direction of their walk was leading them to the other side of the lagoon. Chief Himber looked up at the cliffs. "No. She didn't fall from up there.''

"There's something I wanted to ask you. How can you be sure that she drowned? Suppose she was, well, not strangled—you could see marks on her neck in that case—but suppose she was suffocated and then pushed into the water, just as an example?''

He smiled. "I think I want to recruit you for the force—you have a deductive mind. But she did drown. The doctor pressed on her chest, and quantities of water poured from her nose and mouth.''

"From her lungs?''

"Right.''

Imagining it, Vivienne felt sick. "I don't think I have the stomach for forensic detail.''

"Oh, I think you've got plenty of guts. Stepping right in the water where you found the body—not too many people would have the stomach to do that.''

"Thanks, but I was such a coward before. I went running for Matt and didn't even turn the body over to see who it was."

"You're not supposed to turn bodies over. That causes problems."

"Oh, that's right! But suppose she'd been alive?"

"It was obvious she was dead, wasn't it?"

"Yes."

MacGuffin was dancing around her ankles with another stick in his mouth. She took it from him and threw it; he raced away over the dunes.

"Let's walk back the other way," Vivienne said. "I need to pick up my shoes."

They circled the sandbank in companionable silence, heading toward the big driftwood log.

Vivienne thought of another query. "You told me there were no signs that Sisu Potter's death was anything but an accident. What did you mean by that—how would you know that? I guess that would mean there were no marks or bruises on her body, wouldn't it?"

"That's what it means."

"Could she have been held under the water? But then the person who held her would have been soaked. They would have had to change their clothes, and no one at the party did that."

"Theoretically, she could have been. But, as you said, no one at the party changed their clothes or appeared to be wet. And I assume if she *was* held underwater, she would have put up quite a struggle—if she was conscious."

"Conscious?"

"She'd been drinking heavily?"

"Yes, but that water is cold, almost as cold as the ocean. It would wake anyone up—worse than a cold shower, I would think."

"Good point. If she passed out and fell in, the coldness of the water would probably have brought her back to consciousness."

They reached the log, and Vivienne sat on it and slipped her shoes back on. Suddenly, she remembered the most important question of all. "What time did she die? Was it during the party or later?"

Chief Himber sat near the end of the log with his hands resting uncomfortably on his knees. "She didn't drown first thing in the morning, that's for sure," he said. "They think it was some time between 11 P.M. and 3 A.M."

"The party really got started around eleven, and Sisu didn't arrive until later. I saw her briefly, shortly after she arrived, then not again. I know Matt talked to her, but I don't know what time that was. Early on in the party, I would think. People just kept roaming around, disappearing, coming back."

"Except for those who didn't come back."

"Yes."

"Miss Potter and Miss Everett."

"I haven't been able to talk to Edwinta since all this happened. She doesn't ever seem to be at home."

"A talented girl. I remember her from years back at the Dockside Theatre. Highly convincing portrayal of a psychopathic child. I still remember the expression on her face when she looked out at the audience at the end of the play after she'd killed all those people. Bloodcurdling! But they say kids are natural actors. Didn't the little girl in the play—"

Vivienne turned to him, interrupting. "Drown someone. Mr. Himber, I've known Edwinta Everett since she was a child. Believe me, that girl couldn't kill anyone. She may not have had the happiest time growing up, but she has a wonderful spirit. She's full of life. For her to kill someone—that's just not possible."

His intelligent blue eyes seemed to bore into her own. "Then why are you so afraid of her?"

She looked away, holding tight to the log under her. "Circumstances. Her disappearing from the party and not coming back. Playing the 'bad seed.' Everyone remembers her in that role. And Sisu giving her such a hard time."

"She did?"

"She and Sisu were sharing one of the big dressing rooms at first. And Sisu had been involved with Ted Reid and resented Edwinta's friendship with him. When Edwinta told me about the problem with Sisu, I had her move her things into my dressing room. That seemed to calm the situation. I think Edwinta ran off from the party because of the scene between her father and her mother."

"Miss Potter certainly seems to have had her enemies, but aside from her being a thorn in several sides, no one seems to have profited from her death."

"Did she have a will?"

"The father says no. The family has money, but Daddy and Mommy took care of her. She was their little girl, they were older, she was going to outlive them. All very sad."

"It must be so difficult talking to the family of someone who—who died."

"Always is."

"Hilly Lawton must have been hard to deal with, too. I heard that he and Sisu were planning to marry."

"He told me they weren't officially engaged but they'd discussed it seriously. And there's no motive there. If they were married, he might have inherited some of her family's wealth on her death, but they weren't."

"Who *could* have profited from Sisu's death?" Vivienne mused. "No one I can think of. Medora Everett inherited her role in the play—but no one kills for a role with a dozen lines! Especially not Medora. She didn't want to do it in the first place, and she's only doing it now to help out."

The police chief looked at his watch. "Excuse me, Miss Montrose, I have to get back. I'm sure we'll be speculating about this again." He rose from his seat on the driftwood log.

"I know there's something else I need to ask you, but I can't think of it." Vivienne got up, called to MacGuffin, and the three began to walk back across the low dunes toward the parking lot. Vivienne saw a police car and two other cars parked in the lot. The sun had risen higher in the sky, and the day was turning warm.

"I know what it is!" Vivienne stood still. "Currents!"

"I'll show you something. Come on." Chief Himber turned and led Vivienne back to the lagoon.

They walked to the promontory on the bank where he reached down and picked up a small piece of driftwood, four or five inches long, thick and flat. He tossed it six feet or so out into the lagoon. Very slowly, the stick began to ripple back toward the shore.

Vivienne turned and looked up at him, her anger rising. "What does that mean?" she asked coldly.

"It means the current is very weak. Where Miss Potter went into the water is pretty much where you found her. She was out a little farther than that when she drowned, but not much farther. She may have foundered out where the bank drops off underwater, panicked, and couldn't get back."

Vivienne was so furious she felt tears welling up. She bit her lip. He knew all this all along, she thought, and he was just playing with me, leading me on to find out what I knew! Fighting back her rage, she glanced up at the police chief. He was looking out toward the center of the lagoon.

"I know you think I've been teasing you and treating you like a child," he said. "I don't blame you for being mad. But this is my job. Don't get me wrong." He turned to her. "I like it that you're this interested. It makes the case more interesting for me, and it's helpful that you're working on it full-time mentally, too. You and Matt Ross, I'm presuming. Between the two of you, you know all the parties involved fairly well. I don't."

Vivienne took a deep breath and started to speak, then stopped herself.

"What were you going to say?" he asked.

"I accept your apology, if that's what it is."

"It is. I'm not sitting you down and telling you everything I know because that's not part of my job, but then you're not telling me everything you know, either."

Vivienne looked at him in surprise. He was absolutely right.

"Frankly," he continued, "I doubt this case is going to go down in the records as anything more than an accident. Suppose someone did push her in, for whatever reason. If we have no witness and no motive—no evidence—in short, there's nothing we can do. Right now, I suggest you and I and your Watson just keep a lookout and see if anything surfaces."

Vivienne didn't look at him. She sensed he was smiling at her, but she wouldn't look up. "That's what we plan on doing," she said, still miffed.

"Which way are you walking?"

"Not through the parking lot," she said. "Down to the beach and up the stone steps—that way."

"Then I'll head out the other way and get my car. Call me if you need anything. Or if you remember anything you want to tell me."

"Thanks," Vivienne said coolly. She called to MacGuffin, and he started running toward her. Men! she thought—thank heavens MacGuffin is a dog!

She walked off down the beach, the wind whipping her hair and her skirts, and MacGuffin running in circles around her.

NINETEEN

THE LITTLE CHAPEL by the Sea was not exactly *by* the sea; in fact, it was at least a quarter of a mile away from the sea, on one of the side streets that wound off Ocean Avenue, Carmel's main thoroughfare. Matt imagined it would be an antique Anglican building of stone and wood, or at the least red brick—a place where Mrs. Miniver or Mr. Chips would have gone to kneel and say a prayer or two. The surprise came when he finally located it and found a Mediterranean-style stucco building, vaguely pink, with high walls and a bell tower resembling the one at the nearby Carmel Mission—sort of a miniature version of a Pebble Beach mansion. Apparently people needed a lot less room to pray than they did to eat, sleep and entertain.

A path of adobe bricks led to the entrance doors, which were large, ornately carved wooden slabs. The heavy front door on the left was slightly ajar, and as Matt cautiously pushed it open, he got a whiff of bitter incense. Inside, the high stucco walls were broken by window after window of stained glass men and women; the two nearest Matt stood holding, respectively, a stained glass sword and a stained glass lily. The sun poured its afternoon light through the windows in the left wall, bathing the interior of the chapel in patches of color. At the opposite end by the altar, a young woman was arranging golden chrysanthemums in a large brass vase.

Matt walked down to the altar where the girl was kneeling as she snipped the stems, and touched her on the shoulder. She started in surprise and threw her head up to see him.

"I didn't mean to scare you," Matt said.

"But you did," Claudia said, rising. "It's that carpet that runs down the center aisle. Everywhere else in the church you can hear a pin drop, but you can't hear anyone if they're walking on the carpet. It's happened to me a few times before, though. I should be used to it by now.'' Claudia finally looked at Matt again. ''Why are you here?''

''Your mother told me how to find the place. I've called your house a dozen times and you're never around. I thought I'd stop by the Playhouse last night for the blocking rehearsal with Mrs. Everett, but then I wouldn't have been able to talk to you alone. So I thought I'd come here.''

''Well, let's go outside then.''

Claudia led the way past the altar and out a side door to the lawn. She stopped and turned back to him.

''I guess you don't want to walk down to the lagoon this time,'' she said.

Matt ducked his head quickly in embarrassment. ''I want to beg off that one,'' he said. ''In fact, I want to apologize for the whole evening. Especially for leaving you alone down there. I went back to look for you and you were gone.''

''Yes.''

Claudia began walking in the direction of a fruit tree at the edge of the lawn, and Matt followed her.

''Claudia, I'd like to spend some time with you. Maybe we could go to dinner at that place you said you always wanted to go to.''

Claudia stopped by the tree and sat, leaning against its trunk. Matt knelt beside her.

''Yes, I *would* like to go to that restaurant with you,'' she said after some moments. ''I'd *like* to, only...''

''Only what?'' Matt was resting uncomfortably on one knee on the grass under the tree, feeling like the classic case of the importunate suitor.

''You live in another world, Matt. For you, everything's black and white, like an old movie on TV. I've watched some of them since I got to know you and,'' she looked at him wonderingly, ''they're so romantic! Everything is grander than life, more heroic, more beautiful. I can see why you love them so much. Only in real life, if someone isn't perfect—if they don't behave or talk just the way you think they ought to—you want to change the channel. Or rewrite the script. My feelings got hurt, Matt, and you can't write dialogue to get around that.'' Claudia's soft voice was emphatic. ''I'm not one of the characters in your book or in some old film; I'm me. Maybe I'll change, but if I do it'll be because *I* want to change, not so I can live up to someone else's ideal. That's what I mean. If I spend time with you, I don't want to feel you've set up some shining ideal on one side, and on the other side—there's me."

Matt sat down next to her. "I don't know how to say this, Claudia. Ever since that night I've been realizing that I made a huge mistake about you. A lot of things have spelled that out in big letters. It's not only that I behaved badly. I know I did, and I kept seeing it reflected in the way other men were behaving—Hilly Lawton, Ted Reid—especially Ted Reid. I thought about what I was throwing away, and I felt sick about it." He reached over and took her hand. "Claudia, getting this far in life hasn't been easy for me. I had to put on rose-colored glasses just to survive. I can't give up my shining ideals, as you call them. That's me. Even the rose-colored glasses are me. I just wasn't looking at *you* through them. I was afraid to look at you. Do you understand that I mean?"

Claudia, looking away, squeezed his hand hard in both of hers, then turned her face to him. Her violet eyes framed by their long, dark lashes were luminous. "I do understand," she said.

"Could we have dinner tonight?"

"I'd like that very much, but everything's so busy now. Today I have to work here until around five, and I need to get back to the Playhouse before seven-thirty to get things set up for the show. I guess you do, too."

"Why don't I come back when you've finished here, and we'll get a quick bite to eat and then go down to the theatre?"

"Okay." Claudia began to get to her feet, and Matt jumped up and helped her.

"How's Hilly Lawton been taking this?" he asked. "Everyone's been wondering."

"He's better now. We were all worried about him right after it happened. He looked so old—as though he'd aged ten years. He came in the day after her body was found to help out here, but we made him go home. He seems to be getting over it now, though. You just missed him; he was here earlier today."

"Do you think he'll want to do the show again?"

"I think it would get his mind off her death, to be busy acting again. He loves the theatre. I suggested to him that he wait till next week, and then come by and see if he's up to doing the show, and I got the feeling that's what's he's going to do."

They began walking back toward the church.

"Claudia, that night—I know you want to forget about it, and I do, too, but I have a question. Vivienne's curious about why Sisu would go walking by herself. She feels Sisu is more likely to have been with someone, or have gone to meet someone. I thought that since you were sitting down there, you might have heard something or seen something—maybe something you weren't even aware of."

Claudia stopped walking and stood silently preoccupied, a troubled expression on her face.

"I heard her voice," she said slowly. "I heard people coming down the slope, and I didn't want to see anyone so I slipped around the other side of your cottage where it was dark."

"What was she saying?"

"She was talking loudly. She sounded like she'd been drinking. She said something about a priest, or priests, I'm not sure which. I couldn't hear her very well. When I'm upset, I have trouble remembering things people say. I'm not like you."

"Usually I remember everything verbatim."

"I know, it's your gift as a writer."

"What was she saying about a priest?"

Claudia looked both anxious and embarrassed. "She was angry. You know how Sisu was when she got angry. She could say really nasty things."

"What do you mean by 'nasty things?'"

"I'd really rather not talk about it, Matt." Claudia seemed to grow more uncomfortable. "As I said, it wasn't nice, what I could hear of it. I don't remember the exact words and I don't want to, but it sounded like she was saying one of the worst things you could say, that's all. I just don't want to talk about it anymore!"

"Okay. I don't want to upset you. I only have one more question. When you were hiding next to the cottage, did you leave first or did she?"

"I'm not sure. I think she did. I heard her voice fading like she was walking farther away. I was going up the hill at the same time, though, so I'm not sure."

"Did it sound like she was going toward the lagoon?"

"She could have been. I'm not sure."

"Have you told this to anyone else?"

"No, not even to my uncle. I didn't want to have to explain why I was down there; I was feeling terrible about it then. I didn't want to have to tell him what she said. I just couldn't."

Matt wanted to change the subject. "It was quite a surprise to everyone, your uncle being the Chief of Police."

She came out of her unhappy reverie and smiled. "Uncle Cor. Quite a coincidence. It was a little family joke."

"A family joke?"

"I probably shouldn't tell you, but Uncle Cor and Aunt Margaret used to go to all the plays Vivienne Montrose was in. They were both big fans of hers. Uncle Cor used to say that his wife—my aunt—was the only woman in the world he wouldn't leave for Vivienne Montrose. We all used to tease him about it, especially Aunt Margaret."

"You're kidding."

"No. It was a little family joke. Then after Aunt Margaret died—that was about three years ago—we stopped teasing him about being in love with Vivienne Montrose. He still goes to see her shows, probably more often than anyone knows, only he doesn't talk about it." She turned to Matt and took his arm. "I don't think I should have told you that. Please don't tell anyone. Especially not Vivienne. It would really embarrass my uncle."

"Believe me, I won't." He paused. "Claudia, will you promise *me* something?"

"What?"

"Don't say anything about what you overheard that night down by the cottage. You can tell your uncle about it, but don't tell anyone else we know. No one."

"I wasn't going to anyway, but why not?"

"If Sisu's death wasn't accidental, I wouldn't want anyone knowing you heard whatever you heard."

"But it *was* an accident! Uncle Cor said there were no signs it wasn't."

"Suppose other people are keeping things secret—the way you were."

Claudia stared at him with huge eyes. "How could you think anyone in our group could do anything like that? I mean, we *know* everyone!"

"I'm not saying anyone did it on purpose. Suppose Sisu fell into the lagoon—you said she sounded drunk—and the person or persons who were with her panicked and didn't pull her out? Shouldn't that come out? Shouldn't the truth be found out and told, if something like that happened?"

"If that happened and nobody's come forward, how could anyone find out about it?"

"I don't know. It just seems to me that if someone asks enough questions, they might be able to come up with some answers. Vivienne feels the same way I do. We've talked about it, about looking into it quietly."

"You and Vivienne?"

Matt took Claudia's hand again. "Unlike your uncle, I am *not* in love with Vivienne Montrose!"

"Remember, I didn't tell you that!" Then Claudia smiled sheepishly. "All right, I guess I know that now, and you know I won't tell anyone, Matt, not even Uncle Cor."

"Claudia, Matt!" A woman was calling them from the path leading from the rectory.

"It's Helen Lawton," Claudia said, as Helen hurried over to them.

"Claudia, you've been working yourself sick and you need a break. We all appreciate it, more than you know, but you're a young girl and you ought be enjoying yourself. Why don't you two go and relax before the show tonight?"

"Helen, thanks, that's really sweet of you," Claudia said. "We were just talking about getting some dinner and now we can take our time."

"Everyone seems to be excited about the show opening again," Helen said, her plain, middle-aged face beaming.

"Medora Everett's going to be wonderful," Claudia said. "At rehearsal last night, I could see that the whole show is going to be different. Much more dramatic."

"Oh, how intimidating! Now that I'm supposed to be understudying her, I mean. But Medora strikes me as a very healthy person. I have the feeling everyone else in the cast would get sick before she did."

"Yes, but then you'd have to do Medora's role all the same," Claudia reminded her gently. "If Vivienne or Bea got sick, Medora would be doing one of *their* roles."

"My goodness, you're right! I suppose this means I'd better learn those lines. Well, at least there aren't too many of them. I just hope we all stay healthy."

TWENTY

On Friday afternoon before the night of the reopening of *A Classic Case of Murder*, Vivienne Montrose got a telephone call from Jonathan Patrick.

"Vivienne, glad you're home. Just a couple of things I wanted to fill you in on. Hilly Lawton is coming back into the show tonight after all. He just called me."

"Jon, I'm so glad to hear that! I hope it doesn't cause him any emotional difficulties."

"It might cause the rest of you emotional difficulties if he doesn't remember his lines, but everyone's used to that. He wants to pitch in for the good of the show the way we all do, and if he has sad memories of Sisu—I think it's kind of touching *someone* does. The other good news is that you're getting the number one star dressing room all to yourself again. Medora Everett asked me to move Edwinta back into the third dressing room with her so you won't be inconvenienced any more."

"Well, that was thoughtful of her."

"We're sold out all weekend and for most of next week. We're going to knock 'em dead, if you'll pardon the expression. Medora was a jewel at rehearsals—so cooperative, no temperament—does a brilliant job with the role! The show will finally be dramatically tight, and I guarantee there will be no foot-long hairs to annoy Bea." Vivienne heard Jonathan give a happy little sigh. "It's a joy going to the theatre at night with no axes grinding between cast members!"

"I guess it will." Vivienne wasn't able to agree unreservedly with this highly optimistic statement. She hung up, wishing she could share Jon's enthusiasm. She had her fears about tonight's reopening show, ranging from the possibility of Bea getting into a snit about the "brilliance" of Medora's performance to the likelihood of Hilly's forgetting his lines and/or breaking down onstage.

The sound of knocking on the front door brought her back to reality. Going to answer it, she expected Matt bearing some further news of their investigation, but when she opened the door she found Edwinta, dressed in pale lavender, her face unreadable.

"I need to talk to you," Edwinta said. "I know you've been trying to call me. Medora told me."

"I have. Quite often, in fact. Come in."

Vivienne walked back into the house with the girl following her. Edwinta sat in one of the smaller chairs that faced the fireplace, and Vivienne sat near her in the big armchair.

"I felt really bad that I went off after the party and didn't even say good-bye. Or thank you."

"I don't mind about the thanks. I *was* worried about you."

Edwinta put a hand to her mouth and bit her thumbnail.

"Everyone was," Vivienne continued. "The men formed a search party, but, needless to say, no one could find you."

Removing her hand from her mouth, Edwinta looked down at her lap and clasped both hands tightly. Then she looked up at Vivienne "I know most people think I killed her, but do you?"

"Of course I don't! Why do you say that?"

"Because Rhoda Penmark drowned Claude Daigle, that's why. And everyone remembers me in *The Bad Seed*." She looked at Vivienne watchfully. "And because I hated her. I'm glad she's dead."

"That doesn't mean you'd kill her," Vivienne said, leaning toward the girl. "Tell me, Winta. What was going on in the third dressing room? What upset you so much in there?"

"She was disgusting." Edwinta shook her head. "Like when I'd walk into the dressing room, she'd say in that phony voice of hers: 'If it isn't little Miss Everett. I wonder if Little Miss's mother knows what she's doing in her spare time?' Or she wouldn't say anything, just put on that gross makeup she wears. Wore, I mean. And make faces at herself in the mirror and watch me with those shifty little raccoon eyes while I got undressed. Ugh! She gave me the creeps! And that hair! It looked like a wig, it was so bleached and teased and ratted. Then she'd start hosing herself down with this huge can of hair spray—like, you needed an iron lung to stay in the dressing room! I'd start to cough, and she loved it!"

Edwinta imitated Sisu's voice again. "'I guess Little Miss is so *natural* and *unspoiled* she isn't *used* to *hair* spray.' What a bitch! Like, I wouldn't blame anyone for killing her." She paused, looking sideways at Vivienne "And I could have done it," she added quietly. "I was on the lagoon beach that night."

"You were! Matt told me you'd gone looking for Ted Reid. He said Ted was supposed to give you a ride home."

"Yeah." Edwinta squeezed her hands together and squirmed in the chair. "That creep Steve told me Ted went for a walk on the beach. So I went down there, to the lagoon beach. I didn't see him, and I came back."

"Have you talked to Ted since then?"

"No." Edwinta twisted in the chair and looked out the window that faced the lagoon beach and Point Lobos.

"You've been awfully hard to get in touch with, Winta. Since you've been out every time I called, I would think Ted might have had the same problem."

"He hasn't called. Not once. He's a creep, just like my father." The girl's lips turned down in an expression of disgust. "Just like him."

"Winta, all men aren't creeps—"

"Oh, yeah?" Edwinta targeted Vivienne with her large brown eyes. "Then why aren't you with one? Why isn't Medora?"

Vivienne wanted to give an answer that wouldn't involve Medora. "I can't speak for your mother. But for myself, it isn't because men are creeps."

"Then how come?" Edwinta stared at her intently. "You aren't a lesbian, are you?"

Vivienne started to laugh in spite of herself. No wonder the girl made people uncomfortable. In her directness, she was so much like her grandfather.

"You're not afraid of asking anything, are you, Winta? No, I'm not."

Edwinta looked abashed. "I didn't think you were. It's just sometimes people say weird things if someone isn't married." She bit her lips.

"This isn't easy for me to talk about, Winta, but I'd like to if I can." Vivienne thought for a simple way to explain a complicated story. "I had affairs with quite a few men. You probably know all that—everyone in Carmel seems to." Vivienne shifted position in the chair, more uncomfortable with the subject than the resting place.

"I went into films when I was very young. My parents were both actors. They acted constantly, off the stage and on. Occasionally reality would peek through, and it wasn't very pleasant. You might think I would have turned out the other way and have had both my feet on the ground, but I didn't. I met some handsome, charming men as a result of being in films. It was hard for me to discern what was real and what wasn't." She paused. "Then again, maybe I could, and for whatever reason what I chose didn't make me happy. Men seemed to disappoint me. A lot of them. I had a second-rate film career and wasted my youth. At the end of it, I was an ingenue has-been with more notoriety than ability. Perhaps I'm being hard on myself, but I think it was true.

"I moved to Carmel to get away from all of that, and I haven't been involved with a man since. That's the way I had to do it. But that's me, Winta. You're a different person. You're very young, and you have tremendous opportunities ahead of you. You're talented and beautiful, and you have a strong spirit. Your grandfather gave you that, and you can't let *him* down. You can't think all men are creeps when you remember your grandfather."

Edwinta put her hands to her face, covering the tears that had started running down her cheeks. "I don't want to let *him* down, but I can't go there and do my scene with that creep Ted like everything's normal. And Medora'll be expecting me to be a trouper and go on with the show and that makes it a million times worse because I'll have to act offstage, too. There's no place to hide. Besides," she sniffed, wiping her eyes with her sleeve, "everyone thinks I drowned Sisu Potter."

Vivienne went to Edwinta, bent over her chair and took her hand. She felt the sleeve of the girl's dress. It was damp from her tears.

"I don't think you drowned Sisu Potter," Vivienne said.

Edwinta sighed heavily but didn't look up. Vivienne knelt next to her and watched her face carefully. "When you went down to the lagoon beach that night, how far did you go? What I'm really interested in is whether you saw or heard anyone."

"I didn't. The moon was going in and out. I could see fairly well when it was out and not too well when it went behind the clouds. I went across the road, through the parking lot and down onto the beach, but I didn't see Ted. So I walked down to the shore where there was some light reflected on the water and followed the shore around to the stone staircase and climbed it back up to the road. Then I walked home."

"You're sure you didn't hear anything?"

"Nothing. Just the sound of the waves."

"The party must have been a nightmare for you."

"Yeah, from the beginning. First it was Ted acting like the creep he turned out to be and then the fight between my mother and father. Oh, before that I ran into this kid, Claudia Kellog's younger brother. He told me he remembered me from *The Little Star That Couldn't Find Its Way to Bethlehem*. He played a shepherd, and he remembered me crawling around on my hands and knees and bleating. He said if I was nice to him, he wouldn't tell anyone about my being a sheep."

"You don't mean that?"

"He was just kidding. He isn't bad. He's a pretty nice kid." She threw a glance at Vivienne, then quickly dropped her gaze to the floor by her sandaled feet, studying the patterns in the Persian carpet. "You know, sometimes I don't understand why Medora married Thorson. He's such a jerk, and he makes her furious."

Vivienne chose to be discreet. Privately, she suspected Medora had become accustomed to using Thorson as a whipping boy and saw no reason to give up the pleasure simply because they were divorced. "It's difficult to know what motivates people," she said.

Edwinta was staring disconsolately out the window in the direction of Point Lobos, her face a study in misery.

"Winta, I know the show is going to be hard for you to do, especially tonight, but I know you can do it. If you're going to be a professional actress, you'll have to get used to going on with the show when you don't feel like it. I know Claudia knows your part, but the show would really suffer if she had to go on for you on such short notice.''

Edwinta whipped around in the chair. ''Claudia knows my part!'' she exclaimed.

''Jonathan says she has the whole show memorized,'' Vivienne said casually. ''And she *is* your understudy.''

''I'm going on!'' Edwinta stood up. ''I've gotta get home and study my lines. I haven't looked at them since last week. I don't have as good a memory as I did when I was a kid. I'd better look them over.''

''I thought you'd see it that way,'' Vivienne said, hiding a smile.

Edwinta started for the door.

''See you tonight!'' Vivienne called out to her.

TWENTY-ONE

THE PLAYHOUSE WAS OPEN but seemingly deserted when Vivienne arrived shortly after seven. The work lights were on in the house, and backstage the dusky light of early evening was filtering through the small window over the prop table. The first two dressing room doors were open. The third door, that of the dressing room now shared by Medora and Edwinta Everett, was closed. Vivienne knocked gently on it.

"Come in." Medora Everett's voice resonated from the interior of the small room.

Vivienne turned the knob and pushed open the door. Medora was sitting in front of the mirror in the place Sisu Potter had occupied, applying mascara to her already dark lashes. A script lay open before her on the long dressing table. She shifted and looked up at Vivienne, mild surprise registering on her face. "You're here early, aren't you?"

"Yes. So are you."

"Annie Watts let me in. I always get to the theatre early, even when I'm familiar with the show, which I'm not now."

"I thought you might be here—that's really why I came early. I know this isn't the right time or place, Medora, but something has been worrying me for the last few days, something I want to ask you about."

"Ask away." Medora continued sloshing the mascara brush in its little trough and daubing it on her eyelashes.

Vivienne sat in one of the two unoccupied chairs. To her left two Medora Everetts sat opposite each other, both with dark hair pulled back from their faces, revealing two pairs of high cheekbones and four cat-like eyes—one Medora in front of the mirror and one in it.

"Years ago we had a conversation at a cast party, late at night. It was right after Easter. We were doing *Family Portrait* at the time."

Medora tipped her head back reflectively. "I remember *Family Portrait* as if it were yesterday. Jonathan Patrick was Judas. With that guileless, boyish face, he was perfect." Medora's luxuriant tones had taken on a sarcasm that was beginning to seep out with every word. "You were the Virgin Mary, and I was Mary Magdalen. We were all perfectly cast."

Ignoring this, Vivienne pressed on. "Edwin had died a week or so before the show opened. If you remember, you told me he'd divided his estate between Thorson and Edwinta—two thirds to Edwinta, one-third to Thorson—with Edwinta coming into her share on her eighteenth birthday."

"I remember telling you. One of those immediately regretted, indiscreet confidences. I was probably drunk. It was a terrible time for me, and I hate cast parties." Medora regarded Vivienne suspiciously. "Why do you bring this up now?"

Vivienne took a deep breath and began. "Ever since Sisu Potter's death, I've been thinking how much alike they could have looked, Sisu and Edwinta, in the dark. When I found the body, my first fear was that it was Edwinta—the blond hair, the white dress—especially after she'd disappeared from the party. She told me that girl, Sandi, hates her violently, and I could see it when the two of them were around each other. Edwinta said that during the party, she walked down to the lagoon beach through the parking lot and came back the other way, up the stone staircase at the near end of the beach. Do you see what might have happened?"

Medora was painstakingly separating her lashes with the tip of her mascara brush, a process she continued as she spoke. "Is this like one of those murder party games Bea Brown is so fond of? How a grown woman can find those things amusing when she has all the money in the world is utterly beyond me. What you're implying then, Vivienne, if I'm correct, is that the little slut who lives with my former husband may have, hard as it is to imagine, become bored with Thorson's scintillating party conversation, and may have gone to the beach, glimpsed Sisu Potter in the dark, thought she was my daughter and pushed her into the lagoon." Medora paused, holding Vivienne's gaze, the brush raised in one hand. "Just how dark was it, that she made such an error?"

"It does sound ridiculous when you put it that way, but it's possible. The moon was going in and out behind the clouds that night. At times it was bright; at times it was very hard to see. Thorson had been drinking. He and Sandi left the party together, but they weren't together for the whole party. There are several possibilities that seem to be worth looking into, especially if—"

"Thorson is Edwinta's flesh and blood," Medora interrupted, turning away from the mirror to face Vivienne. "He may be a lot of unfortunate things, but he'd never harm Edwinta, or be a party to harming her. Sandi's a wretched little tramp, but she doesn't have the brains or the guts to murder anyone. She's living it up at Everett House. Thorson has enough money to keep her in peroxide and grapefruit for a few years, and her kind never thinks beyond next week. She has everything she wants. Why should she want to murder my daughter?"

"When is Edwinta's birthday?"

"In October. She'll be sixteen. That gives Sandi and Thorson two more years to bump her off." Medora returned her attention to the mascara box, closing the brush inside it with a resounding click.

"I thought she was older! She told me she was a senior in high school, and seniors are seventeen, aren't they?"

"She was moved up two grades. She has trouble making friends with the older children."

Vivienne, at a loss for words, sat in embarrassed silence.

"Did you imagine she was conceived around the time Edwin was painting your portrait?" Medora looked like a panther ready to torment a small animal. Her cheekbones seemed to rise even higher, and her slightly slanted eyes glittered. "Just as though she was *your* child, yours and Edwin's. Well, she isn't, is she?"

"Of course she isn't!"

"Vivienne, you have a hell of a lot of nerve," Medora said slowly. "You really do." She began powdering her face methodically, addressing Vivienne in the mirror as she did so. "It's not enough for you to do every role you want in Carmel theatre. It's not enough for you to be Carmel's very own little tin goddess. It isn't enough to have men drool over you for years like you were the last of the red-hot virgins, which we both know is a joke. You went through men like crackerjacks before you moved to Carmel."

"Medora!" In shock, Vivienne rose from the chair.

"Oh, come now! It isn't as though you don't know precisely what you're doing. You've even got a live-in fan club with that boy Matt following you around like you were Garbo."

Medora continued to powder her face, never breaking her flow of words, as Vivienne found herself backing involuntarily toward the dressing room door.

"It's not enough that you teased Edwin, you teased Thorson, you tease every man who gets near you, which I'm sure gives your ego a great satisfaction. No. You have to try to adopt my daughter. Well, much as you might wish it otherwise, she's *my* child. Not yours."

Vivienne backed up against the door as though driven there by Medora's words and leaned heavily against the door jamb. She felt a dull ache across her chest and throat. "I'm sorry," she said slowly. "I felt as though she *was*. Maybe it's the scene in the play. I don't know. It really makes no sense, but I felt as though she was both my child and at the same time, me...as a girl... The feeling was so strong." Vivienne pressed the side of her face against the door. "Of wanting to protect her from the things I suffered. But she isn't, of course."

"No."

With an effort, Vivienne looked directly at Medora. "I owe you an apology. I didn't think I was trying to take Edwinta away from you, but I must have been. I don't understand why..."

"Oh, really?" Medora turned to her again. "I had no idea you were so lacking in perception. Or self-awareness. It took Edwin longer to paint your portrait than it did to do any of his other works. First he did sketches of you. Then he did watercolors of you. Then he spent an interminable time painting you."

"I never had an affair with him."

"No, you didn't. You were probably the only beautiful woman in Carmel Edwin didn't sleep with. I knew you weren't lovers."

"How?"

"Edwin was ga-ga over you for over a year. Usually he went through his women in a few months, sometimes a few weeks." The skin across Medora's cheekbones drew tighter, slackening under her eyes.

Vivienne looked away and saw her own reflection—standing in the pose of her portrait—in the tall mirror behind the dressing table. "I knew that all along," she whispered.

"Of course you did." Medora also stared into the mirror. "You knew how to keep his interest."

"But you didn't." Vivienne spoke quietly, looking at Medora's reflection.

"No." Medora turned her head away so only her dark hair and the right side of her upper body was showing in the glass. "Edwin only really loved one woman. My daughter."

Suddenly the truth hit Vivienne like a boulder, and she spoke almost to herself in amazement, wondering how she could possibly not have known it before. "*His* daughter," she whispered.

Medora swung around in the chair, her cat's eyes flashing. "You and everyone else in Carmel would love to think that, wouldn't you?"

"Thorson must know she's his sister. Somewhere, deep down, he must know. It explains so much! And Edwinta doesn't know. How painful for all of you!"

"You'd really like the satisfaction of knowing what my life has been like, wouldn't you? Vivienne Montrose—poor lonely former film star. Hard to believe anyone else might have suffered but you!" Medora rose from her chair and walked to the costume rack. "It's about time for you to go back to your dressing room and get ready to star in your show. Make your carefully calculated entrance. Have your loyal Carmelite audience at your feet all evening, looking forward to going home and seeing your old movies—badly edited for television—on their little Sylvanias and RCAs." She took her costume from its hanger. "Excuse me," she said with exaggerated politeness. "I have to dress for my supporting role."

Vivienne got out of the room and ran down the narrow corridor. She fumbled her dressing room door open, slammed it behind her and stood, pressing her head against the wall next to the mirror, as tears began to course down her cheeks.

Sometime later she heard a knock on the door and a voice. "Viv, are you there?"

It was Bea. Vivienne didn't reply. By the time she'd turned toward the door, Bea was in the room.

"Honey, what happened to you? What's the matter?" Bea grabbed her by the arms.

"Oh, Bea..." Vivienne's throat hurt so much she could hardly speak. "I can't tell you. It's Medora..." She put her head on Bea's right shoulder and sobbed silently, spasms shaking her body.

"Honey, what did she say to you?" Bea whispered. "It can't have been *that* bad. You haven't been in a dressing room with chorus girls. You don't know how to dish it out. Medora's a barracuda! What'd she say?"

"I can't talk about it," Vivienne gasped. "Or I won't get through the show. I have to have some water. Oh, Bea, I don't think I can go on."

"I'll get you water from the sink down the hall." Bea held her by the shoulders and forced her to sit down. "Viv, I've never seen you like this. What did that bitch say to you?"

Vivienne took in an uneven breath of air in order to speak. "It's not Medora. It's me. I feel like I'm trapped, and I can't get out."

Vivienne and Bea both jumped at a loud knock on the dressing room door, followed by Claudia Kellog's voice saying "Half hour!"

"Thanks, Claudia. We're here!" Bea cried out. "You just sit here a minute, and I'll be back with the water," she whispered to Vivienne. "Don't let anyone in."

Vivienne leaned over the dressing table, holding her head in her hands. In a few minutes, Bea was back.

"Drink this." Bea sat in the other chair in the tiny dressing room while Vivienne drank the entire glass of water.

"Okay, tell me."

Vivienne set the empty glass on the small dressing table. "She talked about Edwin Everett and Edwinta. How he... Bea, Edwinta is his *daughter*. Medora won't admit it, but it's true. I know it! I always knew, deep down. I just didn't realize it."

"Viv, honey, I don't know where you've been for the last fifteen years. That's the worst-kept secret in Carmel. People say

Medora only put the 't' in Edwinta to make Thorson feel better.''

Vivienne pressed her hands to her throat. The ache was there, as strong as before. She sighed softly and looked at Bea. ''Everything she said was true.''

''Honey, I don't know what she told you, but Medora's jealous as hell of you. Now you know why I call her the Spider Woman. That's what I thought was so beautiful about you befriending that kid. She needed you.''

''She said I tried to take Edwinta away from her.''

''Viv, you helped that girl. I saw that. Anyone could see that. Medora's a lousy mother, anyway. Jesus, that poor little kid! She had a grandfather who was her father, and now she's got a father who's her brother! It's sick!''

''Fifteen minutes,'' Jonathan said outside the door. ''Vivienne, Beatrice, you're both in there, aren't you?''

''We've been here for hours, Jon! I'm just helping Viv with her costume!''

They sat in silence until they heard Jon move down the corridor.

''I didn't do it for Edwinta,'' Vivienne said softly. ''If I had, I wouldn't feel like this now. I wanted to help her, to give her the guidance no one gave me. As though that would make it right. As though that would help me.''

''So what's wrong with that?'' Bea exploded. ''Was Medora giving her encouragement or guidance? Was Thorson? That woman has some kind of a goddamned nerve! It amazes me that people have children, and they don't give a damn about them until the kid finds someone to look up to. *Then* they get jealous!''

''Bea, you're such a good friend.'' Vivienne reached out and took Bea's hands. ''I can't thank you enough. But this is very hard for me to face. I love that child. She deserves every happiness. But that doesn't change what's inside me. It doesn't make the mistakes I made— It doesn't make my own fears, my own cowardice—'' She sighed. ''It doesn't make them go away.''

''You and Edwin Everett always had a thing for each other, didn't you?''

Vivienne gave a little laugh. "Bea, you really mince no words, do you?"

"You did, I know it. He was crazy about you, too. As much as I've regretted my, shall we say, intimate liaison with Thorson, I've never regretted it with Edwin. Even when it was over, I felt like a queen. I don't think any woman in Carmel who knew him, and there were plenty of them, have regretted it either."

"I'm glad you feel like that about him," Vivienne said. "I just wasn't up to it. I knew him, I knew how he was. He wasn't a hypocrite about it. He was a widower, he had affairs with many, many women, and I knew he would until the end of his days."

"Well, I enjoyed every minute of it. That's why I look so good in the portrait he did of me. But you and I are different."

"Yes, we are, Bea."

Another knock came at the door. "Five minutes," Claudia called out.

"Oh, Jesus, Viv!" Bea exclaimed, rising. "I'm not even dressed, and I'm on first. Will you be okay?"

"I may not give my best performance, but I promise I'll get through the show. You go ahead and get dressed."

Bea gave Vivienne a quick hug and whisked out of the dressing room.

Vivienne slipped into her dressing gown, put a towel around her shoulders and began to put on makeup. She heard the one-minute call, then the music that played during the dimming of the lights in the theatre, followed by Bea's voice speaking the first lines of the play. She finished her makeup, doing as much as she could to disguise the swollen look around her eyes, and changed into her costume as the first act progressed. Having no desire to run into Medora Everett, even in the dark of the backstage area, she waited until Medora was onstage before leaving her dressing room.

By this time the entire cast was onstage except for Vivienne and Hilly Lawton. Hilly's entrance was coming up in a few minutes, and hers would follow some minutes later. She saw a crack of light under the door of the dressing room shared by

Hilly and Ted Reid, and knocked very softly on it. The light went out and the door opened.

"Vivienne!" Hilly whispered, taking her arm.

In the darkness, they walked through the black curtains screening the vault area and through the vault toward the light of an ancient, many-bulbed candelabra which illuminated the passageway winding past the furniture and costumes.

Vivienne turned to Hilly and spoke softly.

"I just wanted to tell you how sorry I am, Hilly. I hope you know how much we all appreciate your doing the show."

Hilly took Vivienne's hand and squeezed it hard. "Thank you, Vivienne. That means a lot. I had to do the show. Anything's better than sitting at home thinking about it. They told me you found her body."

"I did."

"Something isn't right about it, Vivienne. It doesn't make sense for her to disappear like that—out of the blue—with no word to anyone... Wait a minute! That's my cue!" Hilly pressed her hand again quickly and dropped it, then ran toward the far door in the vault. He stopped, readied himself and disappeared through the curtained doorway.

Vivienne got her suitcase and walked to the far door to wait for her cue. She touched her throat and swallowed. It was still tight and aching. She felt very nervous, as though she hadn't acted in years. She thought of Medora's remark about her delayed entrance and wondered if she should come onstage faster.

Her tension grew as she heard Hilly forgetting all of his poorly memorized dialogue and the others stumbling through. Then Edwinta's voice sounded, giving her cue, "To Persephone!" As the toast was being drunk onstage, Vivienne composed herself, taking a few seconds more time than she usually did before stepping through the curtains of the vault door to make her entrance.

TWENTY-TWO

ON SATURDAY MORNING Matt sat in his cottage drinking coffee and reflecting on the reopening of *A Classic Case of Murder* the night before. The show itself was vastly improved with Medora Everett in Sisu Potter's old role; however, Medora seemed to be the only completely confident person on the stage. The rest of the cast were not at their best, especially Hilly Lawton, who managed to rewrite every one of his lines to the great discomfort of those onstage with him. Matt supposed it was all to be expected and would be forgiven tonight, written off as the consequence of reopening the show so shortly after Sisu's death.

The pall backstage had been thick enough to chop. Except for Hilly, the cast stayed in their row of dressing rooms as though they were ensconced in limousines in a funeral cortege. Poor Hilly was left standing by himself near the light booth, occasionally finding companionship talking to Matt, Claudia or Jonathan when the three weren't busy running the show.

The only time Matt saw Vivienne was when she was onstage or going in and out of her dressing room. She didn't speak a word to him and left right after the show without saying goodbye. He would have thought she had some unknown reason to be mad at him if she hadn't given his arm a squeeze when she passed him once in the darkened corridor.

Ted Reid, hiding from Edwinta, remained in his dressing room when he wasn't onstage, a first for Ted. Edwinta wasn't to be seen offstage either, staying in the third dressing room which she now shared with her mother. Even the usually irrepressible Bea Brown had seemed irritable and worried for the entire show.

Matt hadn't even had a chance to tell Vivienne about his talk with Claudia at the Little Chapel by the Sea. He and Vivienne hadn't spoken in two days, and he was anxious to exchange findings with her.

He was trying to make a list of who-was-where-when at the opening night party when he heard MacGuffin barking outside, followed by a knock on the cottage door. He knew it was Vivienne coming back from her morning walk.

He opened the door and found her outside, standing like a pink bouquet in front of the cypress hedge, wearing one of her shirtwaist dresses with tiny flowers on it and a cardigan sweater over her shoulders. Except for her clothes, she wasn't looking her normal self. MacGuffin was hopping around her feet.

"I want to apologize for not speaking to you last night, Matt," she said. "I was feeling a little nervous about the show, and frankly, things felt very uncomfortable backstage."

"It was obvious, wasn't it? Everyone acted like they'd seen a ghost."

"Maybe they had. Why don't you come up to the house later this morning, and we can catch up on things. We haven't talked in a while."

"Why don't I come up now?"

"That's fine. I can offer you some breakfast if you haven't had any."

"Only if you're making it for yourself." Matt grabbed his notebook from the desk and shut the cottage door behind him. "My list," he explained.

"Let's don't talk about it until we've both had something to eat," Vivienne said.

With MacGuffin, they went up the hill and into the house. Matt sat in the living room trying to remember everything about the night of the party while Vivienne prepared breakfast. She brought the food to the dining room, and they sat at the long table and ate in silence. Matt glanced up at Vivienne several times during the meal. She didn't notice him watching her. She gazed out of the window toward the garden. Her thoughts seemed to be miles away.

When they'd finished eating, Matt helped Vivienne clear away the dishes and silver. He carried the tray of coffee things to the living room and set it on the table in front of the fireplace as Vivienne rejoined him.

"Now," Vivienne said, as she sat in the large armchair. "Tell me about your list."

Matt sat on the sofa. "First of all and most important," he said, readying himself for Vivienne's surprise, "are Sisu's last words."

"Her last words? Matt!" Vivienne's reaction was everything he had hoped for. She leaned forward in the chair excitedly. "Who heard them? And how do you know they were her last, so to speak?"

"Claudia told me. I talked to her yesterday at the Little Chapel by the Sea." He proceeded to relate the parts of the conversation that were relevant to Sisu's death, especially the mention of the priest. "And we know from the timetable the police chief gave you that she must have died during the party, so as far as we know, those were the last words anyone heard. Anyone except the person who was with her, that is."

"My goodness," Vivienne said, leaning back in the chair. "Everything points to Ted Reid, doesn't it? He said he went for a walk by himself on Carmel Beach, but he must have been with Sisu, at least as far as your cottage. Maybe he split off and went the other way and didn't tell anyone." She shook her head. "Ted Reid. It seems hard to believe. As little as I think of the man's behavior, I still find it—"

"No matter who it is," Matt interrupted, "if it's someone we know, it's going to be hard to believe they'd kill someone, but that's what we're pursuing, isn't it? Unless it really was an accident, and she slipped and fell in and whoever she was with panicked and didn't go in after her. *That* I could see Ted doing, but I find it hard to believe he'd deliberately kill someone, even Sisu. As far as I can tell he had absolutely no motive."

"Why do you think he'd be the type to panic? I would think he'd had a great deal of experience with life and death as a priest."

"Last year when we were rehearsing the murder mystery, we had an earth tremor during a rehearsal. Now I admit Ted's not from California, and it *was* quite a tremor. But no one else in the cast bolted."

"Bolted?"

"He turned and ran out of the theatre right in the middle of the rehearsal. The tremor stopped suddenly, the way they do, and he came back. Everyone gave him a hard time about it, and he was embarrassed."

"He seemed so at ease when I saw him coming back from his walk. He was one of the few people at the party who seemed to be enjoying himself."

"He's a good actor," Matt suggested.

"Yes," Vivienne said reflectively. "But then, so are a lot of us. Matt, what do you think about the night Sisu cut her lip on that goblet? Could that have anything to do with all of this?"

"Someone could have switched the glasses backstage. I was in the light booth watching the show during the first act that night. But why? It wasn't fatal; it couldn't have been. Some kind of warning?"

Suddenly Matt heard the sound of knocking, and it irritated him. "Who could that be?" he asked. "I thought we were finally going to get the chance to talk about this."

Vivienne walked to the front door, and Matt, seated on the sofa around the corner from the foyer, could hear a note of surprise in her soft voice as she greeted the visitor.

"I hope I haven't disturbed you by coming by," replied a man's voice that Matt recognized with some annoyance as the police chief's.

"I was in the audience last night," the voice continued. "It's probably none of my business, but you were very disturbed for the whole show, and I wondered if it had anything to do with the drowning."

"How could you tell I was disturbed?" Vivienne's voice sounded strange to Matt. "You don't know me."

"I've seen you in more plays than you might think. I saw you on opening night when everyone's supposed to be nervous, and you didn't seem nervous. Last night you did. More than nervous."

"Well," Vivienne said. Matt heard her pause, then she spoke again. "Please come in. I think I owe you an apology for last time. I was rather rude."

"I don't know about that," the police chief said. Matt could hear them walking through the small entryway. "I've been thinking about—" He stopped speaking as he rounded the corner and saw Matt.

He doesn't want me to be here, Matt thought. Well, that's tough.

Chief Himber walked across the room toward Matt. "Good to see you," he said.

"Actually, this works out well," Vivienne said. "We can all help each other. Please sit down, both of you."

The two men hesitated, standing up until Vivienne sat in the large chair. Then they both sat, with different degrees of reluctance, Matt on one end of the sofa and Chief Himber on the other.

"Matt, why don't you tell . . . ah, Chief Himber what Claudia told you?"

Once again, Matt related the relevant portions of his conversation with Claudia, again leaving out their discussion of "Uncle Cor's" long-standing crush on Vivienne Montrose.

The police chief looked thoughtful and spoke when Matt had finished. "Interesting. What do you suppose Claudia thinks is the worst thing you could say about a priest? She'll never tell me, that's for sure."

"Maybe she'd tell another woman," Vivienne said.

"Much more likely."

"I wouldn't mind asking her, with your permission, Matt."

"My permission?"

"She did tell you in confidence, didn't she?"

"She did, but I don't think she'd mind my telling you that part of our conversation."

"Then I will when I have the opportunity, unless you can talk her into telling you, Matt. If you impress on her how important it is."

"The man who was with Ted Reid was another priest, wasn't he?" Chief Himber asked.

"Yes. His name is Steve. He's supposedly an old friend of Ted's from Texas," Matt volunteered.

"Hmm." The police chief was obviously mulling something over, but he had the ability to keep his thoughts private. "So Miss Potter could have been talking to Ted Reid, or to this Steve, or to someone else about either or both of them."

"The other priest, Steve, was with Bea Brown the entire evening," Vivienne said. "Up until the time she ran into Matt, and then all of us were together, and Sisu had been gone for some time. Bea told me."

"A copybook alibi," Himber said. "'I was with a priest.'" His normally serious face cracked into a smile. "What else have the two of you come up with?"

"We were just discussing an incident involving a broken goblet," Vivienne said, and related it to him.

"This is the first time I've heard about it." He shifted his large frame on the sofa. "Do you think it was an accident?"

"When it happened, yes," Vivienne said. "Now we've been wondering."

"If it wasn't an accident, if someone did it on purpose, it seems like it was meant to frighten Sisu," Matt said.

"Did it?"

"It seemed to, for a day or so, anyway," Vivienne said.

"As I recall from seeing the play, the maid puts the glasses in place on the table. That's Helen Lawton, isn't it?"

Matt and Vivienne both nodded their heads apprehensively.

"After that, there's a lot of activity around that table. Mrs. Brown checks it over, adjusts a few things, then people sit down."

"Five people," Matt said. "Going around the table, it was Bea at the head, then Hilly, Sisu, Ted and Edwinta. Sisu was between Ted and Hilly."

"The table is small," Vivienne said. "There's a lot of confusion as everyone sits down. If the whole thing wasn't just an unfortunate accident, and the cracked goblet was purposely put at Sisu's place, Hilly or Ted could theoretically have switched the glasses. That is, if either of them had planted the glass backstage with the props."

"Or the glass could have been placed by Mrs. Brown or Mrs. Lawton," Himber added.

"Could Edwinta have reached over and changed the glass?" Matt asked.

"I think the whole thing was an accident," Vivienne said quickly. "I always did."

"What about Annie Watts?" Matt asked. "She's always lurking around backstage. Suppose she cracked a glass to see if one of the actors might end up getting hurt. Just for fun."

"Matt, I know you think Annie is some kind of monster, but she isn't," Vivienne interjected. "She's just an unfortunate, obese woman."

"She spooks me," Matt said. "And there's something scary in those tiny eyes hiding behind those thick glasses. Annie Watts would be my first choice for pushing anyone into the lagoon except that I saw her at the refreshment tables all night—feeding."

"It's hard to imagine anyone going for a walk in the moonlight with her," Chief Himber commented.

"You men!" Vivienne exclaimed.

"I didn't mean to offend you, Miss Montrose," Himber said, his face unreadable. "You're an unusually beautiful woman. Maybe that's why you don't understand."

"I don't understand how a woman feels?" Vivienne asked icily, facing Chief Himber.

If Matt didn't know better, he would have thought he saw the police chief flinch almost imperceptibly.

"No, you don't understand how a man feels," Himber responded quietly.

Matt, surprised at this new side of Vivienne, felt strangely glad that she was angry at the police chief and in sympathy with the man at the same time. "Vivienne, he means you don't see how, for a man, the difference between looking at a woman like you and looking at a woman like Annie Watts is enormous. I don't think you can hold it against either of us for being repelled by a woman who looks like Annie, and talking about it is more honest than not talking about it."

"I guess I've never understood men," Vivienne began coolly, then to Matt's astonishment, she smiled ruefully, melting into a vulnerable young girl in front of them. "But I suppose now is a good time to start trying."

Matt felt his heart squeeze and an overpowering desire to be thirty years older. Then he thought of Claudia, and it began to subside.

Himber slowly turned away from watching Vivienne and looked at Matt. "Who else at the party never left your sight, Matt?"

"Well, Jon Patrick, Helen Lawton, Thorson Everett. Sandi, although she disappeared and reappeared again. Claudia, but she and I took a walk, and I was away from the party for maybe half an hour. The only other people I saw at that time were Bea Brown and Steve from Texas. They were talking near my cottage. After that, I was up and down the hill to the cottage several times, looking for Claudia, and then looking for Edwinta and Sisu.''

"I think I should tell you both a few things," Vivienne said, her expression darkening.

"You already have." Himber's voice was serious but his eyes were twinkling. "I don't know if we can stand any more. I know I can't."

Vivienne looked at him in surprise and then gave a little laugh. "No," she said. "I wanted to tell you both about talking to Edwinta Everett and—and to Medora."

Chief Himber sat forward on the sofa. "Please do."

"Edwinta is afraid everyone thinks she drowned Sisu because she played that character in *The Bad Seed*. She's also afraid because she was on the lagoon beach that night."

"That's how her sleeve got wet!" Matt said.

"I don't think so," Vivienne said.

Himber looked at Vivienne. "I haven't heard about this."

"That's because I didn't tell you," Vivienne said, meeting his gaze.

Matt explained. "When I ran into her on the way to my cottage to look for Claudia, I touched her arm, and the sleeve of that white dress she was wearing was damp."

"I know how suspicious that seems, but let me explain," Vivienne said. "First of all, I'm sure the sleeve of her dress was wet because she wiped her eyes with it. She was crying. She went down to the lagoon beach looking for Ted. She told me she didn't see anyone on the beach. She said she went down to the water and then came back via the staircase. Now, my thought was that someone might have followed her, followed that white dress in the dark, lost track of her, and then seen Sisu in a similar white dress near the lagoon."

"Do you suspect a particular person?" Himber asked.

"Yes, I do. I suspect Sandi, Thorson Everett's girlfriend. I had my facts confused when I went to talk to Medora. You see, Edwin Everett's will leaves the bulk of the estate to Edwinta when she turns eighteen, and I thought she was older, but she's only fifteen now…" Vivienne trailed off, looking confused and troubled. "Anyway, Medora scoffed at the whole story, but I still think it could have happened."

"Sandi hates Edwinta," Matt said. "That was obvious at the party. She does seem to have a mean streak, but she's no hundred-watt bulb. I can't see Sandi plotting much of anything beyond how to keep a year-round tan."

"She'd do anything Thorson told her to do," Vivienne said.

"Kill his own daughter!" Matt said in horror. "He's a jerk, but not that!"

"Will you both promise not to tell this to anyone?" Vivienne looked at the two men, her expression pained. "I'm only telling you because if there's any chance Edwinta's life is in danger over the next two years, until she turns eighteen, I have to say this. Medora wouldn't tell me so in so many words, but from the way she acted, I know it. Edwinta is Thorson's sister."

"Wow!" Matt said, realizing the facts involved.

Chief Himber kept looking at Vivienne, unsurprised.

"You don't believe me?" Vivienne asked Himber.

"I do believe you," he said, regarding her inscrutably. "I've always suspected that was the case." He leaned toward her and spoke softly. "What brand of champagne was it?"

Vivienne jerked her head back and gave a little gasp, her eyes flashing quickly around the room and returning to the police chief. Then she stared at him and spoke so softly she almost whispered. "It was domestic."

For a few seconds, Vivienne and Himber stared so intently at each other that Matt jealously thought he might as well not be there. The policeman had an understanding of Vivienne that Matt didn't, and Matt didn't like it one bit.

Vivienne was the one to break the gaze and look away.

"She's jealous of you, of course. That's why," Himber said. "She must have been rough on you."

"I guess everyone needs a dressing-down every now and then," Vivienne said, still looking away. "She called me a little tin goddess."

Himber shook his head. "A base metal. That's going for the jugular."

Vivienne looked back at Himber, smiling shamefacedly. "She said I acted like the last of the red-hot virgins."

Himber threw his head back and laughed, a hearty, infectious laugh. Amazed, Matt watched Vivienne begin to laugh, too—so hard tears started from her eyes, and she had to use a napkin from the coffee tray to wipe them.

"I'm sorry," Himber said. "I wasn't laughing at what Mrs. Everett said to you, only at the way you related it."

It took a few seconds for everything to get back to normal.

Then Himber spoke reflectively. "So Edwinta is the daughter of Edwin Everett. Poor little girl. She didn't know he was her father while he was alive. When she finds out, it's going to be rough for her. She'll have to mourn all over again."

"I just want to make sure she lives long enough to find out," Vivienne said, her beautiful face grim. "I don't trust Thorson and Sandi."

"I'll do everything I can," Himber said simply.

"Do you have children?" Vivienne suddenly asked Himber. "You seem so understanding of Edwinta."

"Two sons. My wife died when they were twenty and twenty-three, so they were able to have both parents until they were grown. Unlike Edwinta Everett, though she doesn't know it yet."

I'd like to be able to convey my precise marital status to a woman and then segue back into the conversation again that coolly, Matt thought. It struck him that his presence was enabling Vivienne and the police chief to speak to each other with a freedom they wouldn't have if he weren't with them.

"I have another question," Vivienne said, gazing at Himber with the cool, truth-seeking look she had sometimes. "Why are you a policeman in a little town like Carmel? You're one of the most perceptive people I've ever met. It must be a boring job 90 percent of the time. I don't see how you find any stimulation here."

"Oh, I get my moments," Himber said wryly, and Vivienne quickly turned away, a slight flush coming to her cheeks. "I fell in love with Carmel when I came here on a visit years ago," Himber continued. "I'd found the most beautiful place in the world, and I didn't want to live anywhere else. But unless you have a small business or an independent source of income, it's almost impossible to live here. Opening a grocery store didn't appeal to me, so when a job on the police force came along, I took it. Occasionally, it's very interesting. And I have free time for other interests. I do a lot of reading."

"I see." Vivienne shifted uncomfortably in her chair. "Well, we've gotten off our subject, haven't we? Where were we? Should I try to talk to Claudia tonight and find out just exactly what she heard?"

"Sounds like a good idea," Himber said. "May I make a suggestion?"

"Of course."

"Talk to Jonathan Patrick. My hunch is he knows where a lot of bodies are buried."

"You're absolutely right," Vivienne said thoughtfully. "He would."

"I've got to be going now." The police chief stood up. "I want to thank both of you for your help. We'll talk again, I'm sure."

"Let me see you to the door," Vivienne said, rising. She and Himber walked toward the foyer while Matt remained on the sofa, listening.

"Thank you," Matt heard Vivienne say in her gentle, clipped tones. "You made me laugh about my scene with Medora. I really needed to do that."

"You're welcome." Himber's voice sounded businesslike. "Tell me about your talk with Jonathan Patrick."

Matt heard the door close behind Himber, and during the minute or two that passed before Vivienne returned, he heard a car start up outside and drive away. When Vivienne walked back into the room, she seemed preoccupied.

She sat down opposite Matt again. "Well, Watson, what do you think of our Inspector Lestrade?"

"That's a joke. The guy's no Lestrade. He's got *us* running around in circles. He's right about Jonathan, and I never thought of it. Jon sees and hears everything."

"'The gift of omniscience, it's a curse,'" Vivienne said. "I'm quoting Jon. I'll call him. Maybe I can have lunch with him today."

"Okay." Matt got up. "I'm going down to the cottage. Call me if you need me." He started for the stairs leading to the back door.

"I will," Vivienne rose from the chair and called after him. "Matt, thank you for being here this morning. Talking to the two of you has made me feel a hundred times better."

"I'm glad," Matt said, turning back. "I didn't realize it was talking to Medora that got you upset last night. I wish I could have done something to help."

"You have," Vivienne said.

TWENTY-THREE

"So I know where the bodies are buried," Jonathan Patrick exclaimed, "according to the Chief of Police! You know, he was at the show last night, and I've seen him a lot. He's a Playhouse regular."

"Apparently so," Vivienne said.

They were lingering over a late lunch at Anzel's, a café hidden in a courtyard of little shops topped by artists' lofts where painting classes were held. Vivienne and Jonathan sat at one of the small tables in the tiny, vine-enshrouded restaurant garden, which was frequented in large number by hummingbirds, bees and spiders, and in smaller number, by local artists and show folk. Since becoming director at the Carmel Playhouse, Jonathan had eaten untold lunches at Anzel's, many bought for him by aspiring thespians during the torturous and often prolonged process of casting shows. Today, Jonathan was treating Vivienne, and due to the slow service at the restaurant, the remains of their lunch lay on the red-and-white-checked tablecloth before them, a prime target for bees and ants.

"Which body do you want to know about first?" Jon asked. He was wearing a green shirt and trousers and appeared even more like a tall elf.

Vivienne regarded him across the table. "Why is Bea so frightened about all of this? I know she's afraid of a scandal, but she hasn't exactly lived her life in fear of scandal, if you know what I mean."

"I do. Bea has her fears. Some I know of, some I don't." Jon paused, carefully shooing away a bumblebee hovering over a large chunk of banana in the remnants of his banana cream pie. After the bee sputtered away, he looked back at Vivienne. "Body number one is Bea's affair with Hilly Lawton."

"No," Vivienne said, aghast. "I didn't know!"

"I know you didn't, and Bea told me not to tell you. She said those things just upset you."

"Well, they do! I could see Bea getting hurt time after time, so after a while I asked her not to talk to me about them anymore."

"Anyway, Bea and Hilly's romance dated from the time of the murder mystery last year up until fairly recently. As far as I can tell, it ended when Hilly started paying court to Sisu."

"Of course," Vivienne said. "I'm so stupid not to have seen that." She thought for a moment. "What about Helen? It must have been awfully difficult for her."

"Not really. Hilly and Helen had been uneasy companions for some time. They were separating about then—just before or just after the affair with Bea began. They're fine now, as you know. No animosities. Helen told me they'd stayed together until their daughter was grown and away from home. The daughter inherited some money from Helen's sister and went off to college back east. Helen says it's a relief not to be married anymore. She likes being single, slaves away over at their church, loves the Carmel Playhouse. As you know, she's an enthusiastic worker for us, a real gem. Every now and then small roles come along that she's suitable for, and I cast her. I know she gets a kick out of doing them."

"Helen has always been very pleasant to me," Vivienne said, her mind on Bea Brown. "So Bea is afraid if it came out, it might be thought that she'd killed Sisu out of jealousy."

"It seems so. In any case, she's scared silly. Your interest in the cast as some sort of detective game has also frightened her. She's afraid it might bring it all out in the open."

"You know I'd never do anything to hurt Bea! I know she couldn't have had anything to do with Sisu's death. I do feel something isn't right about it, though, that it should be looked into, and that's what Matt and I have been doing."

"You as Sherlock and Matt Ross as your Watson!" Jonathan seemed to be repressing a grin. "Excuse me, Vivienne, but it's so fitting. Matt is the only person I can think of in Carmel who's more naïve than you are, with the possible exception of Claudia Kellog."

"Why do you say I'm naïve?" Vivienne resented Jon's description.

"Because you are. Vivienne, stop bristling. I love you—I'd do anything for you and you know that. I'm not saying that deep down inside, you don't know exactly what's going on around you and always have. I think you do. It's just that for the time I've known you, anyway, you haven't looked beneath the surface of anything. It's the way you've chosen to live, for whatever reasons. With the exception of your performances. In them, you go very deep. That's probably kept you sane, Vivienne, and I'm serious." Jonathan gazed at her with a worried face. "Please say you'll speak to me again after this."

"I will, Jon." Vivienne swallowed, feeling a lump in her throat. "I know you're telling me this because you care for me. It was a risk. You could have jeopardized our friendship, and on another occasion you might have."

"I know. Some bizarre instinct told me it was the right time. The wine at lunch could have helped."

"You do have the gift of omniscience."

"In this case I hope it's proved not to be a curse."

Vivienne sipped the last of her coffee. "So, counting me as body number two, now for body number three."

Jon reached for his wine glass and drank off its contents. "Okay, shoot."

"What do you know about Medora Everett?"

"A very talented lady, also an embittered one. I don't think much in her life turned out the way she wanted—her acting career, Thorson, et cetera. All she really has to show for herself is that children's theatre troupe and Edwinta."

"You're very perceptive, Jon." Vivienne paused. "What do you know about her personal life?"

"As far as I know, she doesn't have one. If she does, it's a big secret, and you know how hard that is to pull off in Carmel."

"How about Thorson Everett? What do you think of him?"

Conversation stopped, and they both flinched as a hummingbird dive-bombed their table on its way to the ivy-covered wall behind them.

"Thorson, Son of Thor," Jonathan said. "You were the one who called him that at lunch at Brown Hall that day. So true. Small son of big father. Riddled with insecurities he covers up with bravado."

"Yes, but would you think him capable of murder if he thought his life would be changed drastically? If he thought he might lose face, or lose wealth?"

"Maybe." Jon was thinking. "Maybe so. I could see him lashing out, doing something, but what, I don't know. Depends on how big a loss it would be. I don't really know Thorson that well. Who wants to?"

"Jon, what do you think is the worst thing a priest could do?"

"Have sex with a German shepherd."

Vivienne laughed in surprise and Jon immediately blanched. "Sorry, Vivienne, it just popped out. Seriously now, the worst thing. Well, get a girl pregnant, I guess. That would be one of the worst things a priest could do. Affairs with girls or boys are pretty standard. Pregnancy's different. Or child molesting. Usually boys."

"Jon!"

"I'm serious, Vivienne. Happens more often than anyone knows."

"Do you think Ted is capable of murder?"

"Murder's too definite for Ted. I can't see it. Killing someone accidentally, maybe."

"Maybe Sisu Potter—accidentally?"

"I could see it, but I can't see him being this cool about it now."

"He's a good actor."

"Not that good. There'd have to be a crack somewhere, a chink. So that someone who really knew him could tell."

"Does anyone really know Ted?"

"Matt Ross, maybe. Edwinta Everett, formerly."

"Then you know he isn't seeing her anymore. Matt told me Ted said Edwinta was too demanding, that she was just a child."

"You see! Child molesting—I told you so!"

"Jon, I know you're half serious, but I don't think so. Edwinta would have told me."

"Vivienne, I don't know if you've noticed it, but you not only walk around sporting a halo—you glow in the dark! You are the last person in whom I'd confide things I've done that I'm ashamed of, and I'm certain Edwinta Everett is no different."

"I'm not really delighted with that description of me either, Jon," Vivienne began coolly.

"Whoops! There I go again." Jon stretched his long legs under the table. "Let's change the subject. What else can I tell you—about other people, of course."

"Is there anyone else you can think of who might have wanted Sisu dead?"

Jonathan used his napkin to squash an ant wandering too close to the remains of his dessert. "Let's run through our gang," he said. "Edwinta Everett—hated her. Bea Brown—hated her. Ted Reid—former lover. Hilly Lawton—recent lover. Knowing Sisu as we did, he could have killed her out of sheer frustration. Helen Lawton—possible jealousy, albeit well-hidden. Medora Everett—wanted to take over Sisu's twelve-line role. Thorson Everett, former stage director—could have killed her out of distaste for her acting performance; ditto, this director. Claudia Kellog—no discernable motive. Ditto, Matt Ross. Vivienne Montrose—ultimate suspect—killed Sisu Potter in order to have a subject to dine out on."

"Jon! You're terrible!"

"I know. And I have to get back to the theatre. I can't leave Annie alone in the box office too long or she loses count." Jon made a move to indicate he was getting up so Vivienne could rise first.

Vivienne stood up. "Jon, what about Annie Watts? Did she know Sisu?"

Jon rose, wearing a pensive look. "You know, Sisu was very cruel to Annie behind her back. Not to her face, of course. I wonder if Annie could ever have overheard her?" He put money for the waiter on the table next to their bill. "She might have heard something and not realized it. Annie's quite simple, not very brigh.."

They began to walk through the courtyard toward the street, and Jon spoke again. "She was right by the food all night, Annie was, undoubtedly *sans* several trips to the bathroom."

"Jon, please—"

"I'm serious. She was always around—she's a presence everyone's used to. Maybe we could have thought she was there when she wasn't, just because she's always around. I'll admit I can't see her making the dash to the lagoon and back in a flash and living to tell the tale. That's too strenuous for her."

Reaching the sidewalk, they began to walk in the direction of Vivienne's car, which was parked a short distance down the block.

"How old do you think Annie is?" Vivienne asked as she took Jon's arm.

"Mid-thirties, around Sisu's age. Sisu's former age, I mean. It's still hard to believe she's gone. It's difficult to tell how old Annie is with all that fat, but I think that's what someone told me, maybe Mrs. Whetstone. She's kind of a pitiful character, Annie. I guess that's why we all put up with her."

"Do you think she would be capable of—of cracking a prop goblet so that one of the actors might get cut?"

Jon turned to Vivienne, looking horrified. "I hope not! Sometimes she brings me cookies!"

They reached Vivienne's car.

Jon gripped Vivienne's arm and looked at her, his features suddenly grave. "The oddest feeling just struck me, Vivienne. I've been playing detective with you for the fun of it, but something in our conversation has regurgitated on me. Not the lunch," he added hastily.

Vivienne was immediately riveted. "What could it have been?"

Jon looked as serious as Vivienne had ever seen him. "I think Sisu's death was an accident," he said. "Or if it wasn't, no one will ever find out. But I have this spooky feeling—I don't know why—if things keep getting stirred up, someone might really end up murdered." He pressed her arm again. "Be careful, Vivienne."

She circled the front of the car to get to the driver's seat. "I promise I will, Jon," she called over the hood of the car. "I at least plan to live through the run of the show."

"I'm delighted," Jon shouted at her as he began to walk down the street in the direction of the Playhouse. "But what a shame for Medora!"

TWENTY-FOUR

VIVIENNE WAS AT HOME Sunday afternoon awaiting Bea Brown, who was dropping by for tea before the show that night. In the last twenty-four hours, she thought, her detective ability had proved sadly lacking. She hadn't been able to talk to Claudia Kellog on Saturday; Claudia was busy and Vivienne had realized it was too difficult a subject to bring up under those circumstances. Earlier, before last night's show, she had returned home after her lunch with Jon and picked up the phone to call the police station and report the conversation to Chief Himber.

The whole thing had started off poorly. Himber had answered the telephone himself, which flustered her. She recognized his voice as he came on the line, saying "Police station," and in her confusion she asked for him anyway.

"This is he, Miss Montrose," he had said, obviously recognizing her voice.

"You asked me to call you after I'd talked to Jonathan Patrick. So I am. I have."

"I'm by myself here at the station for a few hours so I can't come by and talk to you." His voice was friendly.

"That's all right," she had replied, a little too quickly. "I really didn't learn much of anything, but I said I'd let you know."

"No buried bodies?"

"Not really. We just discussed people we knew. I can't think of anything to tell you that might help."

There was silence at the other end of the line for a few seconds, then Himber spoke again. "Why don't you think about it for a while and maybe something will surprise you."

"All right, I will."

"I believe in you," he had said reassuringly. "In my estimation you know more than you think you know. I'll talk to you soon."

Not too soon, I hope, Vivienne thought as she hung up the phone.

She was trying to shake this particular conversation of yesterday from her mind when she heard Bea opening the front door.

"Hi, Viv!" Bea called out. "Where are you?"

"Out here," Vivienne said, and picked up the tea tray from the kitchen counter. She carried it into the living room.

Bea was dressed in red slacks and two navy and red sweaters—a pullover and a cardigan—her usual expensive, simple clothes. She was wearing small ruby earrings that sparkled through her curly auburn hair.

"Oh, good—sandwiches!" Bea exclaimed as her eyes lighted on the tray. "I admit I had lunch, but I'm starving, as usual."

They sat near the fireplace, Vivienne in the large chair and Bea on the sofa with her shoes off and her feet up. Bea munched a sandwich as Vivienne poured the tea.

"A true heart-to-heart," Bea said. "We haven't done this in ages. What further intimate secrets can we possibly share?"

Vivienne prepared a cup of tea and put it on the table in front of Bea. She sat back in the chair and faced her. "You could tell me about your affair with Hilly Lawton."

Bea almost choked on her sandwich, sat up and coughed. She reached for the teacup and took a swallow.

"Boy, did you surprise me, Viv," she said after she'd recovered herself. "Them ain't the rules. How come?"

"Maybe I made some rules that ought to be changed," Vivienne said slowly. "I'm not much of a friend to you if something like that was going on for a year and you didn't feel you could tell me."

"Jon told you."

"Yes. Don't be angry with him."

"I'm not." Bea gave a slight shrug. "He wouldn't tell anyone else, only you." She took another sip of tea and leaned back on the sofa. "He's loyal."

"Tell me about it," Vivienne said.

Bea stretched out on the sofa and began, as if reciting a school essay. "'My affair with Hilly Lawton, by Beatrice Brown.' There's not much to say. Pretty typical. It went on for about a year. One or two days a week. Afternoons. It was over a while back. I don't think much of him anymore. I could understand his finding someone single after he got divorced, but not that bargain-basement blond bitch. Like I said, my estimation of him went way down.''

"How did Helen Lawton take it? Are you still friends?"

"Oh, sure," Bea said casually. "She and Hilly just lived together as roommates for years, until the daughter was grown up. Helen has her own interests."

"Apparently so did Hilly."

"Yeah, well, I don't think Helen was ever very interested in sex, and you know what men are."

"They haven't changed?" Vivienne asked, her mouth crinkling.

Bea laughed.

"Seriously, Bea, no one's ever going to learn about you and Hilly. He's not going to tell, I'm not going to tell, and neither will Jon or Helen, for that matter. So I've been wondering what you've been so scared about. You've been terrified, haven't you?"

Bea squirmed on the sofa, her eyes wide.

"No one thinks you killed Sisu Potter," Vivienne continued, "and you were with the priest practically the whole night she died. Why have you been so afraid?"

Bea leaned forward grimly. "Viv, this has got to be strictly between us. Promise."

"I promise I won't tell anyone."

"Remember the auditions for the show? I got there late and told you something weird had happened?"

"Yes! I'd completely forgotten that, Bea! But I thought it just had to do with—"

"I know. Me and one of the five hundred guys. That's why I didn't tell you. That was the day the first one came in the mail."

"The first one of what?"

"Buster started getting notes."

"Notes?"

"Poison-pen letters, they used to call them. They came in the mail on odd days—there was no predicting when they'd come. They stopped after Sisu drowned."

"*Buster* got them?" Vivienne asked, horrified.

"No, thank God, he never got one. I intercepted 'em and burned 'em. But they were addressed to him. If he'd ever seen one—" She shuddered.

"What did they say? Were they about you and Hilly?"

"That's the funny thing. They weren't. They were about me and every man, woman, child and animal in Carmel, but not Hilly. I figured that one out. Sisu just plain hated me, was jealous of my money, whatever—but since she was going with Hilly, she wanted him out of it. Hilly and I had broken up right before the first one came."

"That's probably when you stopped speaking to Sisu."

"It was!"

"I see. She retaliated."

"Yeah, I guess you could look at it that way," Bea said grudgingly. "The other way of looking at it is that she was a bitch. I was scared of her, Viv. That's the truth. That's why I didn't rip her to pieces after she pulled that bit with the hair on her costume during my big speech. I didn't know what she'd try to pull next. Maybe send a telegram to Buster." She leaned back on the sofa, her mouth curling up at one corner. "The joke is everyone thought she was scared of me, and I was scared as hell of her."

"What did they look like, Bea?" Vivienne asked. "The poison-pen letters?"

"They were classic. You know, words cut out of the newspapers or magazines. Letters cut and pieced together when it was a word that wouldn't be printed in a newspaper or magazine, if you get my drift."

"I wonder if anyone else got these things. Edwinta, perhaps. That would make sense if they were truly from Sisu. I'm going to ask her tonight."

"You won't mention me!" Bea look terrified.

"Of course not! I'll just ask if she ever got anything of the sort."

"Jesus!" Bea said. "Remember, Viv, you promised you wouldn't tell anyone."

"And I won't."

"Jon says you've been playing detective. He said you and Matt have been talking to the police chief. That's why I made you promise."

"I won't tell him. I'm not even sure I want to speak to him again." Vivienne twisted in the chair and looked out the window. "I've been having the strangest reaction to him."

"Oh, yeah? Well, policemen scare me on principle. When you've been plotting to kill your husband for years, you see one of those guys and you just instinctively jump. It's a knee-jerk reaction when you're a murderess *manqué*," Bea grinned. "I'll bet you didn't think I knew that word. That's what Jon says I am. Now about this guy. When I saw him at your house before I knew he was the Chief of Police, he seemed nice."

"Oh, he is. It's not that. I can't explain it." Vivienne turned back in the chair uncomfortably. "He's come by to talk to me several times, and I've gotten really angry at him on two occasions. I don't get angry at people unless it's something serious, and in these incidents I wouldn't have been angry at someone else. Isn't that odd?"

"Sounds like he's getting to you for some reason. People get mad at people when they're getting to them."

"I *have* felt vulnerable lately, not like myself." Vivienne sighed, images racing through her mind. "Ever since I found that body, I haven't been sleeping well at night. I wake up around four, and I can't go back to sleep for hours. Everything keeps passing in front of my eyes—that drowned body, the show, Edwin Everett—the whole Everett family..."

"And this police chief? Him, too?"

Vivienne was silent for a few moments, and then looked back at Bea. "He stopped by my house yesterday morning after the reopening. He told me he'd been in the audience that night. He said he knew I was upset during the whole show."

"Pretty observant."

"More than that." Vivienne's voice dropped and her thoughts turned inward. "He guessed why."

"He guessed Medora had gone for blood?"

"Yes."

"Pretty perceptive."

"It's frightening."

"He's probably just in love with you like every other guy in Carmel."

"Oh, no, Bea! He isn't. Men get that moony look when they're infatuated; this man just looks at me as though he's trying to solve a puzzle. Sometimes he's so warm and so charming in his way that I ... And yet I've ended up getting angry at him all the same.''

"Are you attracted to him, Viv?''

Vivienne stiffened in the chair, her heart beginning to pound. "Of course not! That's the last thing I'd need! I'm not sleeping at night, I've been having the most terrible dreams, sometimes I'm afraid something's going to crack inside of me—I'm not up to being attracted to anyone!''

"Viv, honey, whether you're up to it or not, are you? I met the guy, I can see how you could be attracted to him. He isn't café society—I guess they call it the jet set now—but you've had all that. He's not bad-looking, he has to be real intelligent if he's got you this intrigued, and he's probably a decent person. He's Claudia's uncle, and that's a nice family. Truth time, Viv.'' Bea watched her closely. "I think you're attracted to him.''

Vivienne looked at Bea as though she had to announce her own imminent death from a fatal disease. "I am.'' She put her hands to her face and closed her eyes.

"Viv, you know I wouldn't set up my life as a shining example of you, and I'm not trying to.'' Bea's voice was gentle. "But what you've been doing, however many years it's been since you were with a man, just hasn't been normal. You're probably gonna look great for the rest of your life—little old men'll probably be throwing themselves at you out of their wheelchairs—but will it be any fun then?''

Vivienne threw her an imploring glance.

"It could be fun now,'' Bea said.

"I'm not up to it, Bea.'' Vivienne's heart was in her throat. "I'm terrified.'' She rose, almost jumping out of the chair and propelling herself toward the fireplace. "I don't even know if he has the same feelings. Sometimes I think so, sometimes I don't,'' she said, addressing the mantelpiece. She turned back to Bea grimly. "I can't wait till this whole thing is over so I don't have to see him anymore.''

"Why don't you move to Alaska? Then you can be sure of never seeing him.''

"Bea!''

Bea settled back on the sofa with another sandwich. "Look, Viv, my lips are proverbially taped shut about this. You never told me. Do what you want to do. I heard he's a widower and his wife's been dead a few years, so he'll probably find someone and get remarried soon, and then he won't bother you anymore."

"Beatrice Brown!"

"I'm only saying what I'm supposed to say, aren't I?"

The phone rang.

Vivienne almost ran to pick it up and then stopped as she reached it, afraid of who might be at the other end of the line. She picked up the receiver slowly.

"Vivienne, it's me!" It was Matt Ross. "I just talked to Claudia. I can't believe this has happened all over again."

"Oh, no! *What* has happened all over again!"

"Problems with the show because someone else died. No one you and I know," Matt added hastily. "The minister at Claudia's church. He had his second heart attack inside of a month, and this time they took him to the hospital and he died. Claudia's very upset, naturally. Says she, Helen and Hilly won't be able to do the show tonight because of Father Drew and because it's Sunday. She was confused. I wasn't able to get a lot of sense out of what she said."

"What does Jonathan say? He won't want to cancel the show if he can help it."

"I know. I haven't talked to him yet; Claudia just called me. But if the three of them are out of it, it's impossible. Jon could do Hilly's part, but with Claudia and Helen gone, there's no one for the maid."

"Couldn't you do it and make it a butler?"

"Vivienne—that's a great idea! But then who would run the show? Maybe—I'll talk to Jon—maybe we could pull it off."

"Let me know, Matt. Or have Jon call me. Bea's here, too, so you can confer with both of us." She hung up the phone.

"What the hell was that all about?" Bea was standing up by the sofa, staring at Vivienne.

"I'm starting to think this whole show is cursed," Vivienne said, walking back to her. "Matt just said the minister at the church Claudia and the Lawtons go to died of a heart attack,

and he thinks the three of them aren't going to do the show tonight."

"Whew! When you said 'What happened again,' I was
thinking the worst. Like maybe Medora decided to move into
a better role. Except you and I are both alive."

"I don't know if I should try calling Jon or wait for him to
call me." Vivienne started to pace.

"Wait, Viv. He'll call. He knows I'm over here with you."
Bea began to eat her third sandwich, then made a sudden,
muffled noise with her mouth full. She chewed rapidly and
swallowed. "Viv, the guy who died—was that Andrew Mortimer?"

"Matt said it was a Father Drew."

"Boy, is that something." Bea sat again on the sofa
thoughtfully. "Drew Mortimer. That stupid Little Chapel by
the Sea is his church. Looks exactly like a little dinky Mortimer mansion—every bit as ugly as that big pink pile next to
Brown Hall only a lot smaller and with stained glass windows."

"That's right—he was a Mortimer," Vivienne murmured.
"I've known that for years and forgot all about it."

"The last of the breed, as they say. The guy was a regular
Saint Francis of Assisi without the birds, or was that the Bird-
man of Alcatraz? The movies came out right around the same
time and I always got the two mixed up. Anyway, I wouldn't say
the guy renounced the Mortimer fortune, but he lived very
simply over at the church. Tweeds and loafers rather than
sackcloth and sandals, but you get my meaning. No family, just
his little congregation. Some new people own the Mortimer
mansion; he hasn't lived there since he was a kid. I have no idea
if all his dough's given away already or what. There was a lot
of it, though. The Mortimers were real old money."

"How interesting," Vivienne said.

The phone rang again. This time it was Jonathan Patrick.
His voice was harried but cheerful. Vivienne stopped expecting the worst.

"Vivienne, Bea's over there with you, isn't she?"

"Yes, she's right here, eating."

"Bea's appetite is like the Pyramids; if they're still standing
and she's still eating, I'm reassured all's right with the world."

His tone changed. "Contrary to speculation, the show will go on tonight *sans* only Helen Lawton. She'll be taking care of things at the church. Claudia and Hilly have promised to do the show. I threatened them with another death if they didn't— mine! Claudia will play the maid, and when she's onstage, Matt will run the light booth. Can you believe all this? We do a murder mystery, and death haunts us all!"

"It *is* odd, Jon."

"At least it wasn't another cast member. Things have progressed so badly I've run out of sick death jokes. I'm not calling anyone else in the cast—Ted and the Everetts don't need the news until tonight."

"Thanks for letting us know, Jon."

"Of course you two would be the first. I'm afraid I need to make this short, Vivienne. I've got to call Matt and relieve him of the fear that he has to don a maid's uniform."

"Why don't you let me do that? I need to speak to him myself, and I'm sure you're busy."

"Vivienne, thank you! I'm in your debt forever, or at least until tonight."

Vivienne clicked the receiver down and dialed Matt's cottage. Matt came on the line, and she related Jon's information.

"That's a relief," Matt said. "I'm tired of Claudia always working over at that church, anyway. I think they take advantage of her."

"Matt," Vivienne said carefully, "Father Drew Mortimer wasn't just their minister."

"What do you mean?"

"The Little Chapel by the Sea is Episcopal. Father Drew was an Episcopal priest."

"Priest number three!" Matt's voice was hushed with excitement.

"Exactly. That's been right in front of us all along. I, for one, have been completely dense. There were at least three priests Sisu could have been referring to, that we know of."

"Priest number three," Matt repeated again.

"Matt, have you been able to ask Claudia exactly what she heard that night?"

"She says she doesn't remember, and I believe her. But in a roundabout way I know it's something to do with sex. I guess even a priest would have trouble giving that up."

Vivienne gripped the phone. She knew Matt was oblivious to the meaning of what he said as it reflected on her, but it still seemed as though the gods had been making sport of her recently.

"It's something to think about," Vivienne said. "I'll talk to you tonight."

TWENTY-FIVE

VIVIENNE ARRIVED AT the Playhouse at seven-thirty, the time the actors were "called." Everything appeared normal. Annie Watts hailed her from the box office as Vivienne passed on her way to the stage door. Annie's gigantic form filled the lower half of the window. Her wide, doughy face and pale curls allowed a partial view of the box office bulletin board through the upper portion of the pane. The evening sunset glinted off her thick glasses.

"Hi, Miss Montrose! Heard about the changes tonight?"

"Yes, Annie. Thank you for mentioning it. I'm prepared." Vivienne walked ahead to the stage door, hidden around the corner from the box office.

"I put some cookies backstage for everyone. Back in the vault," Annie bellowed. "They're chocolate chip!"

"Thank you," Vivienne shouted back. Hoping Annie wouldn't open the inner door of the box office and continue the conversation, Vivienne opened the stage door and made a quick dash down the corridor to her dressing room. Once safe inside, she put her purse and sweater down and straightened her things. She left the room and walked down the corridor to the third dressing room.

Reaching the door, she knocked softly.

"Come in," Medora's voice answered from inside.

Vivienne opened the dressing room door several inches. She caught a glimpse of Medora in the mirror. She was patting powder on her face and seemed surprised to see her.

"Is Edwinta here yet?" Vivienne asked, facing the real Medora.

"No. I expect her any minute," Medora said pleasantly. The confrontation of Friday night appeared to be completely forgotten.

"Would you ask her to stop by my dressing room? I have something I need to speak to her about."

"I will," Medora said.

As Vivienne was closing the door behind her, she heard Medora's voice call out, "Good show!"

"Good show" indeed, Vivienne thought. "Break a leg" is more likely, and I think she'd mean it.

Walking back to her dressing room, she almost bumped into Edwinta, who was running down the corridor, late for the call.

"Sorry!" Edwinta stepped back, embarrassed.

"I was just down the hall looking for you," Vivienne said. "Can you drop by my dressing room for a few minutes? There's something I need to ask you."

"Yeah—just let me tell Medora I'm here or she'll hit the ceiling about my not being professional." Edwinta flew past her.

Vivienne went back to her dressing room, put on her robe and began making up. She heard Edwinta's knock a minute or two later.

"Come in."

Edwinta opened the door and squeezed into the room. "My old dressing room," she said wistfully. "It was a lot more fun being in here than it is being with Medora. I feel like a little kid in there. She's a lot tougher on me here than she is at home. She just gave me hell for being late."

"She wants you to be as serious about the theatre as she is."

"I am," Edwinta said firmly. She sat in the other small chair. "What is it?"

Vivienne looked at the girl sitting opposite her. Edwinta's smooth, young face was eager now, showing no sign of the pain she might have been spared if she had learned the truth about her father while he was still alive. Vivienne wished with all her heart she could tell her, but instead, she returned to her subject.

"Winta, did you ever get anything in the mail that was—" Vivienne paused, unsure of how to explain herself. The old-fashioned way seemed the best. "Have you received poison-pen letters?"

Edwinta grimaced. "Oh, yeah—Sandi. I didn't know she could spell that well, but I guess she can. Some words she sure knows how to spell. I'll bet she knows how to do them, too." She looked away, her lovely face contorted with disgust.

"Has one come recently?"

"Not for a couple of weeks. Why?"

"I just wondered. When did you start receiving them?"

"Well, like, they weren't addressed to me. They were for Medora, but I go to the post office every day for the mail, and the first one looked weird, so I opened it."

"How did it look?"

"It was typed, the envelope was, and there was no return address. Also no post office box. Just Medora Everett, Carmel."

"Was it postmarked Carmel? Actually, did you keep any of them, and how many did you get?"

"No. I ripped them up and flushed them down the toilet, where they belonged. I noticed they were from Carmel because I couldn't see how they could have made it here with such a weird address if they weren't. I got four."

"What did they say?"

"They were about me and Ted. I mean, really, really bad. Disgusting."

"Do you think they might have been from someone other than Sandi? What about Sisu Potter?"

Edwinta stared at her, startled. "I didn't think of that. It didn't seem like it came from an adult. It was like it was from a mean, nasty, disgusting, evil little kid." She thought. "But one who could spell."

"None have come since Sisu's death?"

"No." She looked at Vivienne almost defiantly. "If she *did* send them, that's another reason I'm glad she's dead."

"I can understand why you'd feel that way," Vivienne said gently. "Thanks, Winta. You've told me some things I needed to know."

"No problem." Edwinta stood up.

Vivienne looked up at her. "You've been giving a wonderful performance despite the difficulties lately. You can be very proud of yourself."

Edwinta smiled lopsidedly. "Thanks. I've really been doing my best. It's been a challenge having to act with that creep Ted and with my mother."

"I hope we have a good show tonight, too. Claudia makes her stage debut."

"Oh, yeah?" Edwinta looked wary. "As what? Not in my role!"

Vivienne hid her amusement. The girl had a lot of Medora in her. "As the maid," she said. "Helen Lawton can't be here tonight. There was a death at her church."

"Well, I think Claudia can handle the maid's part," Edwinta said magnanimously. "I've gotta go or Medora'll really kill me. See you onstage!" She whirled out and shut the door behind her.

Vivienne continued applying makeup. Claudia Kellog came by, knocking on doors and calling the fifteen-minute cue. Shortly afterward there was another knock on the door, followed by Matt Ross's voice.

"It's me, Vivienne. Do you have a minute?"

"Yes, come in," she called out.

Matt stepped inside and closed the door. "Did you find out anything else?"

"A few people had been receiving poison-pen letters, Matt. Since Sisu died, there haven't been any more."

"Wow!" Matt looked even more than usually intense. "It must be tied in with her death. She sent one to someone, and they killed her. Classic—right out of a book! Maybe she was blackmailing someone!"

Vivienne spoke cautiously, weighing her words. "I think I have an idea, Matt. I need to think about it a bit more and possibly get some facts from one other person. I'll talk to you about it after the show."

"I can't wait," Matt said. "I have to get back now. I'm doing a lot more tonight with Claudia filling in for Helen."

After Matt had gone, Vivienne sat for a long while, staring into the mirror without seeing herself. Matt called "Five minutes," and Vivienne was still lost in thought.

The one-minute call came and went. Vivienne heard the music go up and then down again and Bea's voice coming from the stage. Startled, she resumed doing her makeup. She finished it and, still musing, changed into her costume.

Vivienne waited until Medora and Edwinta were onstage with Bea before walking down the darkened corridor and quietly tapping on the fourth dressing room door, the one shared by Ted Reid and Hilly Lawton. The edge of light around the door vanished and Ted opened the door. Behind him, she could see Hilly sitting at the dressing table counter, silhouetted in the dim backstage light.

"Vivienne," Ted whispered. "I can't believe I've seen so little of you since the show opened. The only time I saw you last night was onstage." He pressed her arm with one hand, and Vivienne stiffened slightly. "I've only got a second and then my cue comes up," he said, continuing to hold her arm. "Please come down to the La Playa tonight after the show. It all seemed dull last night without you."

"Thanks for the invitation," Vivienne said coolly. "At this point, Ted, I don't know what my plans are."

"Please try." Ted released her arm and slipped by her, on his way to his entrance.

Hilly rose and came to the door where Vivienne waited.

She whispered up at him. "Hilly, you said you wanted to talk to me about Sisu's death. About my finding her body."

"I do, Vivienne," he whispered back. "Thanks."

He followed her down the hall, past the light booth and through the black curtains into the vault. We can have privacy here, Vivienne thought. Only she and Hilly used the far door in the vault for their entrances. They walked to the interior of the dark storage area, where the sound of the actors' voices coming from the stage was just audible. The standing candelabra glowed brightly, lighting a refreshment table bearing a large vat of bad coffee to be taken outside and forced upon the audience during intermission, some cone-shaped disposable cups, many hideous plastic cup holders, and Annie Watts's chocolate chip cookies in their ripped cellophane package.

"Have some coffee?" Hilly asked, and when Vivienne shook her head, he put a cone-shaped cup in a plastic holder and placed it under the tap at the bottom of the big vat.

"Before we start, Hilly," Vivienne said gently, "I must tell you that I know about the notes."

Hilly straightened, holding the distasteful cup of coffee in his right hand. "The what?"

"The poison-pen letters. She couldn't help it, could she?"

Hilly looked at her dumbly.

"Now that Sisu is dead, she's stopped sending them. Out of fear, I guess. Everyone who received them thinks they were from Sisu. But I know the person who sent those notes had to be Helen."

Hilly let out a small sigh, his shoulders relaxing. "I never thought anyone would guess that."

"I've thought a lot about it, Hilly. I don't know if anyone else would have."

Hilly placed the coffee cup on the table and looked at Vivienne. A deep sadness was in his eyes.

"That's why when Helen's sister died, she didn't leave her money to Helen," Vivienne continued. "She left it to your daughter so she could get away, so she could escape from home. That's the real truth, isn't it?"

Hilly gazed at her, looking strangely relieved. "Yes," he said quietly. "You're one of the few people who's ever realized that."

"None of us thought she was jealous of Sisu, but none of us really knew her, did we? No one ever really noticed Helen. She's one of those people who always stay in the background. We didn't know her very well, but you did, you lived with her. Did she put the cracked goblet at Sisu's place on the table that night as a warning? When she found out the warning wasn't enough, did she have to kill her? Was it jealousy? Or was it something Sisu knew about Helen that she was going to tell Andrew Mortimer?"

Hilly slowly exhaled. "I don't know. Helen wouldn't talk to me about it." He turned away slightly. "It was hell living with her for all those years...everyone thinking...and I couldn't tell them. I was the bad guy and Helen was the angel." He shook his head. "No one saw my side of it."

"I do, Hilly," Vivienne said softly.

Hilly turned back to her eagerly, his handsome face looking years younger, almost boyish. "You do?"

He's a remarkably attractive man, Vivienne thought. It explained so much. She paused, taking a deep breath. Then, as Hilly watched her expectantly, she spoke.

"How long did it take you to get over spraining your back when you threw Sisu Potter into the lagoon?"

Hilly seemed stunned.

"I was sitting in my dressing room, all the facts staring me in the face, but I still couldn't believe you'd done it. Not until

I led you on about Helen and saw you throw her to the wolves. Your own wife.''

Hilly stammered, the look of shock still on his face. "I . . . I don't understand you, Vivienne. What are you talking about?''

"You finally agreed to a divorce from Helen after your sister-in-law left all her money to your daughter. With good reason. She didn't want it going to you.''

Hilly stood silently gaping at Vivienne.

"You had an affair with Bea Brown,'' Vivienne continued, "until she made it clear to you that she got nothing if she left her husband except her jewels and her clothes, and I don't think that seemed like much to you. Especially since you knew that Sisu came from a wealthy family and was eager to get married—to anyone. Sisu's parents in Oklahoma were old, you knew that, and so far they were proving to be frustratingly healthy. You promised Sisu you'd marry her, but you'd been putting her off, not letting her announce it. That was one of the reasons she was furious.''

As she spoke, Vivienne watched Hilly's eyes, more and more certain that what she had surmised was the truth. "You weren't about to lose your ace in the hole, Hilly. You weren't sure when it would pay off, but if you could put up with Sisu and delay marrying her for a while, you might come into two fortunes. You'd been kissing up, as they say, to Andrew Mortimer for years. Until a month ago, you had no idea whether he might be hit by a car next week or live to be ninety. Drew Mortimer understood your marriage to Helen. You kept your other affairs secret. Your dating Sisu openly must have been difficult to explain to him. It must have been especially difficult after he got one of Sisu's letters. A person who would send that sort of thing wouldn't balk at listening in on phone conversations or reading mail. My guess is that Sisu had her facts straight and whatever was in her letter helped set off Drew Mortimer's first heart attack, and made him seriously think about changing his will. The will in which he left a huge sum to you, his lawyer and long-time lover.''

Hilly, standing dumbstruck until now, stepped back. "Vivienne, you must be crazy! This is the craziest thing I've ever heard!''

"No. It isn't. Sisu said as much to you that night, down by the cottage, before she passed out."

Hilly turned away from her, staring into the light of the candelabra.

"But what really gave it away to me, Hilly," Vivienne said, "was your ability to ad lib."

Vivienne felt herself swept into Hilly's arms. In one movement he pulled her right hand to her mouth and covered it, holding his right hand on hers. He pressed her to the right side of his body and gripped her there, holding her immobilized, her left arm pinned to his side. She squirmed and pushed against him to try and break his hold and was amazed at his strength. It was impossible to free herself.

With a kind of horrified awe, Vivienne watched Hilly pick up a stainless steel spoon from the table with his free hand and smash it against one of the light bulbs of the candelabra. It shattered, leaving jagged edges around the standing silver filament. Awkwardly but quickly, Hilly began to break each of the bulbs in turn, leaving one intact and glowing.

Holding her in both arms, he pressed her close to the table. He lifted the lid of the coffee urn with his left hand and threw it onto an armchair piled with cushions that stood behind the refreshment table. Again with his free hand, he grabbed the big urn and tipped it toward her. As though she were outside her body and watching, Vivienne saw the coffee splash against her waist and pour down her legs, spreading in a pool around her feet.

She couldn't feel anything as she looked down at the floor, but she could think, her mind racing at twice its speed. She was standing wet and grounded on the concrete. In the next few seconds he was going to throw her on top of the broken candelabra and electrocute her. It would look as though she'd stumbled, knocked over the urn and fallen against the candelabra. The current would run through her wet body into the concrete floor. Hilly would be innocent, and she would be dead—an accident. Her body stiffened with a violent fear. There was a pounding, ringing noise in her ears. Sweat was breaking out on the palms of her hands and under her arms. It's salt, she thought, and it would kill her.

One of the onstage voices suddenly was audible to her.

"I don't like it. I'll never like it!" It was Ted Reid as Acis.

Vivienne tried to bend her knees to make it harder for Hilly to get her off balance.

"Is she ever coming back? Will we ever see her again?" Edwinta's voice came from the stage.

Bea began speaking. "We hope so, dear. No matter what she's done, our house will always be open to her. After all, she's still part of our family."

They're so close, Vivienne thought. Just beyond the wall of the vault! She could cry out to them if Hilly hadn't locked her own hand around her jaw in such a tight grip. She struggled, using all her strength to press herself down against the force of Hilly trying to push her forward. It was like living a nightmare. There was no noise in the vault other than Hilly's heavy breathing. She wasn't even aware of whether she was breathing or not, only of exerting a tremendous, mad force. She heard Ted's voice again, very loud, repeating his previous lines, "I don't like it. I'll never like it!"

"Is she *ever* coming back?" Edwinta's voice was almost a shout. "Will we *ever* see her again?"

"Isn't this *odd*," Bea's voice was very loud, calling out lines Vivienne had never heard. "I was expecting a *luncheon guest*! Our family lawyer, *Philip Winfield*," she bellowed, "and I've never known him to be *late*!"

Suddenly Hilly took his hand away from Vivienne's mouth and grabbed her by the waist. She knew she could scream, but screaming was useless now. Later, the others onstage would remember the sound as her death cry. With all her strength, she pushed back against Hilly Lawton.

In a split second, she saw Matt Ross coming toward her from the end of the vault near the light booth and calling out to her; then she felt herself jerked away and falling backward. She landed on something, then realized the something was Hilly, who still gripped her in both his arms. As she tried to pull herself away from Hilly, she saw Chief Himber standing above her and training a gun in her direction. His face was pale, the muscles clenched.

Looking behind her, Himber spoke quietly and with forced evenness. "Let go of her, Lawton. Take your hands off her right now or I'll kill you."

Vivienne felt the arms release her. She lifted herself up from the floor and away from Hilly Lawton and ran. It happened to be in the direction of Matt. At the same time, Jonathan came running through the black curtains between the light booth and the vault.

"Where the hell is Hilly?" Jon yelled. "He's on! He's *on*!" He came to an abrupt stop when he saw the scene—Himber training a gun on Hilly Lawton, and Hilly crouching with his arms around his knees, head bent. "What in the hell happened?"

Still pointing the gun at Hilly, Chief Himber's eyes flashed toward Vivienne, Matt and Jonathan and then back to Lawton.

"He missed his cue," Himber said.

TWENTY-SIX

FOR A MOMENT they stood in the vault like five statues. Vivienne, Jonathan and Matt were staring at each other. Himber still had his eye on Hilly Lawton, and Hilly wasn't looking at anyone. Vivienne had a vague awareness of confused noises coming from the house. The audience members were talking to each other.

"He tried to kill me," Vivienne said to Jonathan and Matt. "You and Chief Himber saved my life, Matt."

Matt and Jonathan stared at her in horror.

"I told you, Vivienne!" Jon stammered. "I told you someone else might get killed. But Hilly? Why in the world...?"

They heard a man's voice speaking in the audience outside the vault door. "I'm leaving," he said. "This is the worst thing I've ever seen. No one knows what the hell they're doing up there."

"Look at them!" a high-pitched woman's voice said. "The actors! They're all leaving! Is this the end of the play?"

"What are we doing?" Jon said wildly. "The whole show's falling apart! I've got to go out there and say something! What are we doing?"

"We'll go on with the show!" Vivienne said. "You can do Hilly's part, and I'll—"

"No," Jon interrupted. "We can't finish the show tonight. Not tonight. But we'll run for years! We just had an attempted murder backstage during a murder play! This is the biggest thing to hit Carmel in a lifetime!" He turned, ran toward the vault exit and disappeared through the curtained door.

Himber spoke. "Matt, do me a favor. Go to the phone here and call the sheriff's office. Tell them I want two men to get over here as fast as they can. Explain the situation."

"Okay," Matt said, and turning hastily, almost ran into Bea Brown. He dodged her and ran out of the vault toward the light booth.

"Where the hell is Hilly?" Bea yelled and then stopped dead when she saw Chief Himber holding a gun on the missing cast member.

"Ladies and gentlemen." They heard Jon's excited voice coming from the stage. "Ladies and gentlemen, thank you for your patience. I must apologize, but tonight's performance is canceled."

Edwinta Everett, wide-eyed, rounded the corner into the vault as they all heard murmurs from the audience.

"Something has happened that..." Jon continued. "One of our cast members..." his voice came haltingly. "In any case, your money will be refunded or you can attend another of our performances free."

More unhappy sounds came from the audience. The group in the vault stood motionless, listening to the crowd in the theatre and to Jonathan's voice.

"We're not able to refund your money tonight, but I assure you it will be...it will be forthcoming at your convenience. Now I have to ask you to leave the theatre as quickly as possible because we have to get the...the indisposed cast member out of the theatre."

A shrill woman's voice spoke. "Did Vivienne Montrose die? I'll bet she's dead, just like that actress who drowned!"

"Someone's dead back there, aren't they?" An additional voice chimed in.

"No!" Jon shouted. "Vivienne Montrose is not dead. *No* one back there is dead. Everyone back there in that vault is alive!"

Bea, who had been standing as if stunned, was suddenly galvanized into action. "We've gotta do something! It's pandemonium out there, and Jon can't handle it alone. Viv, go out there and sign some autographs—it'll calm them down, and they'll go home."

"All right, I will. Winta," Vivienne called out. "Please go tell Claudia to put on the house lights."

Almost afraid to glance at them, Vivienne walked past Himber and Hilly Lawton, out the vault door and down the ramp into the audience. It *was* pandemonium in the house. Some people were standing up, others were sitting, and a muttering crowd was going out the two double exit doors. Jonathan stood in the midst of a group of angry people. He caught sight of her and looked as if she had thrown him a life raft.

"Vivienne, thank God!" he cried out. "Ladies and gentlemen, Miss Montrose will autograph your programs."

Scribbling as fast as she could, Vivienne autographed some two dozen programs before she heard the siren of a police car approaching, the wail getting progressively louder and higher, and finally descending in pitch and stopping outside the theatre. She autographed a few more programs and then saw two men in uniform come through the left double door.

"They're back there," Jon shouted, pointing at the vault entrance.

The audience members remaining in the small theatre gawked as the two policemen went into the vault and emerged with a handcuffed Hilly Lawton. The three passed Vivienne. Hilly looked straight ahead, as though he wasn't really the person being arrested.

The last of the audience left, and Jonathan walked across the stage. "Vivienne, you're soaking wet!" he exclaimed.

Vivienne heard Bea's voice and turned toward the vault ramp.

"Viv, what the hell happened, anyway? No one knows. Hilly wouldn't talk and Chief Himber says we have to ask *you*." Bea approached her. "What have you got on your costume?"

"It's coffee," Vivienne said. "From the vat back there. Don't worry, it was lukewarm, as usual. I'll go backstage and change."

"I'm coming with you," Bea said.

Vivienne led the way. In the corridor, they met Medora on her way to the stage.

"I'll be out there," Medora said. "Now that the autograph-signing is over, I'm waiting for the epilogue."

"Jesus," Bea said under her breath after they passed her. "It's like you did it on purpose to steal the limelight from her."

They both went into the first dressing room. Bea quickly closed the door behind them.

"Viv," she whispered, facing Vivienne, "it was him, wasn't it?"

Vivienne spoke gently. "Yes, Bea."

"He tried to kill you, didn't he?"

"Yes."

"Jesus!" Bea leaned back against the door and pounded her fists into it with a backward stroke of both hands. She looked up at Vivienne. Her eyes were wet. "I've gotta go out there with everyone," she said, her voice thick. "I've gotta get myself under control and if I stay in here with you and think about what that son of a bitch tried to do to you, it's not gonna happen. I can't let anyone know out there about Hilly and me, so I've gotta keep myself under control. Okay?"

"Of course, Bea. I understand completely. Go ahead." Vivienne took her dress from the rack. "I'll change and be right out."

Bea left the room, and Vivienne changed clothes. She took off her stained stockings and wiped off her shoes. The coffee hadn't soaked into them so they were still fairly dry. She left the dressing room and walked along the dim corridor to the entrance by the light booth.

Coming through the door, she saw all of them waiting for her. The cast was seated onstage. Jonathan sat in a chair in the house, and Chief Himber sat in the front row next to the aisle leading to the double exit doors.

Everyone turned and looked up at her.

"To Persephone!" Edwinta Everett said quietly.

Vivienne felt tears start in her eyes. "Thank you, Winta." She stood on the step by the door and bit her lip, trying not to cry.

"You know, Vivienne," Jonathan said, "your delayed entrances are always very dramatic."

Everyone laughed.

"But we've all been waiting here, dying to know what went on back there and why."

Vivienne walked to the center of the stage and Jon quickly picked up one of the house chairs and placed it so Vivienne could sit where everyone could see her.

"Sight lines," he explained, setting the chair down, and they all laughed again.

Vivienne sat in the chair and looked at the people on the stage. Jonathan was to her left in the house seats in front of her, just in the glow of the stage lights, an expectant look on his face. Edwinta sat erect in a chair in front of the desk on the stage, looking at her with Edwin Everett's eyes. Ted, Claudia,

Matt and Bea were around the small table, and Medora sat to her right, half turned away from her as if to show she was only moderately interested. Himber was in her peripheral vision to her left in the audience. She felt him watching her. "It's difficult to know where to begin," she said.

"We've all figured out that Hilly killed Sisu and that he was trying to kill you back in the vault," Matt said. "But how did you guess that Hilly was a murderer and why would he try to kill you back there in the vault with all of us out front?"

"That's exactly what surprised *me*," Vivienne said. "I never thought he would try to harm me back there, with everyone else so close. I thought the vault was the one place I could have the privacy to voice my suspicions to him, and be safe."

Chief Himber made a noise that sounded like several indistinguishable words, and Vivienne turned to look at him.

"Lawton isn't a stupid man," Himber said, his expression again enigmatic. "What did you say to him to make him risk trying to kill you backstage?"

"I tricked him. It was an impulse. I had no idea it would go as far as it did. I implied that I thought Helen had killed Sisu. I knew Helen couldn't hurt a fly, and if he turned on her, it would prove he was really no good, and that's exactly what happened. Then I did something you told me about the first time I talked to you."

Himber's eyes narrowed a little as he sat watching her.

"I could see how he'd attracted people," Vivienne continued, again aware of everyone on the stage. "I could see his charm and at the same time see through it because I was convinced of his guilt. When he thought he had me on his side," she looked at Himber, "I 'got the subject off guard,' just as you said when I first met you."

Himber smiled.

Vivienne turned back to the others. "You see, what really gave it away to me was Hilly's ability to ad lib. You've all had the horrible experience of being onstage with Hilly when he'd forgotten his lines. You either suffered agonies or you learned to roll with it. Hilly couldn't or wouldn't learn his lines, but he could ad lib so well that he could make the actors who *did* know their lines look as though they didn't. It takes a certain kind of personality to go out on the stage and do that—a complete

disregard for others who are playing by the rules and a reck-
lessness, a kind of daring. Spur-of-the-moment behavior.
That's how he drowned Sisu Potter—on the spur of the moment. He ad libbed.''

''But, Vivienne, how did you know, or guess, that Hilly
murdered Sisu?'' Jonathan asked. ''I mean, we all know Hilly
could fudge his lines, but surely that alone couldn't have given
it away to you?''

The group on the stage seemed eager for her answer, except
for Bea, who was staring hard at the prop vase on the table in
front of her.

''No, of course not,'' Vivienne said. ''There were several
factors. Two people who saw Hilly the day after the drowning
said he looked like an old man. A few days later he was back to
normal.''

''That's right!'' Ted said. ''He looked like a broken man,
and then in a day or two he looked fine.''

Vivienne turned to Claudia, with the intention of ignoring
Ted. ''You saw Hilly the day after Sisu died. You told Matt that
he looked as though he'd aged ten years. What made you think
that?''

Claudia shook her head slightly. ''I don't know. It was just
an impression.''

''How does an old man move?'' Vivienne asked.

Surprise registered on Claudia's face. ''Stiffly! He was moving stiffly—that's why I thought he looked old.''

''I didn't realize how strong Hilly was until he grabbed me
backstage tonight. But he strained his back the night he
drowned Sisu. That's something even a very strong man can do
if he bends or twists the wrong way. Sisu had been drinking
heavily at the party, and she must have passed out somewhere
near Matt's cottage, maybe even on the bench down there.
She'd been stirring up a lot of trouble for Hilly, and on the spur
of the moment he decided to carry her over to the lagoon and
pitch her in, far enough so that even if the cold water woke her
up, she wouldn't be able to get back to shore. He knew she
wouldn't swim. If she'd revived at any point on the way to the
lagoon, or if he'd run into anyone as he was carrying her, it
would look as though she'd passed out and he was carrying her

back to her car or to the party. No one, especially not Sisu, would have been the wiser."

"Her car!" Matt said, suddenly involved in the detective process again. "After he killed her, he went back to where they'd parked her car near your house, made sure no one was watching, and drove it down to the lagoon parking lot! Then he walked back to your house—it only would take five minutes if he hurried—and pretended to be sick from too much champagne. All ad libbing again!"

"Exactly, Matt."

"But there was no proof and no motive!"

"You're right in the first instance, Matt. As far as I know, there was no proof, and if Hilly hadn't tried to kill me backstage, I don't know if we ever would have found him out. But there *was* a motive. Sisu was sending poison-pen letters..." Vivienne stopped for a moment when Bea flashed her a fearful glance.

"I know! I got them!" Edwinta interrupted excitedly. "Or really Medora. Only I flushed them down the toilet!"

"You got *what*?" Medora asked in her deep voice.

"Poison-pen letters," Edwinta replied. "I thought they were from, you know... and you might freak out."

"Next time I get mail," Medora said warningly, "I'd appreciate the opportunity to glance at it before you flush it down the toilet."

"That was Hilly's motive?" Matt asked, still intent. "Poison-pen letters?"

"In a roundabout way they were part of it," Vivienne said. "I suppose it will really come out when Father Andrew Mortimer's will is read. Mortimer left Hilly a good sum of money, probably a small fortune. I took a guess on that, but based on Hilly's behavior in a couple of other instances, I knew it had to be his motive. Sisu was sending poison-pen letters to Mortimer and causing problems in general for Hilly. When she couldn't be personally nasty to someone, she had to strike back another way. She wanted Hilly to marry her, and he'd promised her privately he would, but he couldn't, because of Father Drew. Remember how derogatory she was about Hilly's church? So she used the letters as a vehicle to pay him back. She was threatened by his relationship with Andrew Mortimer; she suspected they were lovers.''

There was a crash as the prop vase from the table hit the floor. Bea, her skin ghostly pale, stood up as if to retrieve it.

Claudia looked horrified. ''No!'' she said. ''No, that couldn't be! Not Father Drew! Not Hilly!''

''Good Lord!'' Jonathan said. ''I knew Hilly was a front-office Christian, but I had no idea his religion profited him so well. Nor to what uses he put it!''

''Bea, are you all right?'' Vivienne called out across the small stage. Bea stood unsteadily, looking very ill.

''I need to find the ladies' room,'' Bea said shakily.

Medora went to her. ''Come on, we'll go backstage.'' She led Bea off through the stage right exit toward the restroom.

Edwinta, Claudia, Jonathan and Ted were left with Vivienne and Himber. They were all strangely silent.

I've upset Bea terribly, Vivienne thought, but the worst is over now that she knows the truth. ''He really fooled all of us,'' she said to the others. ''He was such a convincing actor. A natural.''

''I still can't believe it,'' Claudia said. Her eyes widened with a sudden realization. ''That must have been what Sisu was saying when—when she—'' She stammered, reddening, and Matt reached across the table and took her hand.

''Yes, Claudia,'' Vivienne said. ''It must have been.''

''What was that?'' Ted asked, perking up for the first time since the disclosure. ''What did Sisu say to Claudia?''

''Claudia heard Sisu say something before she disappeared that night,'' Matt said. ''Something about a priest or priests.''

''So you all thought it was me, but none of you told me,'' Ted said slowly, hurt and anger in his pale eyes. ''You were all thinking I killed Sisu! You've thought it all along. That's why you've been treating me like this!''

''We've had other reasons, Ted,'' Matt said. ''I'll tell you about them sometime if you're interested.''

Ted got up from the table. ''I thought you were my friends!''

''Some of us are, Ted,'' Jonathan said.

Ted looked at Jonathan and suddenly smiled. ''It isn't healthy to hold grudges,'' he said. ''I forgive all of you.''

There was an embarrassed silence in the house.

"I'm going down to the La Playa," Ted said. "Anyone want to go with me?"

Edwinta ignored him.

"Maybe later, Ted," Jonathan said.

Ted started for the exit aisle. "Hope to see you down there later," he said as he passed Vivienne and Jonathan.

All of them except Edwinta watched Ted leave the theatre.

Medora came through the stage right door, followed by a still pale Bea.

"What happened to the man of the cloth?" Bea asked, a little too loudly.

Jonathan rose from his chair. "He left for the La Playa," he said.

"He's another one who's light in his loafers, if you ask me," Bea said. She walked toward the table.

"Bea, are you sure you're all right?" Jonathan asked.

"Sure. Something I ate didn't agree with me, and in the excitement it acted up on me. I'm okay now." Bea bent down behind the table and came up with the flower from the broken prop vase. "Too bad," she said, waving it at everyone cheerily. "We could have sent this to the funeral."

Medora ignored this macabre bit of humor. "Are you ready to leave?" she asked Edwinta.

"Why don't you two come out for a drink with us, Medora?" Bea asked. "We could all use one, and the kid here could have a Coke," she added affectionately to Edwinta.

"I'd like to go," Edwinta volunteered.

"You may if you wish, Edwinta, but I won't. I teach an early class tomorrow." Medora picked up her purse from the bench and stood up.

"I need to speak to you for a moment in private, Medora," Vivienne said. Then she walked with Medora up the aisle. When they reached the theatre doors and were away from the others, Vivienne spoke quickly.

"Please tell Edwinta the truth. For her sake, not for yours."

"I appreciate your concern, Vivienne," Medora said coolly. "I know you genuinely care for my daughter. And I know that what I say to you will remain in confidence. Edwinta will receive a letter from her grandfather on her eighteenth birthday. I haven't read it. I don't know what is says, only that it says everything he wished her to know. Please respect that." She turned, opened one of the double doors, and was gone.

Vivienne, left standing by the exit doors, turned and started back down the aisle toward the others.

"Let's go," Bea was saying, beginning to usher them all toward the doors.

Matt turned to Claudia. "Do you feel like going down there tonight?"

"I think I'd like to be with people for a while," Claudia said. "I don't want to go home and... My family—I don't know how I'm going to tell my family... about..."

Cortland Himber, who was still sitting in the audience and had been silent thus far, spoke, "I'll tell them."

A look of relief and gratitude crossed Claudia's face. "Thank you, Uncle Cor! I couldn't have faced that."

"Don't worry about it. Go out and have a good time," Himber said.

"If there's one thing I need right now, it's a drink," Bea said. "Jon, shut things down so we can get out of here."

Jonathan hurried across the stage toward the light booth.

"Drinks for everyone are on me at the La Playa!" Bea called out, starting for the doors.

Matt and Claudia had neared the exit. "Claudia and I are going for a walk first," Matt said. "We'll join the rest of you later." He and Claudia went out the front doors.

The stage lights went off, leaving only the glow of the work lights illuminating the small stage. Vivienne, Edwinta, Himber and Bea were alone in the darkened house.

Jonathan reappeared from the light booth. "Once everyone gets to the front doors, I'll turn the work lights off," he called out.

Himber stood up. "I'd like to talk to you for a few minutes," he said to Vivienne.

"Okay, Jon. C'mon, Edwinta," Bea said. "If I'm not sitting at the La Playa drinking an old fashioned five minutes from now, there's gonna be another death!"

"I guess you can switch off the work lights yourself, Vivienne," Jonathan said quickly. "When you go, just pull the door tight and you'll hear the lock click." He passed her on his way to join Bea and Edwinta. "Remember, you're our heroine," he said and gave her a quick kiss on the cheek. Then he bounded up the aisle.

"C'mon, Edwinta," Bea said on her way to the doors. "We'll both go down there and snub that creep with the turned-around collar. If he says something, we pretend we don't hear. I'm great at that. The last person I did that to died!"

The theatre doors clicked shut behind Edwinta, Bea and Jonathan, and Vivienne and Chief Himber were alone in the theatre.

The worst is over, Vivienne thought. If I haven't been through fire, I've been through water, or, in this case, luke-warm coffee. I should be able to live through this.

Himber was standing at the center edge of the stage. She moved closer to him.

"What did you want to speak to me about?" she asked.

"Several pieces of unfinished business. The goblet at the re-hearsal that night—who do you think cracked it?"

Vivienne walked slowly onto the stage and under the work lights. "Well, there were two people at the table who really despised Sisu, but neither of them would have deliberately done something like that. I've always thought it was an accident. I still think it was."

Himber looked at her without speaking for several moments. "Well, Miss Montrose," he finally said, "you solved a crime and almost single-handedly apprehended a murderer."

Vivienne smiled. "Not very single-handedly. If you hadn't come in when you did, you and Matt . . ."

His expression changed. "Almost too late," he said. "You wouldn't have been subjected to that if I'd been less interested in you and more interested in Miss Potter's death."

Vivienne stood absolutely still, feeling a pulse in her throat. "What do you mean?"

"You know what I mean," Himber replied quietly. "You know I'm a fan of yours. I've seen you onstage more times than I'd like to admit. You've always represented something extraordinary to me. Obviously, I was too bowled over by you to think straight about this case, and you almost paid for it. So did I."

"I don't care about that," Vivienne said. "I'm alive now, and we wouldn't have been able to catch him if he hadn't tried to kill me."

"You're probably right, Miss Montrose. You're also being kind."

I'll sit down, Vivienne thought. That will make this easier. She walked to the small bench downstage left and sat on it. She looked back at Himber, almost the hardest thing to do. The very hardest was next. "What do you feel about me?" she asked. "Off the stage?"

Himber began to walk toward her, while looking at the rows of empty seats to his right. He sat in a chair in the front row of seats, facing her.

"That's a tough question. It's obvious I've tried to be around you as often as I could. I'm in love with the onstage Vivienne Montrose."

Vivienne froze.

His eyes flicked to hers. Then he looked away. "Off the stage, I don't know you that well."

Vivienne turned away from him. She felt hot and cold and shaky all at once. It was like having a bad case of influenza. She had an almost overpowering desire to run out of the theatre, drive to her house and never come out again.

"There's more," he said, "as you know. I'm extremely attracted to you. When I saw you wading around in that lagoon . . ." He stopped. "I'm also somewhat in awe of you. I probably always would be if—if I saw more of you." He cleared his throat. "I wouldn't like it if I didn't see you again after this, except to run into you on the street or see you on the stage, but that's up to you. If you wouldn't like to have dinner with me, or anything standard like that, I'd like to go walking on the beach sometimes with you and your dog."

Vivienne felt her throat tighten. "I wouldn't like it if I didn't see you again either." She took a quick breath. "My heart is pounding right now, and I'm afraid I'm having trouble speaking. This is very hard for me, Cortland."

"That's the first time you've ever used my name," he said, sounding as though he was also having trouble speaking.

"I know. I must be honest with you. I don't act on feelings the way I did twenty years ago. I don't have the emotional stamina for it. The way you've expressed yourself has touched me, and I have to admit it's stirred me. But I wouldn't be comfortable... What I'm trying to say is that I'd rather you joined MacGuffin and me on our walks for a while, maybe a long while, before anything 'standard' happened. Do you understand?"

For the first time since their conversation began, he looked her straight in the face. "Yes. I do."

"I usually take MacGuffin out around eight in the morning."

"Which beach are you going to tomorrow?"

"I think we'll try the lagoon beach again."

"May I meet you there?"

She smiled. "You've never asked before; you've always just turned up."

"I had an excuse then."

"Don't you now?"

Looking at her, his face relaxed at last, his blue eyes finally cleared, and he smiled. "That's all I wanted to talk to you about," he said, rising from the chair. "You probably want to get down to the La Playa and meet your friends."

"Oh!" Vivienne said, taken aback. "I forgot."

They walked across the stage and up the aisle, Vivienne ahead of Himber. She could feel the tension building inside of her. She shoved against one of the double doors, and Himber, behind her, pushed it all the way open. He stepped outside.

"I have to turn off the lights," she said, and while he held the door open for her, she reached inside and pulled the switch, leaving the theatre in darkness. She joined him outside, and he pulled the door shut behind her. It closed with a click.

A strong breeze was blowing up from the ocean. The night was clear, and moonlight and the street lamp lit the drive in front of the theatre.

I'm angry at him, Vivienne thought. That's what this is, this feeling; I'm furious! She turned to Himber, the words bursting out of her.

"An hour ago I was almost killed, and you're going to walk off casually into the night! I'd think you'd at least have the decency to tell me you're in love with me!" Then she stood aghast, stunned by her own vehemence.

A delighted smile spread across Himber's face. "You're wonderful," he said. He looked down at her for a moment. "I wasn't going to walk off casually into the night. I was planning to walk you down to the La Playa so you could join your friends. And as for the last, it wouldn't be difficult, but it would be stupid of me, wouldn't it, Vivienne?" He put his hand to her forehead and pushed back a strand of hair that had been blowing across her face.

She felt a wave of warmth sweep through her, and completely forgot the question he had just asked. "Yes, I guess so," she stammered.

"I can't think of a quicker way to make you turn and run." His hand rested on her forehead for a moment.

Vivienne looked up at him, almost in a daze.

"I have patience," he said quietly.

As though by mutual accord, they turned and began to walk down the drive.

They stopped for a moment as a small, smudged rectangle of paper blew in front of their feet. It was edged in black and read, "In Memoriam: Celia Susan Potter." Then the ocean breeze picked it up and carried it away.

"Suspenseful tale features Gothic atmosphere and a small-town Southern setting."
—*Booklist*

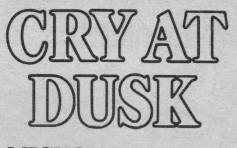

CRY AT DUSK

MIGNON F. BALLARD

A woman comes face-to-face with her darkest nightmare when she returns to her small hometown to investigate the death of her cousin and learns the secret of not one murder but two.

Take 2 books & a surprise gift FREE

SPECIAL LIMITED-TIME OFFER

Mail to: The Mystery Library
901 Fuhrmann Blvd.
P.O. Box 1867
Buffalo, N.Y. 14269-1867

YES! Please send me 2 free books from the Mystery Library and my free surprise gift. Then send me 2 mystery books, first time in paperback, every month. Bill me only $3.50 per book. There is *no* extra charge for shipping and handling! There is no minimum number of books I must purchase. I can always return a shipment and cancel at any time. Even if I never buy another book from The Mystery Library, the 2 free books and the surprise gift are mine to keep forever.

414 BPY BPS9

Name   (PLEASE PRINT)

Address   Apt. No.

City   State   Zip

This offer is limited to one order per household and not valid to present subscribers. Terms and prices subject to change without notice.

MYS-BPA5